NOBLE BRIT

IN THE SHADOWS - BOOK 9

P. T. MICHELLE

LIMITLESS INK PRESS

NOBLE BRIT

IN THE SHADOWS - BOOK 9

In the Shadows Series
Reading Order

Mister Black (Book 1 - Talia & Sebastian, Part 1)
Scarlett Red (Book 2 - Talia & Sebastian, Part 2)
Blackest Red (Book 3 - Talia & Sebastian, Part 3)
Gold Shimmer (Book 4 - Cass & Calder, Part 1)
Steel Rush (Book 5 - Cass & Calder, Part 2)
Black Platinum (Book 6 - Talia & Sebastian, Stand Alone Novel)
Reddest Black (Book 7 - Talia & Sebastian, Stand Alone Novel)
Blood Rose (Book 8 - Cass & Calder, Stand Alone Novel)
Noble Brit (Book 9 - Mina & Den, Stand Alone Novel)

Black and Red (Book 10 - Talia & Sebastian, Stand Alone Novel - Coming December 2019)

Note: Mister Black is the only novella. All the other books are novel length.

DEAR READERS*: The* ***In the Shadows*** *series must be read in the following order:* ***MISTER BLACK****,* ***SCARLETT RED****, and* ***BLACKEST RED****. Sebastian and Talia's happy-ever-after is contained within books 1-3. Cass and Calder's epic love story follows in books 4-5 with* ***GOLD SHIMMER*** *and* ***STEEL RUSH****. Be sure to read books 4-5, since you'll also get to visit with Sebastian and Talia as they play key roles in Cass and Calder's story. The rest of the books in the series:* ***BLACK PLATINUM, REDDEST BLACK, BLOOD ROSE,*** *and* ***NOBLE BRIT*** *are all stand alone novels.*

Sometimes it takes losing yourself to find the right person to put you back together.

COPYRIGHT

Print ISBN-13: 9781939672452
Print ISBN-10: 1939672457

To stay informed when the next P.T. Michelle book will be released, join P.T. Michelle's free newsletter http://bit.ly/11tqAQN.

Cover credit: Cover designed by P.T. Michelle
V06262019

NOBLE BRIT SUMMARY

Dennet Barasa. British. Former MI6. Bodyguard. Controlled and cool under pressure, he's about to meet his match in a petite heiress, who will be his toughest assignment yet.

When I lost everything I ever cared about, guarding the Blake family became my life. I've spent years protecting the wealthy family like they were my own.

Until I was assigned Mina Blake.

Beautiful and intelligent, she's infuriatingly stubborn as she challenges me. She's also a delightful storm, tearing up the roadblocks around my heart faster than I can rebuild them.

But someone is after Mina, and as the danger closes in from all sides, I'm finding it harder to separate my head from my heart.

She is everything I thought I would never have in my life. And I will do whatever it takes to keep her forever.

Dear Readers: NOBLE BRIT is a stand alone story set in the IN THE SHADOWS world.

IN THE SHADOWS SERIES:

Mister Black (Book 1 - Talia & Sebastian, Part 1)
Scarlett Red (Book 2 - Talia & Sebastian, Part 2)
Blackest Red (Book 3 - Talia & Sebastian, Part 3)
Gold Shimmer (Book 4 - Cass & Calder, Part 1)
Steel Rush (Book 5 - Cass & Calder, Part 2)
Black Platinum (Book 6 - Talia & Sebastian, Stand Alone Novel)
Reddest Black (Book 7 - Talia & Sebastian, Stand Alone Novel)
Blood Rose (Book 8 - Cass & Calder, Stand Alone Novel)
Noble Brit (Book 9 - Mina & Den, Stand Alone Novel)
Black and Red (Book 10 - Talia & Sebastian, Stand Alone Novel - Coming December 2019)

CHAPTER ONE

MINA

"Meeeeena" The haunting sound carries on the cold wind lifting my hair and whipping it around. I halt my brisk walk and pivot, quickly shoving the long strands away from my face. *That... sounded like my name.*

People brush past in both directions on the busy Manhattan sidewalk. The end of the day is upon them. As is mine. When a woman knocks my shoulder as she strides by, I glare after her and zip my thin coat tighter against the frigid air.

Turning back in the direction I'd been heading, I frown at the clouds above as they quickly blot out the last bit of afternoon sun's warmth. I'd been looking forward to checking out a couple of new shops all week. I'm not letting this suddenly crappy weather ruin the little bit of "me" time I'd carved out. I have forty minutes before I have to pick up Josi from daycare, so I'm making the most of it. Just two more blocks.

The last of the sun fades, heralding a vigorous gust of wind whistling fiercely in and around the tall buildings. Its intensity carries with it an eerie, sing-song rhythm along with the darkening sky.

"Meeee-na, Meeee-na, Meeee-na."

I pull the coat's collar tight around my ears and focus on the shop windows as I pass. Anything to distract me from the feminine pitch. It's so achingly familiar, an unbidden shiver runs the full length of my spine.

"I'm losing it," I murmur and stop in front of a boutique custom shoe shop. As I force my gaze to focus on the high heels in various fall shades so I can tune out my hearing, a woman's reflection in the glass jolts at my racing heart.

Mom?

I gasp and glance across the street. A layer of sweat quickly coats my body, and despite the cold making my teeth chatter, I dig my nails into my palms and scan for my mom's thin frame, blond hair, and cool blue gaze. A part of me dreads the moment I'll find her standing in the crowd, while the daughter in me is desperate to know the image in the glass was real and not some figment of my imagination.

My gaze darts back and forth, and I blink to ward off

the sudden wooziness in my head. *She's gone. I know this. Why am I even hoping for a glimpse?* Closing my eyes for a brief second, I sigh, then start walking. At least I don't have to dodge around so many people now. For whatever reason, everyone seems to be heading toward the steps down to the trains.

Why are they all going there at the same time? Is a bad storm coming? I look up and find the clouds churning a dark, angry brew. Just as I pick up my pace, someone calls in a raspy voice, "Mina!"

I stop, my heart thudding. My whole body jerks to the crazed rhythm as I slowly turn.

My mom is standing across the street.

Her loose-fitting dress is covered in soot and half her face too. She looks thinner, her hair a dirty, matted mess. But it's the sight of the smoke slowly rising off her clothes and hair that makes me start to shake.

"Come to me," she says, lifting her hand.

Her voice is as clear as if she's standing right in front of me, yet she's a good thirty feet away. *You know this is wrong, Mina. This isn't real. You need to run. Now!*

Gulping out a sob, I take off toward the closest train station. Tears blur my vision and my toes jam painfully into the points of my high heels, but I don't care. I can't deal with my own fucked-up mind right now. That woman is a mirage, conjured by wistful thoughts and regrets.

I reach the entrance to the subway, but before I can descend, someone yanks my arm and a scream tears out of me.

Molten heat radiates from my mother's tight grip. Even through my jacket, I can feel my arm singeing. "You're hurting me!" Pain blurring my vision and scared out of my mind, I try to tug free, but only manage to drag the searing heat along my arm.

"Stop..." she snaps on a harsh wheeze. Anger flares as she tries to catch her breath. With each rise and fall of her chest, her face cracks, the fissures widening, exposing burning embers shimmering beneath the surface.

Tears track my cheeks. "Let me go," I plead, trying once more to pull away from the pain.

"Stop running, Mina!"

What does she mean? The sharp smell of charred flesh makes my stomach roil. Is it hers? Or mine? How did she survive that explosion? And where has she been? Self-preservation trumps my need for answers, and I finally yank free of her hold. The moment I pull away, Mom's gaze narrows and her face cracks all the way across. I gape in terror, frozen in place by the horrifying sight. My mom reaches for me once more, but the moment we connect, she explodes. Screaming, I jump back, my hands flying to my face to shield it from flying bits of fiery, bloody flesh and bone.

I yank awake on a low, horrified wail and quickly

shove the blanket off to smack at imagined hot embers still scalding my skin. Sitting up on my couch, it takes several breaths to calm down as the low hiss of the warm fire in the hearth buzzes in my ears.

"You're awake," I say to myself on a relieved rasp and shake out my hands, trying to get a grip on my emotions. *What the hell was that?* That dream was a straight up horror freak show!

Josi's steady breathing in the baby monitor is the only comforting thing in the room, so I focus on the sound for several seconds to help me calm down. "Love you, Josi-Bean," I whisper my appreciation.

Raking my hands through my damp hair, I stand and approach the mantle to stare at a picture of my mom. "You might be gone, but your presence still lingers around every corner." The reflective glass impedes my view, so I pull it down. Sliding the photo from behind the glass, I set the empty frame back. The fire below pops and crackles. Normally it would evoke fond childhood memories of campfires with my rowdy older brothers and parents at the Hamptons in the fall. Instead, tonight I wiggle my nose to rid it of the burning wood smell and study the thin blond woman in a couture dress. Her light blue eyes are sharply aware as she smiles for the camera while holding my baby girl.

I remember that moment so clearly.

After Josi's christening was over, Mom saw the

photographer coming, so she took my baby out of my arms and turned to pose for several shots. The moment the photographer moved on to take photos of other guests, she immediately handed Josi back to me. That photo of Isabel Blake with her first grandchild, Josi, ended up in the next issue of NY Style Magazine. And, of course, my mom made sure I had a framed copy.

I rub my thumb over my mother's face and realize just how true that old saying about hindsight is. With time and distance, the 20-20 sharpness can haunt you with vivid clarity. "I know you had your bitchy moments," I murmur and lift the picture up so we're at eye level. "But how could I have been so blind to not see how truly self-serving you were?"

The dead don't answer. They just haunt your mind on an endless loop with all the things left unsaid.

As I toss the photo into the fire, Josi sighs and rolls over in her crib, her movements coming through the speaker clearly. I glance down at the sweet image of her clutching her blanket in the monitor's video display on the coffee table, and as a smile tilts my lips, I notice I have a new text on my phone.

Hey, girl. Stopped by, but you weren't home. Just wanted you to know I'm thinking of you. Give me a call when you get a moment.

My gaze strays to the kitchen table where I'd unwrapped

the gift I found at the front door with a red and white striped bow. Whenever I've needed cheering up, Laura always found a way to remind me that she's there for me. This went all the way back to middle school where she dressed up as a candy cane with me in a school play just to support my crazy effort to get to know the lead of the play, Parker Hudson.

I pick up my phone and tap out a quick text.

Thank you for being so thoughtful and such a wonderful friend. I'll give you a call next week when I'm feeling better.

You'd better. Rest up and take care of yourself. Kiss Josi for me.

I send her a kiss emoji and set my phone down, glancing at the tea. A couple weeks ago, she'd left me an Earl Grey set. And today it's a chamomile blend. It's totally like her to never say a thing about it, but it was so sweet to think of a way to help me relax. I'll have to drop off a gift for her one day soon, just because.

I pick up my mug of chamomile tea and mutter, "I wish I could sleep as soundly as my baby." Taking a sip of the now cool tea, I sit on the sofa and lean back, tugging the blanket onto my lap. Normally I'd pick up my sketchpad and go to town with my charcoal pencil, drawing images of things I'd seen throughout the day: people, animals, nature. But I just haven't had the energy lately. Too little sleep has messed with my creative mojo, taking away the one relaxation tool that had always worked for me.

The photo I tossed into the fire has turned to ash on top of all the other photos I'd already dropped into the flames before I fell asleep. Yawning my tiredness, I shake my head. "That's the last one in the house, Mom. I need you out of my head once and for all."

CHAPTER TWO

DEN

"You've got a solid plan, Gavin," Sebastian says as his half-brother pushes his seat back from the conference room table. "It's just too fast for all that you want to do. Adding an additional person and stretching out the implementation to six months from your proposed three should make the transition smoother."

"I appreciate your thoughts." Gavin shakes his dark head and stands, sliding his phone into his pants pocket. "Though it really pisses me off that Dad asked you to be here for this meeting. It's like he just can't let go of the fact you turned him down to take over once he retires. I'm doing my best to let that go, but he's got to stop being so damn controlling and let me run Blake Industries the way I see fit."

"It's still Adam's company." Sebastian rises to meet Gavin, using his couple of inches height over his brother to his advantage. "He's not retired yet. If I hadn't attended today, you would've missed out on some salient points. I've had years to build my business. BLACK Security is thriving and expanding, so check your ego and take the free advice. That will make Adam happy, and once he sees you're willing to listen to other viewpoints, he won't keep bringing me into meetings where you're planning to make big changes across the company he spent a lifetime building."

A text from a London number draws my attention from their debate.

Den! Hey, mate. It's been a bit. I need to have a chat with you. You've got my number now, so ring me.

The moment I see the text, my chest tightens with unbidden anger. *Why the hell is Hugh trying to contact me?* I haven't heard from him since my MI6 days. Whatever he wants, I'm not biting. Since I didn't return his voice message from a week ago asking me to get in touch with him, that should've been my answer. He needs to stop. This time, I block his number, then slide my finger across the screen, deleting the message with ease. Shifting my gaze to Talia, I tune back into the brothers' conversation.

She's calmly gathering papers and putting them in folders as if she's not really paying attention to their discussion, but I know she's listening intently. Her mere presence keeps the brothers' tones even, and I mentally snort at how completely unaware they are of this fact. Talia wants all the Blakes, half or otherwise, to accept each other. With such strong personalities, Sebastian and Gavin will continue to knock heads from time to time, but Talia's the one who will bring them back to seeing reason if necessary. She might be a Blake only by her marriage to Sebastian, but she is absolutely the family's Queen.

She hasn't always exuded serene calmness. There was a time when I saw pain and betrayal in her eyes, and deep sadness too. We shared an unspoken bond over tragic pasts, and at that moment I knew if Talia ever needed me, I'd help her. She's one of those rare people who sees the good in all those around her. I rub my jaw, wondering how she'd label our unique relationship. Despite the paycheck I receive from BLACK Security, she and I have never had a traditional employer/employee dynamic. Talia's like my smart-as-a-whip younger sister, who knows I have flaws I'll never share and she accepts me anyway. We exchange a look as Gavin tries one last time to argue against the timeframe Sebastian suggested.

I lower my fingers from my jaw: three, two, one just as Sebastian ends the discussion in a final tone.

"Six months, Gavin. If you buck it, I guarantee I'll be called in a meeting later where you'll have to explain to Adam why you thought three months was plenty of time."

While Gavin backs down, Talia smiles her amusement that I nailed it. I'll never tell her that I consider her family, but I think deep down she knows.

From a pure entertainment perspective, watching the oldest Blake siblings interact amuses me, but I'm still unclear as to why Talia asked me to attend this meeting. As her bodyguard, I'm not usually involved in the day-to-day BLACK Security business she runs with her husband. And attending a meeting at Sebastian's father's business, Blake Industries, is definitely not the norm. My job is to watch Talia's back, so I only get involved when there's a security-related issue. Doesn't mean I don't notice a hell of a lot going on around me at both companies. When you're an observer for a living, it comes with the territory.

After Gavin leaves, Sebastian glances at his watch. "Guess Mina's running a bit late."

Talia shakes her head. "She has got to stop being late for meetings, Sebastian. She knows we won't be back here until next week. There's too much going on at BLACK Security."

Sebastian rubs the back of his neck. "After Josi was born, Mina figured out how to handle the single mom thing, but I think Regan's betrayal, on top of losing her mom, is taking longer for her to adjust."

Talia lifts her eyebrows. "I know she's been through a lot. Maybe she came back to work too soon and should consider only coming back part-time for now, but if she's going to set up meetings, she should be here on time. This is the fourth instance this month. There's no excuse."

I silently applaud Talia for not giving Mina a pass like the Blake men in her family tend to do. Mina is brilliant and a savvy marketer. I've seen her work a boardroom with deftness and class as effectively as she does a party. Yes, her life has turned to shite recently, but work is often the best way to help a person buffer themselves from tragedies they don't want to face. Regan, her best friend, embezzled millions from Blake Industries before she disappeared into thin air. That probably played a part in Mina's erratic behavior, but that doesn't give her an excuse to leave everyone hanging. Life is hard. When it beats you down, you fight back. Deal with it, don't avoid it.

Talia starts to hit the button on the conference room speaker when an email alert pops up on her phone. As she looks down, her all-business expression shifts to a sympathetic one. "James Martin's wife thanked us for the get-well flowers we sent, but she just passed on the sad news that he died of unexpected complications after a successful surgery last night."

"I'm sorry to hear that." Sebastian's brow furrows as he buttons his suit jacket. "Now I'm really glad you suggested we set up that scholarship fund for his kids' college. At least that's one less thing his wife has to worry about."

"Me too." Talia nods solemnly as she types on her phone. "I'm making a note to send flowers for the funeral."

Frowning, I glance Sebastian's way. "Was he the chap driving the limousine that blew up during your wedding rehearsal?" At his slight nod, I continue, "If you hadn't pulled him out of that burning car, he might not have survived at all."

Sebastian shakes his head, his mouth downturned. "If only we could've saved Isabel too. James had a long road to recovery. He was finally doing better. It's a damn shame that later complications took his life."

The room goes silent for a moment, and I can tell the last thing Talia wants to do is continue her earlier discussion about Mina's absence on the tail of such gloomy news. Clearing her throat, she pushes the speaker button and dials an extension.

When Mina's phone goes straight to voicemail, Talia looks at her husband and slides the speaker phone his way. "Buzz Sarah's extension."

"Mina Blake's office," the admin says in a cheery tone.

"Sarah, it's Sebastian. We're waiting in the main conference room for Mina. Can you please ask her to join us for this meeting?"

"I would be happy to, Mr. Blake, but Mina just left the office a couple minutes ago."

His gaze narrows with irritation. "My sister called this meeting. Did she say where she was going?"

"I'm sorry, she didn't. She received a call, then a few minutes later hurried out of the office. To be honest she seemed pretty distracted."

"Is my niece okay?" Sebastian immediately asks, his brow furrowing with concern.

"I'm pretty sure it wasn't the daycare. They know to call my number during office hours if they need to get in touch with Mina."

"Thanks, Sarah." Hanging up, Sebastian retrieves his phone from his pocket and dials a number. Listening, he looks at Talia. "It's going straight to voicemail."

Talia exhales a sigh and looks at me. "Den, I'd like you to discretely follow Mina and find out what's going on—"

"Talia—" Sebastian begins.

"You know Mina hasn't been herself for a while now." Auburn eyebrows elevating over determined green eyes, Talia ignores her husband's warning look. "Whatever is going on with her seems to be escalating. I'd like to make sure she's okay. If there's something that we can do to help her, we should."

Sebastian and Talia are usually in sync about most issues, but he definitely has a blind spot when it comes to his little sister. And now I know why Talia asked me to attend this meeting. As I stand, Sebastian scowls at me. "You should at least pretend to wait for my 'okay' on this."

The last thing I want is to chase after an heiress who's been pampered to the point that moments like this are even necessary, but I agree with Talia. Buttoning my suit jacket around my gun holster, I meet his challenging gaze. "Have Elijah send me your sister's location."

Walking out, I smirk as he calls after me, "You're fired!"

CHAPTER THREE

DEN

This is Mina's last location.

As I log the street and general direction she's heading into my phone, another text comes through from Sebastian.

From now on, each time I fire you, I'm docking your pay.

A new text comes through from Talia.

Ignore him.

Not this bloody time. I send Sebastian a text back.

This is a favor for Talia. Next time, I'll send you my bill.

After I hit Send, I pull out of the parking lot. If my BLACK Security employment status was a relationship, it would absolutely fall in the on again/off again category. Considering I only told Sebastian as a courtesy that I was

Talia's new bodyguard, I'm not sure why he thinks he can fire me.

Arrogant Brit! Just keep an eye on my sister and report back.

My gaze flicks over Sebastian's quick response before the text disappears from my phone's screen. The fact I don't need this job seems to go right over his head, yet I know my association with BLACK Security will only last as long as I successfully continue to protect the Blakes.

Mina's family might shelter her from life's hard knocks more than they should, but my loyalty to Talia extends to the whole Blake family. As long as I can accommodate, I will.

Even if those family members make questionable life choices.

My jaw sets as I pull to a stop across the street from the dodgy hotel, Eastend, just in time to see Mina stride toward its main door with determined steps. As I stare in disbelief, she walks inside, her head held high.

She might not appear coerced or tense, but my gaze automatically skims the few cars in the parking lot near hers for possible threats. I can't believe she would ditch her family and work responsibilities for a tryst in a cheap hotel. She's attractive and smart. With long, honey-blond hair and warm brown eyes, she attracts men's attention like bees to the brightest flower. Regardless of the wealthy Blake family name, she could easily have any guy she wanted. *So what the hell kind of low-class wanker is she hooking up with?*

My first instinct is to walk in there, kick open the room door, and punch the guy for not having more respect for her. Then I'd yank her pampered, self-absorbed arse out of the hotel. And after resisting the urge to spank her for not having more respect for herself, I'd tell her to "grow the hell up and become the formidable *Blake* I know she's capable of being" before I took her home.

I keep my hands on the steering wheel to hold myself in place. Acting on those instincts would definitely get me fired. Permanently this time.

Rational thoughts prevail and I focus on memorizing every vehicle's make and model around the hotel and in the parking lot, along with any visible cameras. I'm not surprised I don't see any cameras. A hotel like this would make sure not to have any.

A sudden shadow in my right periphery has me quickly pulling my gun. Finger right next to the trigger, I narrow my gaze on the man standing on the other side of the passenger window's glass. The stubborn set of his jawline makes the two-inch scar on his chin stand out. He taps the glass and nods toward the window.

I lower my hand, but keep my gun trained on him as I hit the button to crack the window. "What are you doing here?"

"Nice to see you too, Den." Hugh's dark eyebrows

elevate, his gaze dropping to my gun. "Right cagey, aren't ya?"

The last eight years have taken their toll on my old MI6 comrade. Gray peppers the temples of his buzzed dark hair. He looks leaner, his face a craggy display of sharp angles and mission-experience grooves. Even his blue gaze has grown darker. No matter his motivation for seeking me out—just seeing him twists the hot poker in my chest, stirring the embers of regret and guilt into a new level of pain—I sure as hell don't want him to see Mina. "I'm working," I grate. "You need to go. Now."

"Surveillance on cheating wives? What has America done to you, mate?" He gestures to the seedy hotel and snorts. "I'm sure she'll be busy for a bit. You can spare a minute or two."

Why is he purposefully ignoring my I'm-going-to-end-you-in-two-seconds expression? The fact that he's seen Mina is bad enough, but his assumption about her infuriates me. "Piss off. We have nothing to discuss."

He scowls. "You need to listen to—"

All I can think about is the past, when I'm supposed to be focusing on Mina. I don't know what the hell he wants, but I won't risk him learning who she is. Or anything about her. I lift my gun again, my tone deadly. "Walk away. Right. Fucking. Now."

Hugh always was a stubborn bastard, but he steps

away from my car, his hands lifted in "calm down" mode. "Fine. I'm leaving."

I track his every step and watch him get into a car down the street. It's too far for me to see the license plate, but I register the make and model. After he drives away, I let up on my clenched jaw and tuck my gun away, mulling over why he's here in the US. He didn't mention a case, so what's his angle? The moment I turn my attention back toward the hotel, I see Mina driving out of the parking lot, her foot heavy on the gas.

Bloody hell! I start my engine and put the car into gear, grumbling, "He lasted like, what? Twenty minutes max? Doesn't seem worth her trip here." *What was she thinking?*

Just as I turn my wheel, a line of city buses drive past at a snail's pace, cutting me off.

Once the seven buses finally clear, I rev my engine and veer into the lane, dialing Elijah's number.

"Hey, Den. What's up?"

"I need you to track Mina's location."

"Sebastian pulled it earlier. Buzz him for the info."

Annoyed, I keep my voice even. "Ping it again."

"Lost her already? That's got to be a record." Elijah chuckles. "I know Sebastian wanted to keep tabs, so I'll have him pull the data and text you. Two birds, one stone and all that."

"You'll *be* the dead bird in this scenario if you don't get me the info right bloody now!"

"*Someone* skipped their morning coffee," he mutters as typing sounds in the background for several seconds. "Okay, she appears to have stopped moving. I'm sending the location to your phone now."

"Thanks," I say in a calmer tone.

"Will Sebastian want this too?"

"No, I'll update him later." Ending the call, I shake my head and mumble, "I'll probably be working for free by next week."

CHAPTER FOUR

MINA

How am I supposed to move forward when ghosts from my past won't let me? I lift my phone up and my hands shake as I hover my finger over the name. Derrick's number.

He said he wants to be involved, Mina. Now's your chance to find out. Can you trust him?

Swallowing my nerves, I scrub at my face, hoping the tear stains are mostly gone. I don't know where I finally found my calm state. I must be in shock right now. Otherwise, normal me would be screaming through my emotions. Instead, I gnaw on my bottom lip and set the phone down once more to take a long sip of my wine. *I can't believe this is happening.*

The female bartender in a slick black ponytail calls to

me as she passes by with a tray of beers for a half dozen guys at the end of the bar. "Just let me know when you're ready for another."

The game has drawn a crowd. Loads of men are standing in and around the bar, watching the TV on the back corner wall, which is fine by me. It's easier to get overlooked in the excitement and less likely guys will think I'm there to be hit on. I've got enough going on in my life right now. I take another sip and savor the taste. Wow, this wine is good, stronger than I expected, but good.

God knows I haven't been myself lately, but how could I have hit rock bottom like this? I stare at my clean hands and think about how dirty they became overnight. All it took was walking into that hotel. I knew better. I knew I shouldn't have gone, but I had to know. So I went. As the memory washes over me, my body starts to shake and my stomach twists into knots. I swallow a few times to settle the nauseous churning. Holding up my half-empty glass, I reply to the bartender on her way back, "I'll just order another now."

The moment she nods her understanding, I down the rest of the contents. *Liquid courage, don't fail me now.*

My stomach buzzes and my head suddenly feels all warm and fuzzy, making it a bit easier to pick up my phone and hit the dial button.

"Hey, Mina. It's good to hear from you. I knew you'd eventually call."

His smugness annoys the crap out of me, but for now I need him. "Hey, Derrick. I'm going out on a limb here, but if you were serious about wanting to be involved, then I need you to do me a favor."

"Sure, what can I do for you?"

"Can you pick up Josi at daycare today? I'll have to call them and update the permissions listing—I still haven't even taken my mom off since she passed away—but if you could—"

My phone is unceremoniously swiped from my hand. I frown to see Den speaking into it in a low, authoritative tone. "Miss Blake no longer requires your help."

Before I can counter his statement, he hangs up. "Off you go."

"Give that back," I snap. "What are you doing here?"

"Saving you from yourself."

As he slips my phone into his inside jacket pocket, the bartender approaches, grinning at his imposing size. "What'll you have, handsome?"

Any other day, I would have been intrigued to be the subject of Den's sudden undivided attention. The six-foot-five, well-dressed, self-contained man with striking lion-colored eyes has always secretly fascinated me. He's so steadfast in his loyalty, not just to Talia, but to our family as a whole. His work ethic has kept him at an unapproachable distance, only allowing me glimpses of his sexy accent and rock-solid presence from afar.

Until now.

Now, this Brit is being a royal pain in my ass. I think I liked it better when he ignored me.

"Go away, *Noble Brit*. I'm not going anywhere. And give me my phone before you leave," I finish, holding out my hand.

"I'm only here for *Lady Mina*," he answers the bartender's question at the same time he leans over and scoops me off the stool, straight up into muscular arms.

"Put me down, Den," I say, squirming to be free of his steel hold.

The bartender's eyes widen in alarm and she picks up the bar's phone. "If you don't release her this instant, I'm calling the police!"

Despite the fact that every eye in the room is watching us, Den looks at me, his tone unconcerned. "Do you want her to call the police?"

Quickly shaking my head, I wave my hands. "No, it's fine. He's just my...driver, trying to take care of me." I don't want my father to find out Den had to haul me out of a bar in the middle of the day, let alone on a workday. *God, my head is so woozy. How did I get so buzzed off one glass of wine?* It's bad enough Den is staring at me with a judgmental gaze, I don't need my body wimping out on me like this.

Wait...*why* is Den here?

The bartender's brown eyes dart between Den and me, her expression tense. "If you're suuure," she says slowly, phone still held aloft.

Nodding, I lean over and grab my coat and purse from the back of the chair, then quickly pull out several bills. "Seriously, I'm good." I drop the cash on the counter and glance up at Den. "Put me down. I can walk on my own."

He doesn't even look down at me. "I don't trust you'll keep your word."

A part of me is insulted by his comment, but another part knows he's right. I'd sit right back down on that barstool and consume the second wine I ordered in the hopes it would help me decide what to do. I fold my purse and coat to my chest, knowing he won't back down. "Fine. Let's go."

Den starts to turn when the bartender says, "Look, if you let her walk out of here of her own accord, I won't have to report this to those police officers on their way into this bar."

He frowns at the glass door and the two cops approaching, then glances my way, his tone low, but firm. "The last thing your family needs is a spectacle, Mina."

I nod my agreement.

His stance tense, he sets me on my feet, takes my coat

and holds it out until I put my arms inside, then rumbles, "After you."

It's amazing how sober you can act when you need to. I nod and smile at the police officers as I follow Den out. The moment we're outside, I turn and head for my car, ignoring Den's irritation as he calls after me. "My car is this way."

The cool fall air blowing against my face makes me feel a bit light-headed, but I keep walking. I need space right now. Time to come up with a plan to—I halt at the sight of a woman about my mom's height and with a similar hairstyle standing next to my car.

Her back is to me, but I don't want to see. Not after last night's surreal dream. My breathing ramps and my pulse begins to race, so I quickly pivot, intending to take Den up on his offer for a ride. Instead, I bounce off his rock-hard frame.

As I stumble back and he grabs my arms to steady me, I frown up at him. "Are you *following* me? Is that why you walked into that bar?"

"You needed a ride. Isn't that what drivers do?"

I don't miss the sarcastic edge to his comment as he releases me, but before I can reply, he bends slightly at the waist and gestures toward his BMW diagonally across the lot. "After you, Lady Mina."

I eye him, unsure if he's blatantly mocking me or if he's just being British-polite, but when I see several people gathering at the bar's main window to watch our interaction, I sigh and do my best to keep from swaying as I follow him to his car.

Considering he's keeping up the pretense of being my driver, I'm surprised he opens the front passenger door, but I don't argue and slide into the seat.

I haven't looked back toward my car to see if the woman near my car has turned around. And honestly, I don't plan to. I'm too busy trying to clear my vision that has started zooming in and out like a telescope, while Den slides into the driver's seat and starts the engine. *Am I drunk? How's that possible? I only had one glass of wine.* Shaking my head in confusion, I decide to focus on something other than my own issues. Like the fact I'm annoyed with Den for hanging up on my ex.

Granted, calling Derrick for help wasn't easy. After he backed out on the whole marriage and fatherhood package, it took time to adjust to his rejection before I fully embraced being a single mom. I love being a mom, but other areas of my life have been full of grief, crushing disappointment, and shocked resentment, so when he started calling a couple months ago, asking to see his daughter, I said yes. Josi only knows him as a friend of mine, which is how I prefer it.

Until today, when my life turned into a complete mess.

Derrick is the one person who can handle Josi for a bit

and who also wouldn't ask me any questions. It's not like he has room to judge. But then Den went and blew that for me, cutting my time to figure out a plan in half. I have to pick Josi up in less than two hours. How am I supposed to deal with this now?

"I'm your driver?"

Den's obvious offense draws me out of my worried musings. My head swims when I look his way, so I blink to try and settle it. "Would you prefer I said you were my bodyguard?" I close my eyes and pinch my nose, hoping my head will stop feeling like it's stuffed with alcohol-soaked cotton. "I'm pretty sure that answer would've drawn even more curious gazes."

"You mean more than the *entire* room watching?"

I open my eyes to see he's cut a mocking gaze my way.

Who knew the guy had such a sardonic streak? Despite my wooziness and frayed nerves, I cross my arms, my back straightening. "I'm pretty sure it was the massive guy practically cave-manning me over his shoulder that drew all the attention."

Den takes a right turn, his expression unapologetic. "If people didn't recognize you when you walked in, they certainly knew who you were by the time you left."

Ugh, at least there wasn't any paparazzi around. My father would flip. Score one for Noble Brit. Unable to think of a comeback, I glance out the window and realize that I don't recognize this road. Not that I have any intention of going back to work right now, but why aren't we heading toward my apartment? And why does it feel like the car is moving super slow? I don't remember Den driving like an old man.

"This isn't the way to my apartment."

"That's correct."

"Where are we going?"

He turns onto another street, this one a quiet side street with rows of expensive brownstones. Glancing into his rearview mirror, he hits a button on the bottom of it, then slows to a stop. As a garage opens, he says, "To my place."

If anyone else deviated from where I expected them to take me, I would flip out, but Den has guarded our family for years. It's in his DNA to protect. Despite my tense nerves, seeing him relaxed in his own home, is suddenly appealing. Who is this man behind his bodyguard persona, who also happens to live in a brownstone with a freaking garage? I know it had to cost a hefty price. My brother must be paying him very well. Den's so private...so controlled. I'll bet his place is minimally decorated. Probably modern.

Ugh, why am I even speculating about this? Because you're avoiding dealing with what happened earlier. My first instinct was to call Sebastian, but I quashed the thought. An hour ago, I refused to call my brother, not about this. But now, I've run out of time for alternative options. My stomach churns with my failure, but I know my family will support me. "Take me back to my car, Den. And give me my phone."

"Not yet."

When he cuts the engine, I frown in confusion. As a bodyguard to my father first, and then to Sebastian and Talia's family, Den has always done what was asked of him, even if he didn't agree with it. He has never challenged a request, at least none that I can recall. What gives? When Den hits the button to close the garage door behind us, a sudden thought hits me and I narrow my gaze. "Did Sebastian send you after me? Is that why you showed up at the bar? Is this some kind of big brother by proxy thing? Give me my phone so I can rip him a new one!"

"You skipped out on your meeting."

My jaw falls open. "Skipping a meeting doesn't justify invading my privacy. Also, not that it's *any* of my brother's business, but I had something important I had to do. That..." I pause and sigh. "I've turned into a mess."

"Obviously not your best choice," Den says in a low tone. Stepping out of his car, he leans over to look at me in my seat. "This wasn't the first or even the second time you've left Sebastian and Talia hanging."

What's he talking about? Before I can respond to his comment, he shuts the door, cutting me off. When he walks up the stairs and disappears inside, leaving me alone in the garage, I gape. Did he just judge me?

I jerk open the car door and yelp in pain when the weight of it yanks my arm, pulling me halfway out of the car. Leaving my coat and purse in the seat, I slam the heavy-ass door closed before stomping loudly up the stairs. The noise helps drown out the buzzing in my head, and at least my vision has stopped zooming. I still have to grab onto the handrail a couple of times before I reach the door, but otherwise my head feels a bit clearer. Good thing, because I'm ready to cut that arrogant bodyguard off at the knees.

The moment I walk through the door and snap, "I wasn't done talking, Den!" he grabs my hand and yanks me forward, hauling me over his shoulder.

"What the hell! That cave-man comment was a joke. Put me down, so I can yell at you face-to-face, damnit!"

"You have to pick up Josi soon," he says calmly as he starts climbing a flight of stairs.

"I know that. No thanks to you!" I shoot back. As much as I want to pummel his lower back with my fists, or better yet, bite the hell out of his hard butt to get him to put me down, when my world tilts and I spy wooden steps through my wild mess of hair, I panic and wrap my arms around his muscular waist instead. "Don't you drop me, you overgrown Brit." Scared to death, I press my face into his perfectly pressed dress shirt, growling in anger. "My brother is going to kill you for scaring the shit out of me!"

"He should be giving me a bloody medal," he grumbles just before he steps onto a level floor, then walks into a room. "You need to stop depending on your family to clean up after you. And it's going to start with taking care of your own obligations and responsibilities."

"How dare you judge me! You have no idea what's going on in my life." I try to see where I am, but all I can make out is a herringbone-patterned hardwood floor as he yanks my heels off my feet and tosses them down the stairs.

"Those are thousand dollar shoes!" Furious, I kick my bare feet harder as he turns and takes a few more steps, then quickly sets me down on a hard, cold floor.

Just as I push my tangled hair out of my face and righteous fury hisses through my teeth, I'm hit with a pounding spray of cold water.

"Uuuuuuuuggh!" I screech and swing my fists. My hits bounce fruitlessly off his hard shoulders as he holds me under the full blast of the shower. Sputtering against the water hitting my face, I yell, "Are you insane? My brother is going to kill you!"

"Your little girl is expecting you to pick her up." I shiver as he continues, his expression as unyielding as his hold. "And you're going to do so sober."

"I'm not drunk, you judgy asshole!" I bellow at him

and manage to yank on his ear before he pulls back with a grunt. "I had a glass of wine before you arrived. One freaking glass. Turn off the water, Den!"

He scowls, his brows pulling together as he turns the faucet off. "You could barely keep your eyes from rolling in your head in the car. Your pupils were dilated. Are you high too?"

"Hell no, and fuck you!" I yell, trying my best to get free.

"Your hands shook like a junkie waiting for his next fix," he continues, unaffected by my fury. "You were definitely drunk enough that you called the man who didn't even bother to show up for Josi's birth."

I'm so surprised that Den knows that about my ex that I'm struck speechless for a second, until a shiver of cold rips through my body. "Wh—why do you even care?"

Den's golden eyes soften and he loosens his tight hold on my arms, his warmth seeping through my dress sleeves' cotton material. "Do you not realize that if he learned you were drunk today, that could give him ammunition against you? He could claim you're an unfit mother and file for custody."

My stomach tilts and my lips begin to quiver. His statement hits me harder than a jolt of ice water ever could. "He would never do that. He didn't even want to be a father."

"Your daughter is worth *billions*, Mina." The judgment in his expression shifts as his fingers flex on my arms. "What were you thinking?"

Somehow, I liked his anger better. The disappointment lacing his tone twists my stomach with guilt. Even if sleep deprivation contributed to my inebriated state, there is no excuse for jeopardizing my daughter's well-being. Before I can speak, he sighs and shakes his head.

"Skipping out on work meetings for a rendezvous in a seedy hotel, then getting pissed during work hours? Whatever's going on with you? Whoever this chap is? He's dragging you down. Ditch him and get your life sorted. You don't need Sebastian. You need to do this yourself. This is your mess to fix, Mina. Get yourself straight for Josi."

Oh, shit! He knows about the hotel? My body tenses all over again. His perceptive gaze is lasering through me... as if he's sifting his way through the ugly bits of my mind that I've hidden from the world, especially from my family. They don't know how messed up I am. How little I sleep. Too many dreams that turn into nightmares. Nightmares that feel so real. They would lock me up and take my daughter away from me.

"So you *were* following me," I say in a much calmer tone than I feel as I swipe my wet hair away from my face. When he nods, I feel like such an unworthy failure that my righteous anger saps right out of me. All I want to do is draw on the solid strength of his hands holding me. "You don't understand. I wasn't at the bar to get drunk. I was there trying to form a plan to deal with this myself. I just can't figure my way out of this." My bottom lip starts to shake, so I bite it and look away, hoping he can't see that I'm barely holding it together. "I don't want to go to jail."

CHAPTER FIVE

DEN

"Jail?" My gaze snaps to her mouth where her lip is twitching nervously, and I frown that I notice how soft her lips are. "What would you be arrested for?"

Her brown eyes slide to me, fear swirling, before she glances away once more and whispers, "Murder."

My hands instantly tighten on her slight frame, my protective instincts kicking in. I expected possibly a lovers' quarrel. Or maybe the bastard broke it off and that's why she was so upset, but not murder. *Bloody fucking hell.* I grab my towel off the rack, my movements quick and efficient as I wrap the oversized length completely around her. "Did you accidentally hurt someone at the hotel?"

"What?" Her eyes widen and she quickly shakes her head. "No. I didn't hurt anyone, but..." Tears spill down her cheeks and she starts to shake all over. "I messed up so much, Den. I should never have gone."

I quickly lift her in my arms and carry her into my bedroom. Sitting on the end of the bed, I set her on my lap and push her hair back, my tone calm even as my whole body tenses with worry. Something is very wrong. I need to get her talking before I can bring Sebastian into this. "I can't help you if I don't know what happened. Start from the beginning."

She takes several breaths to calm herself, then closes her eyes, speaking slowly as if playing it all back in her head. "I was at work, preparing to come to the meeting with Sebastian and Talia, when someone I never expected to hear from called my office phone." Her eyes fly open and she looks at me. "I *needed* to know, so I went."

"Who called you?" My brow furrows. "And what did you need to know?"

"I lost..." Mina cups a shaky hand over her mouth and her gaze glazes over with tears. "There was so much blood."

I cup her jaw and make her look at me. "What happened, Mina?"

She opens her mouth to speak, but her teeth start to chatter and a hard shudder rips through her. I stand and set her down on the floor. "You need to get into some dry clothes. I'll put your dress in the dryer."

When she nods, I step over to my closet and pull out a

clean sweatshirt and casual trousers. She takes one look at the trousers and shakes her head. "I'm at least ten inches shorter than you. A pair of shorts might work better."

Nodding my agreement, I grab a dress shirt and new tie, then hand her the sweatshirt and athletic shorts before I walk downstairs.

While I wait for Mina to change, I put her shoes by the couch, then slip into a dry shirt and tie. An image of Mina sputtering her fury in the shower flits through my mind as I put on a kettle for tea, but I refuse to feel guilty for giving her the wakeup call she obviously needed. Evidently, even more than I realized. *What the hell happened in that hotel?*

I check my phone for the first time since Elijah sent me Mina's location and see a new text from Sebastian.

Where's your update on my sister?

Any truths I provide at this point will result in him storming over here to demand answers. I send a general response.

Mina met a friend, then ran some errands.

Who did she meet with?

Evasive is best.

My job is to keep Mina safe, not report her every move.

You definitely want to be fired.

I think one person asking Mina questions is enough. She might shut down with too many of us demanding answers, so I ignore his last response. Just before I slip my phone back in my trouser pocket, another text pings. This one is from Talia.

Do we need to be worried, Den?

I won't lie to her, so I send the only answer I have.

I don't know yet, but I'll stay with her until I have answers.

I'll give them feedback once I have something to report. Right now, all I have are questions. And growing concern by the minute.

Just as I glance at my watch, Mina walks down the stairs carrying her wet clothes.

Without a word, I take her clothes and put them in the dryer. On my way back to the living room, I find her standing in front of the gas fireplace holding her hands out to soak up the flames' warmth. With rolled up sleeves and the hem of my sweatshirt hitting her mid-thigh, she looks so petite as she lifts on her toes to stare at the landscape artwork on the wall above the mantle.

My lips quirk at the appealing sight she makes with the fire as a backdrop. I'm not afraid to admit that I'm glad she passed on wearing my shorts. They'd be trousers on her and it would be a sin to cover up such attractive legs and tiny ankles. She might be my charge, but I'm not blind or dead.

I am, however, a professional, so I clear my throat and start to speak when the kettle begins to whistle.

Mina turns at the sound, a quick smile suddenly tilting her lips. "You're making tea?"

She doesn't wait for an answer, but instead pads out of the living room and into the kitchen. "Everybody I know drinks coffee," she rambles on as I lift the kettle from the stove and pour the hot water into the two mugs I'd set on the small island.

"We Brits enjoy our tea." I slide the box of tea toward her as well as a couple of biscuits on a small plate. She needs food in her belly to counteract the alcohol.

Mina flips through the bags, settling on Earl Grey. "It's one of my favorite black teas, but I drink chamomile at night." She starts to take a sip, but pauses as I pour cream into my cup. "I've never had tea that way before. Is it good?"

"It's the only proper way to have a cup of tea." I lift the container, eyebrows raised. When she nods that she wants it in hers as well, I pour some in, then push the tin of cubed sugar her way. "Your choice. I usually go without."

"So you have sugar for guests?" she asks, picking up one and dropping it into her tea.

With wide eyes and her towel-dried blond hair falling over her shoulders in soft waves, she appears genuinely curious. Most likely she's trying to avoid discussing what happened in that hotel. I straighten my shoulders. "I'm always prepared."

"You sound just like my brother," she mumbles around a bite of biscuit. "Such Boy Scouts."

Needing answers, I set my mug down. "Tell me about the phone call you got at work."

Mina stirs her tea a couple of times, then looks at me as she tucks her hair behind her ear, a slight smile crooking her lips. "Oxford, huh?"

My gaze instantly drops to my uni's logo hugging the swells of her breasts. She's perfectly proportioned. Well curved, but not too big for her tiny size. Glancing down briefly, I take a step back and fold my arms in a relaxed stance to hopefully set her at ease. "Yes, I went to Oxford."

"Interesting. I never would've taken you for an Oxford alum. You seem more like a Cambridge guy." She thumbs over her shoulder toward the living room. "Then again, your house is far cozier than I expected. I pictured you with modern decor...all bold lines, chrome metal, and black, white and red. Not the dark leather furniture and soft cream pillows. And that artwork over the fireplace; it's so peaceful and mesmerizing. All that lush green land. Where was that painted?"

She's definitely avoiding. "We need to talk about what happened in the hotel, Mina. You said you didn't hurt anyone earlier, but you mentioned a lot of blood."

Mina takes another sip of her tea, then her hands start to shake and her calm expression breaks. "Regan called."

Every muscle in my body tenses, but I keep my tone even. "What did she want?"

Her hands tighten around the mug as if she's trying to soak in all its warmth. "She sounded weird...a bit off, and really anxious. She told me that she needed to explain her actions. I wanted to yell at her for betraying my family's generosity, *my* trust. I got her that job and she stole from us using my log-in access, but I worried if I said all the angry thoughts rushing through my head, she'd hang up and disappear for good." Mina's eyes brim with tears. "I needed to know why, Den. How could she throw away a lifetime of friendship?"

Twenty-three million of Blake Industries' money is ample reason, but what I'm concerned with is *what made Regan suddenly grow a conscience?* It's been months since Sebastian uncovered Regan's embezzlement, but by then she had already disappeared. We tried and failed to find her. It's like she never existed, no trail to follow, nothing. I don't believe the flimsy excuse she gave Mina. There's no way unloading her guilt could be worth the possibility of getting caught and having to rot in prison for her crime.

"Did you two get into a fight?" I push off the counter, straightening. "I don't remember seeing any scrapes on you, but is that how she got hurt?"

"It wasn't like that." The moment Mina glances away from my intense stare, the dryer shuts off. Heavy silence fills the room, highlighting her evasive answer. As Mina walks out of the room to retrieve her clothes from the dryer, she calls over her shoulder, "I don't think I can handle describing it." Returning with her clothes in hand, she nods slowly. "It'll be easier if I show you. Once you see, then..." A shaky breath escapes, as if the weight on her shoulders just grew heavier. "We can call the police."

CHAPTER SIX

MINA

I stay quiet as Den drives us back to the hotel. Despite my shower dunking, which I will never admit helped sober me up like a jolt of adrenaline, a truce seems to have fallen over us like my warm clothes right out of the dryer and a fresh scent of peace.

It's been so long since I've let myself depend on someone enough to share my flaws and trust them to back me up. Family doesn't count. Blakes always support each other, no matter what. Den is different. He has no reason to help, but he is, and I don't know what to do with that fact. So instead, at least for this car ride, I close my eyes and let go of my worry of picking Josi up on time. Den has her back too. Taking slow breaths, I push away the anxiety that awful scene in the hotel conjures, along with the tragic loss of my friend. For now, I just exist. Den's years of field experience and calm approach will help keep me grounded when I call the authorities.

My eyes fly open at the sound of a phone ringing inside the car.

"Hey, Den. How's everything going at BLACK Security?"

He's calling my father? My whole body tenses and panic rises in my chest. The warmth quickly evaporates and I shake my head in fast jerks, but Den completely ignores me. "Good afternoon, Mr. Blake. Everything is fine. Talia and Sebastian have asked Mina to work on a time-sensitive project, and your daughter asked me to call and see if your schedule would allow you to pick Josi up from daycare today so she can finish her part."

"I'll be happy to pick Josi up," he says, his voice full of pride. "As a matter of fact, since it's Friday, I hope Mina will be okay with me making it a weekend with my granddaughter. I was going to call tomorrow and ask if I could take Josi to the new animated movie *An Adventure in Atlantis* that just came out. Let Mina know that it's age appropriate and I've got everything Josi needs at the house. Between Helena and myself, she'll have a wonderful time."

Helena's back? Thankful mist blurs my gaze and I quickly nod my approval to Den's questioning look. As my nanny, Helena practically raised me. I was so sad when she moved to the West coast to be with her mother after I left for college. I don't know when she returned, but she couldn't have come back at a better time. Josi will adore her, and she's going to get the biggest hug from me.

"I'm sure Mina would fully approve of her daughter having some quality time with her grandfather," Den says as he reaches inside his coat pocket, then hands me my phone.

"Good! Once she's done with her project, tell my daughter I said to go out and do something frivolous. She should enjoy the rare treat of having the whole weekend to herself."

I tense at the thought that I could be sitting in a jail cell soon instead of a spa.

"I'll convey the message. She'll be in touch with you later, Mr. Blake."

Den hangs up just before he turns into the hotel's parking lot. Cutting the engine, he looks at me. "Now that Josi's in good hands, we can focus on what happened earlier. Do you have a key to the room?"

I nod and open my purse to retrieve it. "Regan said she was exhausted and needed a nap, so she'd leave me a key at the front desk. All I had to do was give them her room number. The desk clerk didn't even look up from the graphic novel he was reading as he handed me the key card." My voice shakes as I drop the card in his hand. "Sh—she's in room 410. I don't know if I can go back in there."

"It's best if I go in alone. Stay here," he says, taking the card from me.

I watch Den walk inside and despite the fact that I'm wearing my coat, I start to shiver. Anxiety knots my stomach as I imagine the look on his face, the judgment in his eyes that I somehow played a part in what happened to Regan.

I jump when my phone rings with a call. My fingers fumble as I answer.

"Hello?" I say, my voice cracking.

"I need you to come to the room," Den simply says.

I don't bother asking how he has my number. How else could he have tracked me to that bar? "Should I dial 9-1-1 or call the front desk first?"

"Don't do either."

"But, shouldn't I—"

"Don't speak to anyone, Mina. Understand?"

My back stiffens at his curt tone. He's already judging me. "Yes, I'm coming."

I walk right past the front desk. The guy is still engrossed in his novel. That's some great customer service right there. The ride in the elevator seems to take forever, but the moment it pings on the fourth floor, my whole body fills with dread. Taking a deep breath, I clench and unclench my shaking hands and swallow several times to prepare myself for seeing Regan again. I reach the door and quietly knock, whispering, "I'm here."

Den opens the door, his broad shoulders filling the frame. The look of concern on his face worries me even more. His job depends on him remaining expressionless. I step into the room and he quickly shuts the door behind me. When he steps to the side, I turn, refusing to look toward the bed. I can't see my friend like that. She might've decided to take the easy way out, but I don't understand why she needed me to see it. *Why did you do this, Regan?*

I blink to stay calm and keep my gaze locked on Den's face. "I know I need to be here when we call the police, but I wish we could've done it from the car. I just don't want to revisit the horror of it, Den."

His brow furrows as he briefly glances in the room. "What do you think happened here, Mina?"

I gesture toward the bed, upset that he's asking me to describe what I think happened. "Isn't it obvious? Regan committed suicide. And for whatever sick reason she wanted me to find her. When I walked in and saw all the blood, I thought maybe I got here just after it happened." Choking up, I blink past the rush of tears and take a deep breath, then bow my head and close my eyes. "I know it was wrong to run, but I was scared out of my mind." Lifting my gaze to his, my words pour out in a tumble. "It hit me that this could've been Regan's last *fuck you* to my family. That she called me here to set me up. I mean, what if the police didn't believe me and they thought I did it for what she did to us—"

"Mina," Den clasps my shoulders and turns me around. "There is nothing here."

I gape at the empty room. The neatly made bed. *Where's Regan?* I jerk my gaze to his. "There was a food tray on that table over there. And she was *right here,* lying on the bed. Blood was splattered on the comforter and the pillows. Some was even on the headboard." Den's staring at me like he's watching a wounded animal and trying to figure out how to approach it.

My heart races faster and faster. "Don't look at me like that. I swear to you, she was right here. When I saw her like that, I held back a scream, then leaned over her to see if I could feel air coming out of her nose. There was nothing. She wasn't breathing."

I fall to my knees and lift the comforter, looking for proof that might've been left behind. A shoe, a sock. Anything. All I see is dust. Standing, I frown. "Do we have the right room?"

"The key would only work on the correct room," he reminds me.

Rubbing my suddenly throbbing temples, I whisper, "I promise, she was here."

"What makes you think it was a suicide? Could you tell how she killed herself?"

At least he's asking more questions instead of

looking at me like I've lost my mind. "There was a lot of blood, but she appeared to have wounds in her chest. Here," I say, pointing to my heart. "And the engraved letter opener that I gave her for her first year anniversary at Blake Industries was on the bed beside her. Underneath all that blood, my prints could probably still be on it."

I shake my head and begin to pace, tears tracking my cheeks. "I don't understand this. My best friend died in this room."

"Was the room registered in her name?"

I halt and glance his way. "She said she registered under another name. A place like this doesn't care who you are as long as you have cash."

"Which begs the question: why would Regan choose to stay in such a cheap hotel? She stole a fortune from your family."

I part my lips to answer, but don't have one. He's right. It doesn't make sense. I look around the room, bewildered. I know what I saw, but...did I?

It was Regan, right? She looked like she'd lost some weight, but I didn't look too closely at her face. Walking in and immediately seeing all that blood freaked me the hell out.

"The call I got sounded like Regan. The woman looked like Regan. And she had her letter opener. I—" I pause, unsure what else to say to convince him.

"Let me take you home. Once you get some food in your belly, your mind will clear."

"But..." I gesture to the room, bewildered.

"We can't report what's not here, Mina." Opening the door, he calmly says, "We should go."

Den probably thinks I was having a hallucination. I wasn't high earlier like he assumed, but what I don't want to admit is that I could be wrong. Before I walked into this empty room, with its clean bed and neatly tucked tacky floral cover, I would've sworn up and down what I saw was real, and not some freaking nightmare. Then again, I've seen my dead mother while out and about in the city the last few months too. Or someone I thought could be her. So maybe I'm not the best judge of what's real or not.

Den's right about one thing. I can't report a crime that doesn't exist.

Exhaling a shaky breath, I walk out of the room and wonder if I'm losing my mind.

CHAPTER SEVEN

MINA

"Thank you so much for picking up Josi, Dad." I tuck my phone under my chin as I tug an oversized sweater over my t-shirt. It feels so good to slip into comfy, casual clothes. "I hope she's a good girl for you at the movies tomorrow. The last time I took her, she couldn't sit still. I really appreciate you spending the weekend with her. She does have an event I signed her up for at church on Sunday."

"Text me the details for the church thing. I'll get her there for it. And of course I'm happy to do it, Mina. This will be great one-on-one quality time. I do hope you make sure to do something relaxing the next couple of days."

"I'll try. Thank you. Can you put the phone up to Josi's ear?"

"Sure, just a second." My gaze slides to Den glancing

out my apartment window while my father's footsteps echo on the wood floor. "Josi, your mom's on the phone."

"Mama?"

I smile at her sweet voice. I miss her already. "I just wanted to say that I love you, baby girl. Have fun with your Granddad."

"Wuv you, Mama. Bye-bye."

When Dad gets back on the phone, I snort. "I think she's happy to be there."

"That's because Helena is setting up a tea party for her," he says, laughing. "Do you remember that tea set you refused to let your mother throw away?"

"Ah, I'd forgotten all about it." Den peers casually through the curtains to the street below. He's always so vigilant. I tuck my hand in the back pocket of my jeans as I tap the toe of my tennis shoe on the patterned carpet under the coffee table. "Do *you* remember when I used to demand that you come to my tea parties? I was what? Three?"

"Yes, I remember very well. You'd stamp your little foot, scrunch that adorable face surrounded by a mop of flyaway hair, and insist I call you Princess Mina the entire time. How could I resist such strong Blake traits at such an early age?" he says, pride in his voice.

"Guess Princess Mina wanted to rule the room," I say softly. *Where'd that decisive girl go? I don't even trust my own mind anymore.* My gaze lifts to Den's face to make sure he didn't hear the *Princess Mina* part. Who knows what kind of inference he'd draw from my childhood egocentrics. The last thing I need is more judgment today. Thankfully he's still staring outside, completely oblivious. *What's he so interested in?*

"You certainly knew your own mind," Dad says, pulling me back to the conversation. "And Josi's just like you. Helena's the one who remembered the tea set and brought it out. And…it looks like I'm being summoned to the table for a cup."

"Love you, Dad. Please tell Helena I can't wait to see her. I hope you can find a way to convince her to stay. I miss her. Not to mention, who's going to look after you?"

He chuckles. "I've been doing that for a very long time now, young lady. I'll survive, but I sure do enjoy having Josi here, so Helena may have to stick around to remember important little things like tea parties. Have a great weekend and see you on Sunday."

As I hang up, I say to Den with a half-laugh, "Josi was all like, 'Mom who?'"

Den nods. "She feels safe and loved. That's all that matters." He glances at his phone when a new text buzzes through, then lets the curtain fall back into place. "I have an appointment, but Theo has arrived and put your car in its parking spot. He will be just outside your door until I return. If you need anything, ask him."

I can't believe how disappointed I am that he's leaving. I don't want another BLACK Security guy to watch over me. In the middle of my emotional rollercoaster today, the tiny peek behind the curtain of Den's life drew me in and kept me from imploding. And now that I'm completely sober, the last thing I want is to be alone. The idea of a whole weekend ahead of me will give me way too much time to question my sanity after seeing that empty hotel room.

I'd hoped I could convince Den to stick around and tell me about his Oxford days over dinner and another pot of tea—no more alcohol for me for a while. *What was he like in his early twenties?* Has he always been a man of few words? I bet he has some great stories. I'm sure he and his British buddies got into all kinds of trouble.

"Thanks for getting my car, but where are you going?" He pauses as he lifts his overcoat from the chair, his eyebrows raised. *Ugh, that was a bit forward, Mina.* "Um, what I meant was...were you assigned to me for the evening too?" I tuck my hair behind my ear and smile. "I kind of wanted to hear some stories from Oxford."

Den's brief smile transforms his whole face, giving another peek into the man behind the stoic guard persona. "We were an incorrigible lot." Clearing his throat, he seems to pull back into himself, his expression turning serious once more as he shrugs into his coat. "I imagine you'll be asleep by the time I relieve Theo."

"Maybe not." Tilting my head, I smile. "For the first

time in forever, I get to sleep in tomorrow. See you later, Den."

Opening the door, he nods. "Lock it after I leave."

Once the door closes, I do as he says and flip the deadbolt, then move over to the window. As I wait for Den to exit my building and slide into his car, I smile behind the closed curtain, thinking about the deadly combo of his smile with his appealing accent. Is his laugh equally pleasing to listen to? My smile fades when I see my ex pull up in his car across the street from my building. Den stops walking and turns to wait for him. *What's Derrick doing here?*

As much as I don't want to see my ex, I can't have him getting into it with Den. When my gaze lands on the scarf Den left on the chair, I have the perfect excuse to go downstairs and hopefully head off any confrontation. Grabbing the scarf, I quickly slip on my jacket and start for the door, then frown. Theo will adhere to BLACK Security protocol and follow me downstairs, causing more attention than I want. I gnaw on my lip and stare at the fire escape. Yep, that'll be much faster. Locking my phone, I slip it and my keys into my jacket pocket, then open my window.

The last thing I expect to see is Den walking down the sidewalk when I round the corner of my building. His car is still parked at the curb and my ex is nowhere in sight.

What did Den say to chase Derrick away? I really

need to know so I'm prepared if he tries to give me a hard time about it later. I can't have Derrick using Den's protective nature as an excuse to try to get shared custody of Josi in order to see her whenever he wants.

And where is Den going? He seemed a bit on edge right before he left. And why did he have Theo come relieve him? What could he possibly be worried about? There's only one way to find out. I tuck Den's soft scarf around my neck and pull my jacket's hood over my hair as I follow him toward the train station.

As Den gets off in East Village, I do the same. The last place I expect to see him walk into is a popular bar/night-club called Village Venue, known for great drinks and all genres of music. I've been there before with college friends, but I honestly don't remember much about that night. I wait a few minutes before I slip inside, then quickly push my hood back and move over to the only empty table close to the back of the dimly lit room. Next to me, a large group of people in their thirties are holding their beers up and calling out songs they'd like the live band to play in their next set. According to their loud conversation, apparently this band is known for its folksy blues sound.

I peer through the neon lit darkness, looking for Den and sigh my frustration when I don't see him in the crowded room of people drinking and chatting. Where did he go? Is he in a backroom or something?

The sound of a bass guitar being strummed as the band warms up draws my attention to the stage where blue, pink, and deep purple lights shine. My focus locks on Den talking to a man holding a saxophone. The bald guy with a thick, dark beard smiles at something Den says, then points to the stage. When Den shakes his head, the guy shrugs and sits on a stool, wets his reed with his tongue, then pulls the stand up mic closer to his instrument. Giving Den an expectant look, he lifts the mic from its stand.

Den stares at him for a second, shakes his head, then unbuttons his suit jacket. Once he shrugs out of it, and starts to take off his tie, the guy lets out a victorious laugh and turns to speak to his band mates before putting the mic to his lips. "We're back this time with a special guest who came all the way across the pond just to entertain you for a song or two. Give it up for Den, New Yoooooork!"

As the crowd whoops and whistles, I wait for Den to pick up the guitar leaning against an empty stool on the stage. But when he rolls up his sleeves, then takes the mic from the bearded guy's hand, I let out a short laugh of surprise. *He's going to sing?*

The drummer taps his sticks and then the rest of the band jumps in with their bluesy take of Rolling Stone's iconic "I Can't Get No Satisfaction." The audience claps and hollers at the crowd-pleasing choice. The moment

Den belts out the first few lyrics, the whole room goes wild in their approval of his deep, angsty voice. Chill bumps scatter across my skin and I stare in astonishment at his sexy, smoldering rendition of the famous song as the music amps. Clapping my wholehearted appreciation along with the rest of the room, I call out, "Rock it, Den!"

"Hell if I ever knew Den could sing that well," a dark-haired man in his late-thirties with gray at his temples sits in a chair at my table.

His British accent quickly captures my attention and I say over the music, "You're a friend of Den's?"

"I'm Hugh. Den and I have known each other for a long time." A scar on his chin stands out in the darkness as he puts the beer bottle to his lips. Instead of taking a swig, he continues, "We haven't talked in a while, so I'm here to see him."

I gesture to the stage. "I think he should be done soon."

"There's some old wounds." He absently rubs the scar on his chin, his attention never leaving Den. "I'm not sure if he'll be willing to chat."

Unspoken issues with my mom, ones I'll never get to address, swim around in the back of my mind. That's probably why it seems like I see her everywhere lately. I shrug the sudden tension from my shoulders and shift my gaze back to Den on the stage. "Don't wait until it's too late. You never know if you'll get another chance."

The song ends, but Den and the band effortlessly segue into a faster paced tune I've never heard before. I tap my fingers on the table and smile. "This one's new to me, but I really like it."

"You're so young, I'm not surprised you don't recognize this lesser known classic by the Stones, Mina. It's called 'Ride 'Em On Down.'"

I instantly tense that he knows my name. I never said it. Then it hits me...how did he know to sit next to me? It's true my table was the only one that wasn't already full, but still.

"I need to use the restroom. Can you save my seat for me?" I start to slide my chair back, but he puts his foot directly behind my chair legs, stopping my movement as he leans closer to speak over the music.

"You should stay until the song's over," he says smoothly, his gaze still fixed on the stage. "It'll be worth listening to the whole song."

Heart racing like mad, my whole body tenses. Just as I start to push the table forward to free myself, the song ends and the room lights brighten slightly. Oblivious to the crowd's whoops and applause of appreciation, Den's gaze lands directly on me. He hands the bearded guy the mic, says something quickly, then grabs his jacket and tie and walks off stage, heading straight for our table.

If I weren't already a bit tense about this guy next to me, I'd be unsettled by the intense look on Den's face. He nods to acknowledge the couple of people in the crowd who clap him on the shoulder as he passes, but he doesn't take his eyes off us, his determined stride never breaking.

"Let's go," he says, gripping my elbow to pull me to my feet once he reaches the table. Turning his head, he directs a lethal tone at Hugh. "If you come within a hundred feet of her again, I will end you."

The guy holds his hands up, his beer bottle dangling between two fingers. "I'm just here to talk, Den. I really need you to listen. There could be trouble."

"The only trouble is staring right at me." Den looks pointedly at Hugh, then turns to me. "Off you go."

The tension between the two men is so palpable, I let Den lead me out of the club without a word. Once we're outside, he continues to usher me forward, but several steps away from the club, I pull free of his hold. "What the hell was that? Why won't you talk to the guy?"

"He's dangerous, Mina. Trained to kill."

"You mean just like you?" I challenge. When he doesn't respond, I exhale a slow breath. So Den really was part of the MI6 in the past. I always assumed the office rumors were exaggerated and had never asked my dad to confirm when Den first came to work for him. "If Hugh wanted to kill me, he would have. He was there to speak to you."

He looks down at me, the grooves around his mouth

deepening. "Either keep walking or I'll *cave-man* you out of here."

I throw my hands up and follow him farther away from the club. "Is threatening to haul me around like a sack of sand going to be your pattern?"

"Will a total disregard for your own safety continue to be yours?"

We're only a block away from the club, but I'm already panting from taking three steps for every one of his. "Slow down, you long-legged, Brit!"

Den suddenly halts, then lifts an arm to hail a cab.

I study his profile, noticing a small muscle pulsing in his jaw. He's really not happy. "I don't need a babysitter, Den."

The silent "I know *better*" look he cuts my way sparks my defenses.

"Today's crazy-Mina was an anomaly," I say, spreading my hands in innocence. "Normally I'm pretty boring."

The cab pulls up and Den says in a low tone as he reaches for the door. "You're not crazy, nor is there a single boring thing about you. The stubborn Blake blood running through your veins assures that."

Den doesn't speak the entire ride, but I can tell by the way he's resting his big hands on his thighs, fingers spread with a slight grip, that this discussion is far from over.

Fine by me, I'm not done yet either.

THE MOMENT DEN and I step off the elevator, Theo stands up from his chair outside my apartment door. Rubbing a hand through his styled light brown hair, he shrugs his thick shoulders and does a double take. "Are you some kind of ninja, Mina? How'd you leave without me seeing you?" Before I can respond, he looks at Den and shakes his head. "I honestly never left my post."

Den waits for me to unlock my door, then says to Theo, "Your job was to keep others from getting in." He pauses a beat, shifting his gaze briefly my way. "Not to have to keep the person you're protecting from sneaking out. I'll take it from here for the night."

"Do you want me to write the report for this evening?" Theo asks as he shrugs into his jacket.

Den shakes his head. "I'll fill Sebastian in tomorrow."

"Thanks, Theo," I call after him as he walks toward the elevator. I feel bad that he just wasted a couple hours of his time guarding an empty apartment.

"Hold on a sec," Den says to his colleague as I enter my apartment. I leave the men to chat and walk inside, shrugging out of my coat.

My cheeks flame with embarrassed heat when Den closes the door and catches me sliding his scarf from underneath my hair. I set in on the back of my couch. "I um, put your scarf on once I saw you walking down the street. I'd brought it downstairs after you left without it, but you were already heading away. That's why I followed you to the club."

His brows pull together. "You followed me all the way to East Village just to give me my scarf?"

"Of course not," I say, shaking my head. "Before I came downstairs, I saw my ex had just pulled up and you seemed to be waiting on him. By the time I made it downstairs to make sure you two were civil to each other, he was nowhere to be found. I needed to know what was said between you two before he tries to contact me again. My daughter is my priority, and I don't want to mess up our current status."

"Which is?" Den's gaze narrows slightly. "You're not planning on getting back together with him again, are you?"

I give him an "are you kidding?" look. "So what did you say to him to make him leave?"

"I told him you were tired and couldn't be disturbed."

"That's all?" I tilt my head, eyeing him. "I know there's more. What else did you say?"

He steps into the living room and picks up the scarf, his gaze holding mine. "I told him that it's good to see he's finally showing an interest in his daughter, but if he ever tried to manipulate Josi or you for any kind of financial gain, that I would ruin him."

I can only imagine how intimidating Den appeared to

Derrick. I'm so surprised he stepped in to make sure my daughter's father does right by her that I'm speechless for a second. "Thank you for looking out for Josi, Den. I appreciate it."

He dips his head in a quick nod, then holds the scarf out to me, saying gruffly, "There's no reason to take it off, since you're not staying. You need to pack a bag."

On reflex I'd taken the scarf he handed back to me, but I lift my gaze to his, crushing the soft material between my fingers. "A bag? Why?"

Den folds his arms, his serious demeanor making him look every bit the MI6 agent he used to be. "I'm not discounting your story about what happened in that hotel."

"But you said there wasn't any evidence."

"Lack of evidence doesn't mean something didn't happen. At least for tonight, I would like you to stay somewhere that's not easily traceable to you."

"You think I'm in danger?" My pulse starts to race. "Is that why you had Theo stay behind while you went off to sing at a night club?"

He frowns. "That wasn't singing. That was a negotiation."

"Sounded like singing to me. Which was freaking awesome, by the way. But you obviously weren't too worried or you never would've left." Setting the scarf back down on the couch, I walk into my kitchen to retrieve a mug from the cabinet, then tug the container of tea forward. "I'm staying here and making some tea. My best friend, Laura, bought these blends for me. You should try some."

"Mina—" Den says, but I just talk over him.

"While you have a cup, you can tell me some Oxford stories." I start to open the container of tea when Den's hands land on either side of my mug on the counter. His hard body trapping me in, he leans close, his voice rumbling in my ear.

"That wasn't a request. If all evidence was removed that quickly in the hotel room, it could only have been the work of a professional. Bring your tea if you want, but you're not staying here."

My stomach knots and I glance up at him over my shoulder. "A professional? Does that mean you think Regan didn't kill herself?"

Den turns me around and tilts my chin so I meet his gaze. "I'm not sure yet, but I'm not taking any chances with your safety. I want you to come stay with me."

Stay with him? The knots of worry in my stomach morph into excited flutters as the warmth from his touch spreads through me. He's so close, his compelling golden gaze bending me to his will. I inhale, trying to get a grip of my scattered emotions, but his aftershave only pulls me deeper. Appealing notes of leather and woodsy bergamot soak into my senses and chill bumps scatter across my skin, just like when he began to sing earlier.

There's something so primal about Den. He's as hard as steel, but there's a caring quality about him that draws me in. Like the way he protects Talia, and how he considered Josi's well-being first in every instance. I close my eyes against his magnetism, but I can't shut off his actions. He has no idea how much his belief in me, despite any tangible proof, bolsters my battered confidence. I've never trusted a man this much or felt so safe, and it's freaking me out. I've been doing things on my own for a while now. How is it possible to feel like both a failure and adept in someone's presence? I swallow my nervousness and open my eyes, nodding my agreement. "Just so you know, when you ask nicely, the combination of your deep voice and accent is like some kind of hypnotic sorcery."

Den releases me, his low laugh silky smooth. "I'll keep that in mind. Now go get packed."

I walk into the living room, then pause to pull out my phone.

"What are you doing?" Den asks from his leaning position against the kitchen doorjamb.

After a quick search, I click a button, then I tuck my phone away in my back pocket, calling over my shoulder, "Ordering a pair of earplugs."

His arrogant chuckle follows me all the way to my room.

CHAPTER EIGHT

DEN

My gut tells me Mina's in danger. Not a single bit of evidence gives me a reason to think this, but I trust my instincts, and her word, on this one.

She's been quiet on the ride back to my house. Something shifted between us the moment I turned her around in her kitchen. It wasn't my intent to get that close, but she's so stubborn and I needed her to understand. When she lifted those gorgeous brown eyes and looked at me with such blind trust, my whole body tightened with the need to slide my hand down the beautiful curve of her neck, to feel her soft skin and pull her against me. I had to release her and put some distance between us. I can't overstep my bounds. She's my charge. My one job is to protect her.

Yet she distracts me with worry, makes me care for her and Josi's safety. Mina invades my thoughts in ways I swore I would never let another again. I didn't want to let her in, but here she is, winding past my defenses, breathing life into my dead heart, making me think about her. More than I bloody well should.

I don't want the pain, fear, and terror that caring for another can evoke.

I don't want any of it.

But that's exactly what I felt when I saw Hugh sitting beside Mina in that nightclub. I didn't need my gun at the club, so I'd left it in my car for this trip. Which made the gut-wrenching panic I was determined to never experience again that much more visceral, crushing my lungs and jacking my protective instincts. I didn't have a way to defend her from a distance.

All I thought about, all that mattered, was getting her to safety.

I want to fucking kill that bastard for defying my threat, but most especially for having the bollocks to sit next to her. His actions clearly said: I can find you anywhere, anytime. I'll do whatever it takes and threaten whomever I want around you to get your undivided attention.

Once Mina's no longer threatened by this Regan thing, I will hunt him down. I turn into the garage and close it behind my car, shutting off the engine.

Until then, she's safest with me.

"Why won't you talk to your friend?" Mina asks as she follows me into my home.

It's like she'd been reading my mind the whole way there. I set her bag down and shrug out of my overcoat, then put my hand out to take hers, but she shakes her head, refusing to unbutton it. "Why, Den?"

"He's not my friend," I say gruffly. When she just stands her ground, I reach for the button on her jacket.

She puts her hand over mine. "But he used to be."

It wasn't a question. When I nod, she lets me unbutton her coat and slip it off her shoulders.

I'm relieved when she drops the subject and walks off toward my kitchen. "I'm starving. What do you have to eat?"

While I make us steak and mushrooms, Mina prepares a salad. We work easily in the kitchen, as if we've done it a hundred times before. As stubborn as she can be, this ease she and I seemed to have settled in mystifies me. Instead of sitting at the table, Mina chooses to sit on the barstools at the island and immediately digs into her steak with gusto.

"For a petite woman, you eat well." I smirk that she's already eaten half her steak before I've taken two bites.

"I can't help it. This is delicious!" Holding up her fork, she ticks off a list in the air. "Great cook, fabulous singer, exceptional bodyguard. Who knew you were so multitalented?" She spears another piece of meat, then frowns slightly. "I'm starting to feel like an underachiever."

I let out a low chuckle. "I've had decades to perfect said talents."

Mina tilts her head, her gaze narrowing. "How old *are* you, Dennet Barasa?"

"A lot more years than you," I respond before taking another bite of my steak.

She eyes me, scrutinizing my face. "I'd say you're at least Sebastian's age."

"Close enough."

"Close enough? That's all I get?"

I dig my fork into my salad. "You do realize it's rude to ask someone's age, right?"

"Says who? Old people?" Mina wrinkles her nose. "Also, you know it's rude to point out how much a woman eats, right?"

"Touché." I smile, enjoying sparring with her. "Guess I'm old then."

"Nope, just old-fashioned," she says, nodding. "But that's what makes you so appealing."

She's not looking at me at the moment, but just hearing her say that tightens my chest. I can't let whatever is happening between us progress, but damn it's hard to stop it. She's a delightful storm, tearing up the roadblocks I've carefully constructed around myself. A force of nature in a small package I can't stop being drawn to.

"So tell me why you ditched me to entertain a roomful of people tonight." She pulls me from my musings as she takes a bite of her salad.

"I told you, it was a—"

"Yeah, yeah...a negotiation. Must be another old-fashioned term."

I set my fork down and push my plate back. "The bloke playing the sax used to be a crime scene investigator. I asked Travis to go over to the hotel room that I had slipped some cash to the night clerk to assure discretion for the day. In return, I had to sing a couple songs. I didn't tell him anything about the room or why I wanted him to go over it. I suspect he won't find a thing."

"I'm confused." She shakes her head, her brow furrowed. "If you don't think he'll find anything, why are you sending him?"

"Because of the sheer *lack* of evidence. Before you got there, I did a quick sweep with a black light on my phone. I didn't pick up any body fluids. It could be that my phone just didn't see it, but in a hotel like that, there's bound to be some. While other body fluids do, blood doesn't show up under black light. Travis is a professional. He has all the right tools to make any bit of blood reveal itself. If there's anything there, he'll find it."

Mina finishes her salad, then pushes her plate away

too. "So basically you want him to prove you're right? That the room was professionally cleaned?"

I turn toward her, resting my forearm on the counter. "I want to prove *you* were right. And that someone tried to cover up what actually happened in that room."

She blinks a couple of times. "Then what?"

"That depends on what my tech friend finds. We might get lucky and there's proof Regan was there, or even better some clue as to who was there eliminating her presence."

"But I don't understand. Why do you think I might be in danger?"

"We don't know how or why Regan died, but someone went to a lot of trouble to erase her from that room. We can't rule out that they might have seen you enter or exit and consider you a witness."

Mina puts a shaky hand over her mouth. "I didn't even consider that."

My first instinct is to comfort her and tell her I'll keep her safe, but instead of taking her hand like I want to, I stand and pick up our plates. "That's what I'm here for. The more I think like a criminal, the better I can protect you. Are you ready for some tea now?"

Mina blows out a calming breath. "Only if you're ready to share your best Oxford stories. I need the distraction."

I smirk that she found a way to pull some stories out of

me, but the distraction will keep me from thinking about her in ways I shouldn't be, so I grudgingly nod my agreement.

"I just know you have some doozies." Hopping off the stool, she comes around the island while pushing up her sweater's sleeves. "I'll help with the dishes so we can get to you spilling your college days' escapades sooner."

"You do realize you'll have to reciprocate," I say, while filling the sink with hot soapy water.

"Who me?" Mina exhales a low laugh and takes the dry towel I hand her. "I told you that I'm pretty boring."

"Not possible." I pin her with a knowing gaze as I lower the dishes into the sink. "You have to share at least one story."

"Well, there was that brief time in college when I delivered drugs."

Not a lot surprises me, but that certainly does. I glance her way, but hold my silence as I lower dishes into the sink.

"It's not exactly what you think," she hedges, looking regretful that she mentioned it. "But it wasn't my proudest moment either. Around that time is when Talia kind of fell into my life, which was the best thing to ever happen to me."

"Case in point, there's nothing boring about you. I must hear about this dodgy history."

"Are you expecting a quid pro quo?" Her grip tightens on the towel, sudden apprehension evident.

"If you want to dig around in my uni archives..." I smile a ruthless challenge, anticipating the fierce negotiation ahead. "You'll have to share more details."

After Mina settles in for the night in my bed, I set my gun on the coffee table downstairs, then lie back on the sofa in the dark, tucking my pillow behind my head. Tonight after dinner, once I shared a few stories that made Mina laugh at college boy stunts, the longer we talked, the more animated she became. She completely opened up with her own stories and filled the whole room with sunshine.

At one point, she even acted out an entire scavenger hunt from her business fraternity days that involved picking up a box of chicken, but one student took the hunt literally and brought back a box of live chicks. The moment she finished her last story, she laughed at the memory, then crashed on the couch, her eyelids drooping in sheer exhaustion.

That's when I knew the long, emotionally charged day had finally caught up to her. I insisted that she go upstairs, but after several back and forth debates as to who would take the couch, she finally caved to my forceful "no" and walked her sexy arse up the stairs, where she promptly passed out.

Lying here by myself, the living room suddenly feels empty, like it's missing a personality. Now that Mina's wide smile, perky nose, rosy cheeks and golden locks are no longer lighting it up, that's when it hits me...my home lacks an essence.

A heart and soul.

That's not surprising, I suppose. I lost mine a long time ago.

Experiencing unfettered Mina tonight was like watching a pixie flutter around my home, leaving energized fairy dust in her wake. Even now, I'm sure Mina's only taking up a tiny portion of my king-size bed, but she's infusing that bit with her presence. Her perfect little body and tight bum are warming my sheets, while that gorgeous tumble of long blond hair is leaving her sweet smell behind on my pillows. My body tightens as my imagination kicks in and I have to adjust myself, twice.

I grunt my frustration, knowing I need to get her out of my head. So I think back to earlier this evening and conjure my anger at Hugh. Once I'm infuriated all over again, I pick up my phone and unblock his number to send him a text.

You crossed the line the instant you involved those around me. You'd better leave the country while you still can. Once I find you, you'll pay for today's stunt.

After I send Hugh a text, I immediately re-block the number. I didn't send the message expecting a response. I would have to trust him to listen to anything he had to say.

My phone says it's almost one. I thought for sure I would've heard back from Travis by now. The band was only supposed to play until nine. My hope is his report will give us a potential lead to take to Sebastian.

Just before I set my phone down, a text from Travis comes through.

This room has been professionally cleaned. The place was operating-room spotless. But, I'm the best and I didn't give up. It became like a puzzle. I knew that no one was that good. I searched every nook and cranny and found some blood splatter. It was in the piping crease at the top of the cloth headboard. I'll have to run a test against DNA to prove the person's identity...that is if this is about a concern of foul play, which is usually why professional cleaners are brought in. I can tell you this; it was female blood. This doesn't prove much, but it can prove the person's presence. If you're concerned that something went down here, get me a DNA sample so I can do a comparison.

Rubbing my jaw, I send him a text back.

Thank you for your help, Travis. I was concerned that something had happened. I'll send a follow up DNA for comparison tomorrow.

Once the text is sent, I close my eyes. The moment I

let my head rest briefly on the couch, Mina lets out a scream.

The fear in her voice clamps a vise around my chest. Bolting upright, I grab my gun and vault up the stairs three at a time.

CHAPTER NINE

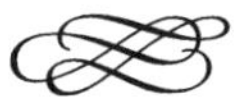

DEN

I enter the room on full alert. My gun at the ready, I survey the dark room for an intruder, but all I see is Mina tossing around under the covers. Tears seep out of her closed eyes as she moans, her voice a raspy whisper, "I don't want to die."

I set my gun on the table and sit beside her. The instant I touch her shoulder, her eyes fly open and she lets out a gasp that sounds more relieved than fearful.

"You screamed in your sleep." Releasing her, I continue to hold her gaze in the bit of light from the street lamppost. "Do you remember what you were dreaming?"

She exhales an unsteady breath as she sits up and shudders, clearly trying to shake off whatever images tortured her sleep.

"I dreamed about Regan in the hotel room."

I pull the oversized t-shirt that had slipped off her shoulder back into place. I blink back surprise at how that small bit of her sleep-warmed skin makes me ache for more. "It's normal that you dreamed about it. That would be traumatic for anyone to walk in on."

Mina slowly nods and swallows. "But this time as soon as I stepped into the room, Regan was very much alive. She was sitting on the bed, leaning against the headboard. When her gaze connected with mine, she let out a crazed laugh right before she plunged the letter opener into her chest. I screamed and ran over to try to stop her, but she yanked the weapon out and plunged it in again and again. Blood spewed everywhere, its warm madness coating my body and clothes. Then she fell back onto the covers in the same position I found her, her body so still." Her voice quivers. "It's like time rewound and put me there just before it happened so I could see inside her head."

"It was just a dream, Mina. It's your mind attempting to fill in the blanks."

Staring straight ahead, she shivers and runs her hands up and down her bare arms underneath the shirt's short sleeves. "There was so much darkness in that room, Den. She wanted me to know."

"What did she want you to know?" I ask, realizing she needs to reason this out so the dream will release its tight grip on her.

She shifts her gaze to me. "That she didn't have a choice."

I want to tell her that she's right, that something happened. But right now she needs her sleep so that tomorrow she can switch her thought process to the fact Regan was most likely murdered. Mina has experienced a horrible trauma. Losing a friend, especially in such a gruesome way, can really mess with your head.

"You've had an emotional shock to your system. Lay back down and try to sleep. You need it to recharge."

She grabs my arm when I start to stand, her hand shaking. "Will you please stay?" When I hesitate, her fingers tighten. "Just until I fall back to sleep."

I fold my hand around her tight grip on my arm, then lift my chin toward the chair near the window. "I'll be right there. Now try to put the dream out of your mind."

Mina nods and once she releases her hold, I move my gun to the small table beside the chair and settle in to wait for her even breathing.

Several minutes pass in the darkness, and just as I close my eyes to briefly rub my fingers over them, I feel the air shift near me. Eyes flying open, I instinctively encircle Mina with my arms as she crawls into my lap. I frown down at her in the darkness, but before I can ask what she's doing, she rests her head on my shoulder and whispers, "Can I just stay here for a little bit? I can't fall asleep."

I tense, unsure how to respond in this situation, until I realize her whole body is quaking. She's still truly shaken.

She's so slight, I barely feel her weight, but I definitely feel the curve of her sweet bum resting on my thigh. Forcing myself to focus on my job and her needs, I curve my arm around her shoulders and cup my fingers around her forehead, tilting her head back so I can look at her. All I want to do is press my mouth to hers, to find out if her lips are as soft as they look, but I stay focused. "Do you want to talk about it?"

I release her and she shakes her head, the scent of vanilla, lavender, and her own arousing smell surrounding me in torturous harmony. "No, please just tell me something to distract me. Tell me about Hugh."

As she flattens her hand on my chest, and lays her head back on my shoulder, snuggling closer against my t-shirt, I exhale harshly. *Where the fuck do I put my hands?* After a couple tense seconds, I settle on resting one on her shoulder, then folding my elbow around her legs to tuck her closer. Needing a distraction to keep from thinking about the fact her sleep shirt has ridden up, exposing shapely thighs, while her breasts press intimately against my ribcage, I mentally recite every single case number I can recall. Getting hard right now would be the height of unprofessional. But bloody hell, I'm not a dead man and she smells so good. Talking about Hugh should kill any bit of lingering desire.

"Hugh and I were colleagues at the MI6. We'd known each other for years, been to weekend parties, work celebratory events together. When he lost his wife in a car accident, he wasn't the same after that. That loss took away part of his humanity."

Mina grips my shirt and I look down at her. "I'm so sorry."

"What made it even harder was that his wife was pregnant with their first child."

Even though she had stopped shaking, tears suddenly fill her gaze. "My God...how horrible for him. Not many people could come back from that kind of devastation."

I lift my gaze and stare into the darkened room. "Agreed."

"What happened between you two? Why do you see him as a threat?"

"Hugh drank to dull the pain of his loss. It's bad enough that he did it after hours because alcohol abuse can destroy lives, but when he was still drunk on the day we had to shut down a terror threat in our city, it was hard to continue holding onto my empathy. When he's not in top form, he threatens the lives of other agents around him. I was frustrated, but out of respect to Hugh, I didn't say anything to upper management."

"That's not good that his issues threatened the lives of his co-workers, including yours. Did you try to talk to him about it?"

"Several times. He just shrugged it off. One evening I had to work late on another case. Hugh had taken the day off, but when I saw him leaning against his car on my street, his body swaying, I knew the bloke shouldn't drive himself home. All I wanted to do was get to my flat. I was only fifty yards away. I was so close, but there was Hugh, blocking my path and so pissed he could barely stand.

"I called a cab and waited with him for it, since he kept asking for his keys and saying he was fine to drive himself. I was in the process of dragging his full-of-drink arse over to the cab, when my building exploded."

"Oh no," she says, sympathy in her gaze.

"If I hadn't had to deal with his self-destructive issues, I might've been able to stop..." I pause and glance away before continuing, "to stop that bomb from going off and save many lives. I lost so much that day. I'll never know if he purposefully kept me away or if he was just that self-absorbed in his own pain. So no, I don't trust Hugh's motives for being here at all."

"What did you lose?"

I don't want to relive the pain, so I stare hard into the darkness. "Are you settled enough to go to sleep now?"

"Guess you're done sharing." Mina sighs, then her voice turns hopeful. "Will you sing something for me?"

"I don't sing," I say in a harsher tone than I intended.

"I'm negotiating." Her comment draws my gaze back to her. "One song and I'll go to bed."

Her smile at the inside joke is hard to resist. I'm glad she's no longer shaking. When I nod, she settles back against my shoulder and I find myself subconsciously pulling her closer as the first strains of Too-Ra-Loo-Ra-Loo-Ral flow from my lips. I've actually never sung the song myself, though I heard it hundreds of times growing up. I'm surprised how soothing it sounds in a deep voice, so I rest my chin on Mina's head and let the rest flow out.

When the last strains fade away, Mina looks up at me, tears in her eyes. "That was wonderful. Since you mentioned Killarney, I have to ask...where did you learn an Irish lullaby?"

"My mother used to sing it to me as a young child."

Her eyes widen in surprise. "Is your mother Irish?"

"Aye, she had the grandest voice," I say in my mother's Irish brogue, the corner of my mouth crooking.

"And where's your father from?"

A couple strands of her hair catch on my overnight scruff. I free them, tucking the golden silk behind her ear.

"Sorry, it's always getting in the way. I've considered cutting it," she says, brushing her hair back.

"Leave the length," I command, then gesture for her to face forward.

When she turns, her complete trust is so unexpected, I smile despite myself as I clasp her hair and quickly twist the golden strands into a thick single braid. Every turn of her soft tresses between my fingers binds me closer, unwinding the vise around my heart. "My father was from Kenya. I guess I inherited my desire to protect from him, though he did his as a Barrister. I've lived my whole life in London, even after my parents passed on."

"Both your parents are gone?" she asks softly.

"It was a long time ago." I reach the end of the long length and hate the idea of the braid unraveling, so I hold fast. Life can be so damned unforgiving. When my gaze drops to the braided cloth bracelet on my wrist, I exhale slowly, then slide it off to wrap it around her braid. "My parents were together when their plane crashed on the way back from a trip to Africa."

Mina glances over her shoulder, sympathy in her eyes. "I'm so sorry, Den." She moves sideways once more and holds my gaze in the darkness for a second before she pulls my handiwork over her shoulder to inspect it. "That's a better braid than I could do on myself. Guess I'll have to add 'hair savant' to your growing list of talents." Glancing up at me, her lips tilt in a soft smile. "So you inherited your light eyes from your mother?"

I nod. "Would you like to hear another song she used to sing, this time in Irish?"

"Yes, please." Smiling her appreciation, she lays her head on my shoulder and tucks her arm around my waist.

The feel of Mina settling against me and sharing this moment makes my chest ache. I haven't thought about my parents in a long time. My mom was a kind soul. She would have been fascinated by Mina's pixie spirit and most definitely inspired by her. I take a deep breath and rest my chin against her temple, tucking her close.

"This song is called Éiníní," I say, then begin the slow, soothing melody, where the singer tries to convince all the little birds to go to sleep. As I call out each bird by name, every breath I take, I inhale Mina's sweet smell. She feels so good in my arms. With her blond hair and tiny frame, so full of inner strength, Mina makes me think of the little willow bird. Her softness and warmth play havoc on my senses, while her essence weaves deep into me, stirring my blood. Filling my soul.

Near the end of the song, I change the name wren to willow and smile. When the song is over, I'm surprised she doesn't make a comment or move to get up. But then I hear her even breathing and mentally chuckle. I might be all wound up, but that lullaby works every single time. It did for me too.

My professional code says I should rouse her, but I'm not ready to let her go just yet. I settle back into the cushioned chair and gather her closer, rubbing my cheek against her soft hair. If this makes me a selfish bastard, I don't give a shite. Right this moment, this little willow is all mine.

"DEN, yer such a good mate. I don't know what I'd do

without you," Hugh slurred as he leaned his whole body against mine.

"You'll be alright, Hugh. Just need to sleep it off." I pulled his arm over my shoulder and hauled him against me, dragging him toward the cab pulling up.

"I just miss her so much. And my child." He stumbled and I had to grab his waist tighter to keep him upright as his voice broke. "Did I tell you they said our baby was a girl?"

"Yes, you told me. I'm truly sorry, my friend." As he dropped his chin to his chest and groaned through his grief, my heart ached for all that he has lost. At the same time I reached for the cab's door, I instinctively scanned the buildings, tracing my gaze further down the street until I saw the warm lights in the sixth floor window. She waited up for me. *I'll be home soon.*

"Go home and sleep this off. We have a busy day tomorrow." I tugged the door open and paid the cabbie after I gave him Hugh's address.

At the same time Hugh flopped into the cab, an explosion and flash of bright light jerked my gaze back down the street. *Motherfucker, my building's on fire!*

No, no, no, no! I took off running. There was so much smoke, I couldn't tell where the explosion was. My heart froze, my lungs filled cold with fear. The faster I ran, the clearer it became, and the more my heart twisted inside itself.

Flames and black smoke had obliterated the warm light that was just there a few seconds ago. I reached the building, but fire fighters and police were already on the scene, keeping on-lookers from getting any closer.

I didn't care if they arrested me. I had to get inside. My fucking whole life is in that flat. I barreled right past two police officers, and had only taken a few steps before the roof of the building collapsed, taking out our flat and the one beneath it as well.

My heart caved, crumbling to pieces just like that roof. I paused and stared in horrified disbelief, then bolted toward the building, yelling, "I'm here! I was right fucking here."

Three officers tried to tackle me, then apparently it took a Taser to finally shut me down. They weren't letting me in that building, no matter what I wanted.

With jolts of electricity shooting through me, I was stuck to the ground, unable to move. All I could do was stare up at the fire and smoke billowing out of that gaping hole in the building with the backdrop of the night sky, and mourn my loss.

I jerk awake, sweat coating my skin. My heart racing under Mina's sleeping head, I instinctively curl my hand over hers pressed against my chest.

Closing my eyes, I exhale a heavy sigh that I dreamed about the last day I spoke to Hugh. I never forgave him for distracting me. It might be irrational, but if I hadn't stopped to help him, I might have prevented the bomb from going off. Or at the very least, I would've died too, instead of my hope dying. That day, my whole life collapsed.

The skills that allowed me to observe details others didn't had served me well while I was with MI6.

Until they didn't.

Everything I loved, cared about, and cherished was taken from me in an instant when my wife and five year old daughter were killed in that blast.

Bren and Enya's deaths shut down my emotional capacity. The man I was before ceased to exist. I became the most professional, thorough, and skilled agent on our team. I lived only to close case after case in order to keep the city safe.

When I received a letter from Adam Blake's recruiter, looking for a bodyguard with military experience, after several years of just existing, I walked away from my old life without looking back. Other than business investments that I could run from anywhere, I had nothing. No attachments. No reason to stay.

Protecting the Blake family was a career I could get my head around. I took my duty seriously for the years I worked for them, but I blame Talia for finding a crack in the armor around my heart. It was a fluke how I learned that she and I shared devastating losses, but a bond formed as I watched her come back from hers. It made me happy to see her bloom with her career, her marriage to Sebastian, and the birth of their first child. They have endured so much as a couple, and are stronger for it, yet she continues to grow. On her own, she's thriving.

She's living proof that it's possible to learn to trust again, if you surround yourself with the right people and give them your utmost loyalty in return.

Mina stirs in my arms.

I glance down at her and my lips quirk. With her hair pulled away from her face, I realize for the first time that her face is heart-shaped. Combined with rosebud cheeks and soft lips, she stirs emotions I thought I was no longer capable of.

She lets out a small sigh, and the moment my body comes to life as she squirms against me, I quickly stand, cradling her in my arms. Damn this is hard. Remaining impartial is my job. It keeps me sharp and always on point. But she's burrowing into my heart faster than I can keep her out.

She mumbles in her sleep, but doesn't wake as her head flops against my chest.

I posted Theo at her apartment earlier as a precaution. The fact that Travis confirmed the hotel room had been professionally cleaned proves someone wanted a woman, who claimed to be Regan, erased from that room completely. Since Mina didn't sign in or give her name, for once, the fact the hotel didn't have any cameras works to our advantage. There's no proof she was there, and no way to identify her for anyone who might ask. Still, I want to confirm that's the case. Once I send over Regan's DNA for Travis to try to match to the blood he found, I'll call Sebastian. It's time to bring him up to speed.

Kissing the top of Mina's head, I lay her in the bed and pull the covers around her. I want the full force of BLACK Security working together to keep her safe.

CHAPTER TEN

MINA

Den seems lost in his own thoughts as he drives us to the BLACK Security office late Saturday morning. I appreciate that he let me sleep in before he informed me that we needed to talk to Sebastian about what I saw at the hotel. But ever since I handed him the bracelet he used on my braid last night and thanked him for letting me borrow it, he remained quiet, keeping to himself.

I look down at the soft waves the loose braid left behind and think about his bracelet. The fabric's worn material and washed out colors of dark blue, white, black, green, orange and red told their own story. At one time, the bracelet would've been so colorful and bright, but it was faded from never being removed from his wrist. It meant something to Den and the fact he used it to help calm me down made me feel guilty and extra special at the same time.

I glance his way, wanting to ask him about it, but then I'd be opening myself up for him to question me. I'm so thankful he never mentioned how I crawled into his lap last night. Or that I bargained with him to sing me to sleep, but God was it worth hearing that lullaby. His voice is amazing and so is he. The man has so many layers that no one knows about, because he's so private. Not once did he ask why I was so upset in the middle of the night, which only makes me appreciate how much of a gentleman he is.

It also makes me want him to see me in the very best light. Even more than my family, I don't want Den to discover how messed up I am. Which is why I didn't tell him the rest of my dream.

After Regan killed herself, my mom appeared beside me in the hotel room. Her smoky form and sharp gaze drilled into me with fiery judgment, filling me with a sense of doom. As she opened her mouth and her face began to crack once more, the smoke around her began to surround me too, yanking the air from my lungs. Backing away, I coughed to catch my breath, my eyes burning. I didn't want to see her torn apart all over again, but this time my chest felt like it was being crushed, as if I was going to be sucked into the volatile vortex surrounding her. I panicked and ran, but before I could reach the door, it slammed closed.

As the room thickened with choking smoke, I coughed and hacked to breathe, blindingly reaching for the doorknob. Hot metal seared my palm and I yanked it back, crying at the throbbing pain. My heart raced as I peered through burning tears, looking around the room for something to protect my hand so I could open the door. The only option thick enough was the blood-soaked cover underneath my dead friend, but I couldn't bring myself to touch her.

While thick acrid smoke clawed its way down my throat and ropes of fog filled every crevice of my lungs, I closed my eyes and wheezed out a low wail, "I don't want to die."

"You'll have to get your hands dirty to save yourself." Mom laughed maniacally and I opened my burning eyes to the room blanketed in blinding smoke.

"I can't," I rasped.

As I fell to the floor, my lungs convulsing with the need for air, the smoke briefly cleared as Mom shoved her face close to mine and smirked. "Then you'll die in here too, just like us."

Swallowing several times to push away the upsetting memory of last night's dream, I wonder what Den would think of my twisted subconscious. At the very least, he would think I'm delusional that I never let my mother go after she died. I'm thankful to be heading to BLACK Security. Not only can Sebastian help us figure out what happened to Regan, but it'll be a good distraction from my own issues. I just wish I knew why my mother continues to haunt me.

One thing I know for sure...once we get to the office, Sebastian will drill me for every possible detail I can remember from yesterday, probably more than once, so it's a good idea to take advantage of the quiet time I have in the car to check on Josi. I grab my phone and start to dial my father's number when I see I have a voicemail from Derrick.

Hitting the play button, I put the phone to my ear.

"Mina, I don't know what's going on, but if you're in some kind of trouble, I want to help. Also, I have a right to know that my daughter's not in any kind of danger. I don't give a damn about your intimidating bodyguard. Get back with me ASAP!"

The last thing I want to do is talk to him while Den's around, so I send a text instead.

I'm fine, Derrick. I was just stretched a bit thin working on a project. It's all good now. I've got coverage for Josi. I'll call you once my project is done.

His reply is lightning fast.

You sounded stressed, Mina. If taking care of Josi is getting too hard, I told you I'm here. You just have to let me in.

Now he wants to swoop in like a hero after the exhausting infant years are over? I don't think so! It's hard not to blast him for his presumption, but I manage to send him a civil reply. *I appreciate your concern, but it's unwarranted. Josi and I are doing very well. Let me see this project through and we'll set up a time for you to come see Josi again.*

As her father this time?

I'll decide when we tell her. You've only spent a few hours here and there with her. A lot more time needs to pass before I feel comfortable telling her anything.

I'm her father, Mina!

You've bailed before. I won't put my daughter through finding out she has a father, then losing him if you decide fatherhood gets too much. Parenting isn't a choice. It's a commitment. I need to know you're here to stay in her life. And time and your actions are the only way I'll know that.

I have rights.

You signed them away.

And I can petition to get them back now that she's two.

My heart ramps with worry. I need to clamp this down fast.

If you're going to go there, you do realize you'll owe me child support back to the day she was born, right? I can pull that trigger at ANY time.

You don't need the money.

As a parent with rights, it'll be your parental duty, by

law. You can't have your cake and eat it too. If you don't want me to go there, you'll follow my lead on when to tell her.

You were the one who called me for help, remember? Makes me question if Sebastian is taking his "parental guardian" role of Josi as seriously as he should.

He has been there for me, and then some. I don't need your help to raise my daughter. Just remember that.

Ready to be done with the conversation, I dial my father's number and force a cheery tone despite the tight knot in my stomach.

"Hey, Dad. I know it's close to lunchtime, but I just wanted to see how Josi did last night. How was the tea party?"

"Josi had the best time with Helena and me. She slept until nine this morning. And by her reaction, I'd say the party was a massive success."

"I can't believe she slept that late!" I say, shocked. "She's always waking me up just as the sun's starting to rise."

"Yep, the little one was exhausted when she went to bed last night. And today it's pancakes for brunch."

"Pancakes? You're spoiling her and now she'll expect them for regular mealtimes at home."

"That's the great thing about being a grandparent, Mina, my sweet. I get to spoil my grandchild rotten, then give her back to her mom."

I laugh, then sigh. "Okay, *Granddad*. Just don't let her have candy at the movies. Share a popcorn with her, but please, *no* soda."

"Shhhh, don't spoil *all* the fun."

"You're impossible." I shake my head, smiling despite the fact he's completely ignoring me. My father spent so much time working while I grew up that I hardly saw him, so it's wonderful to see him spending time with Josi. "Have fun at the movies and thank you for taking her."

"We will. And don't worry. Helena will keep me in line. Mostly."

Hanging up, I roll my eyes. "He's incorrigible."

Den glances my way just before he turns into BLACK Security's parking lot. "Sounds like he's enjoying the perks of being a grandfather."

"Josi's going to be so wired when I get her back."

He shuts off the engine, musing, "Or she'll be completely zonked and barely able to keep her head upright at dinnertime, then go to bed early without a single fuss."

He paints such a vivid picture, I can't help but smile. "Spoken by someone without kiddos, though I like your scenario much better than mine."

"You're correct, I don't have children," Den says in a suddenly serious tone. Nodding toward the handful of cars in the parking lot, he continues, "Everyone's here. Let's not keep them waiting."

He switched from fun banter to all business so quickly, all I can do is nod my agreement and follow him inside.

After my brother rants at Den, laying into him about ignoring his wishes, going off and doing his own damn thing, and generally being an arrogant ass who refuses to listen to orders, I step right up to my brother, my hands on my hips. "I'm just fine. Thanks for asking, Seb!"

When his dark brows pull together in a frown, I shake my head. "You're being over-the-top with this misplaced anger. Den did exactly what was asked of him. He kept an eye on me and kept me safe." Poking him in the chest, I continue, "And speaking of which, *you* have a lot of nerve sending someone to track my every movement. Den took his job seriously. He's a professional. You're the one who invaded my privacy!"

"Actually, it was my idea to send Den," Talia says from the doorway of Seb's office, notepad tucked against her chest. "But why don't we focus on the current issue at hand, because it sounds like we've got one." With a smile, she turns, her auburn hair swaying against her back, as she calls over her shoulder, "Come on. While we're debriefing, there's plenty of coffee, muffins and bagels in the kitchen. Elijah's set up in there as well."

Talia's gentle reminder that we're here because I need their help quickly diffuses my anger. Sighing, I follow her toward their kitchen.

"Did I hear we've got bagels?" Calder comes out of his office, mug in hand, his green gaze already searching for the food.

Den follows behind me, and I notice that he stayed quiet the entire conversation. I don't regret defending him. Not one bit.

After everyone takes a seat at the table with their plates, Den looks at Elijah. "While I explain what brought us here today, please look and see if there are any cameras you can tap into around the hotel's address I sent you this morning. Other than the couple other businesses around that area, nothing else stood out in my quick assessment, but I want to make sure I didn't miss any."

As Den explains yesterday's events, I'm thankful that he leaves out the fact he found me at a bar and had to drive me home. When he starts talking about Travis's findings in the hotel room last night, I jerk my gaze his way. "So he found a drop of blood that was missed?"

Den nods as Talia asks him, "How does he know it wasn't old blood?"

"He doesn't," Den says. "Once Elijah gives me the DNA info on Regan Crawford from our database, I'll send that off to Travis so he can determine if the blood is hers."

Calder looks up from taking a bite of his bagel. "Who covers up a suicide with a cleaner team?"

"I could see a wealthy family doing it to save some

perceived reputation." Seb glances my way, and I know he's thinking about my mom. "But Regan didn't have money until she stole it," he finishes, his expression hardening.

"Mina, can you tell us what you saw when you walked into the hotel room?" Talia leans forward, setting her arms on the table. "Try to think of every detail you can remember."

I describe everything I saw, from the food tray, to Regan in bed not breathing, covered in blood, to the letter opener.

"Based on the way you've described her wounds, it's like she was trying to punish herself." Talia taps her pen on her chin. "Suicide by stabbing is a painful choice for sure. She could've failed in her attempt and passed out before she accomplished her goal. There are much easier ways to go. Statistically with women, it's usually pills." Shaking her head, she continues, "Tell me about the letter opener. Which hand was it close to?"

"It was her right hand, and before you ask, Regan was right-handed."

Writing a few notes, Talia glances up from the notepad. "I know this is hard, Mina, but can you close your eyes and try to see the scene. Does anything else stand out? Anything that doesn't make sense?"

"Other than why someone who stole twenty-three

million dollars from Blake Industries would be in a pay-by-the-hour hotel?"

While Calder grunts his agreement with Seb's comment, I close my eyes and try to see the room again.

My breathing ramps and my heart races at the horrible memory. Den leans closer, his voice calm near my ear. "Separate your emotions, Mina. We still don't have proof yet that it was Regan. Try to think of yourself like an observer."

When I set my hands on the table and take a calming breath, he continues, "Okay, you're standing by the bed now. You said you saw blood on the covers and that she had chest wounds. Was there only blood on her upper chest, neck or face? What about her arms and hands?"

The image of Regan's dead body flashes in my mind's eye. I squeeze my eyes tight and shake my head, not wanting to see it. Inhaling deeply, I flatten my hands on the cool table. "There was blood splatter across her chest and along her neck in a few places. There were only a few drops of blood on her face, but there were more spots on her arm." I pause and tilt my head, recalling how her hands were laying. "Would it matter if her hands were laying palm up on the covers and the letter opener was also pointing upward?"

"Her hands could've fallen palm up," Seb answers. "But if you're going to stab yourself in the chest, it would be far easier to hold the weapon with the heel of your hand toward your chest. Then you'd use your other hand to help give you enough force to drive the knife as deep as it can go. In which case, the knife she used would have the blade facing downward as she withdrew it and let go of it."

"It's possible to hold the knife with the heel of your hand away from your chest and stab yourself," Calder counters. "The knife might not go as deep though."

I gasp and my eyes fly open. "Now I *know* she didn't kill herself."

"You know this how?" Seb says, his attention fully on me.

"There wasn't any blood on her hand next to the letter opener. If she had stabbed herself in the chest, either heel toward her chest or away from it, some blood would've been on her hand or at the very least her wrist and part of her hand, right?" When Seb and Calder nod, I continue, "There wasn't enough blood on either of her hands to have stabbed herself. There were only a few smears."

"Good catch, Mina," Talia says, writing down another note.

Den nods his agreement. "A visual re-walk of the scene is always useful."

"You all might want to see this." Elijah taps on his laptop. "When I put Regan Crawford's name in the system to do a search..." He pauses and cues up a local news station's video report on the main screen in the room.

A dark-haired reporter brushes her hair out of her face as she stands in front of a burned out vehicle, her mic gripped in her hand. "In the early morning, a car barreled into this monument on the edge of Central Park. No one knows if the driver lost control since that wasn't caught on any cameras, but according to witnesses, the car burst into flames upon impact. The driver was the only person found in the badly burned vehicle. Police aren't releasing the person's identity, but they believe it was a woman. They expect to be able to identify her soon."

Seb looks at Elijah. "Are you saying you think that was Regan?"

Elijah nods toward the screen. "The back of the vehicle wasn't as badly burned. I was able to make out the license plate. The license plate is registered to Pamela Boyd Crawford. While we were looking for Regan, I kept a record of family and known friends we thought might help her fly under the radar as well as second homes and property owned by family. Pamela is Regan's mother."

"Her mother died a couple years ago," I say. "If the person in that car turns out to be a woman, Regan didn't have any living female relatives that I'm aware of." I glance Den's way, feeling lightheaded. "Oh God, what if Regan was still alive when I left her in that room?"

Den folds a big hand over my trembling one resting on

the table. "A professional team cleans up loose ends, Mina." He nods toward the video. "If that turns out to be Regan, this car explosion wasn't an accident, but a way to cover up how she really died."

"Who is going to all this trouble to eliminate Regan?" Talia asks while watching the video of the burned out car that Elijah had put on a loop.

Seb stares at the screen for several seconds as well, then turns his blue gaze my way. "Until we can confirm that no one identified you visiting Regan at that hotel, you and Josi will stay with us. After a few days, you can go home, but even then, you'll get a security detail for a while to make sure you're all clear."

"The guy at the desk never even looked up at me when he handed me a key," I say. "Den confirmed that the hotel doesn't have cameras at all. Not even in the parking lot." I look at Elijah. "Can you check out the surrounding businesses to see if I was caught on camera?"

Elijah nods. "I'll scout it out to see if there might be other surveillance that I missed."

"Thanks Elijah. Until then, I'll continue to stay with Den."

"Absolutely not." Seb frowns. "You'll stay with family. I want you and Josi with us."

"Josi's with Dad for at least the weekend, possibly Monday too."

"Adam's *babysitting*?"

"Yep." I nod, enjoying shocking my brother. "And she's having a grand time. For now, she'll be safer and happier there. By the way, Helena is back!" I smile, pretending his scowl hasn't already returned. "You can inform Dad what's going on so he can up security. Hopefully by Monday, I'll be able to pick her up at daycare."

"Until then, *you* will be where I can keep you safe," Seb says.

"It's safest for Mina to stay clear of any known Blake properties, including work, until Elijah can confirm no surveillance puts her at that hotel," Den cuts in, his tone calm and even.

"I disagree with your assessment about the security of my place." My brother turns a narrowed gaze Den's way. "Only family and critical employees know where Talia and I live."

Den leans back in his seat, his arms folded. "*No one* knows where I live."

Seb looks at Talia. When she shakes her head, he grunts. "He gets a check from us. How do we not know where he lives?"

"He gets direct deposit." Talia gives her husband a half-smile. "I assumed we already had it, but apparently I never asked."

Ignoring the tension between the two men, Elijah jumps in. "Since the priority is to make sure there's no proof Mina was at the hotel, I've got the map of the area pulled up on the screen. I've printed copies so we can split the work and eliminate them all quickly. It might take a few of us to cover the whole area to look for any cameras I might've missed in my online sweep."

"I'll get the print outs on my way back from the bathroom." I quickly stand and look at my brother. "Den's place is the most secure location for me right now. I don't want anyone else to get hurt on my account, and I refuse to put your family at risk." Before Seb can debate with me anymore, I turn and walk out of the room.

A couple minutes later, I leave the bathroom and stop at the sound of Talia's phone ringing in her office. *Who calls an office phone on a Saturday?* Thinking it might be important, I walk into her office and hit the speaker button.

"BLACK Security. Talia Blake's phone."

There's a pause on the other end, then a woman says, "Tell Talia that I have important information she'll want to know, that you all will want to know, but first she'll have to help get me moved to another prison."

Whoever this convict is...she's tense, and her voice keeps fading in and out, as if she's looking over her shoulder. "Who is this?"

"Is that you, Mina?" As soon as the woman says my name, I realize who she is.

"Simone?" How is she calling Talia from prison anyway? Do they just let any inmate use a phone whenever they want? Rage fills my body and my hand curls into a fist. "You have a lot of nerve asking for any help! You threatened my brother and Talia's lives. You threatened their baby's life. You killed my mother—" My voice cracks. "You're fucking certifiable!"

"Depends on the perspective, I suppose," she says in a derisive tone. "Your family is going to want to know this information, but I need Talia to use the Blake family influence to get me moved out of this prison first, or I might not live long enough to tell her."

"You deserve whatever karma comes your way, Simone. You're a—"

"I've got this, Mina," Talia cuts me off, her brow furrowed as she walks into her office.

"It's so good to hear your voice, Talia," Simone purrs. "I assumed I'd have to put this request on your voicemail."

Talia hovers her finger over the End button. "There is nothing we need from you, Simone."

"Where's the prisoner? She's not at her assigned job," a man gruffly calls out in the background.

"I don't have a lot of time." Simone lowers her voice, speaking quickly. "I didn't want this call recorded. I don't trust anyone in here. I'm not safe. Get me moved, then I'll tell you. You should know this. It's in your best interest—"

Talia clicks the button, cutting off the call.

"Why would she call you? And how did she?" I can't believe I spoke with the woman responsible for the bomb that killed my mother. Listening to her just now, I can see that Simone is a true psychopath. She's completely self-serving...a narcissist to the core.

"I don't know, but we'll call the warden tomorrow. She should never have been able to make a direct call like that. Calls from prison are usually collect." Wrapping her arm around my shoulders, Talia squeezes me gently. "Are you okay?"

The last thing I needed was to be reminded how my mother died. Having it shoved in my face with that call makes me feel as crazy as that psycho Simone. Why can't I let my mom's memory go? I straighten my spine. "I'm fine." Meeting Talia's concerned green gaze, I nod toward the doorway. "I know Seb means well, but I trust Den. He has my back." I pause and smirk. "He makes sure I carry my own weight. And don't you dare tell my brother this, but it's kind of refreshing for someone to hold me accountable for my own bullshit."

Talia chuckles and silently crosses her heart. "I agree with you on Den. He's an excellent bodyguard and doesn't mince words. Other than Sebastian, he's the only other person I'd want guarding you right now. He lives and breathes his duty to protect. Sebastian knows this. With this investigation into Regan's death, your brother just doesn't like that he can't be in two places at once."

I wrap my arm around her waist and squeeze her back. "I hope he knows how much I appreciate him and all of you for helping. I really did try to deal with this myself." I pause and sigh. "Obviously not very successfully."

Talia shakes her head. "We're family, Mina. Never wait to ask for help. We support each other. And in situations like this, we're pretty dang good at it. For now, let's get back in there and help the guys look for places to scout for cameras." Releasing me, she picks up the map photocopies she laid on the desk and smiles. "I love this wavy hair look on you. It's gorgeous. Come on, let's get back in there. I'm sure you'll be glad to get back to your apartment as fast as possible."

As I follow her, my steps slow a little. *Am I?* I miss Josi like crazy and can't wait to hug her sweet little body once Den thinks it's safe to go back home, but I'm not ready to leave the warm bubble of Den's place. I feel very safe there. With him. The idea of going back home without him around makes me a little sad.

CHAPTER ELEVEN

DEN

"Calder, Elijah, can you give us a minute?"

Once the two guys file out of the kitchen, Sebastian narrows his gaze on me. "My sister thinks she knows what's best. I want you to convince her otherwise."

I take a long sip of my coffee. "So you want me to lie to her."

"Whatever it takes, but I want Mina and Josi with us. She's too vulnerable right now. Too much shit has happened in her life. And now, Regan's murder on the heels of her betrayal just piles on additional stress Mina doesn't need. Make it happen, Den."

I set my coffee mug down. "What exactly are you afraid of? That your sister might actually realize just how capable she is? At some point, you're going to have to let her stumble, maybe even fall, Sebastian. How else is she going to learn how to pick herself up?"

"She's my fucking sister, not yours!" Sebastian barks.

"You're right about that, at least," I say in a droll tone.

"Stop stonewalling me, you damn infuriating Brit!" he grates, his blue gaze laser sharp.

I shrug. "You know I'm right. Make sure Josi's well protected at your father's estate. I'll protect Mina."

As Sebastian gives me a cold stare, Calder says from the doorway, "May we return to the table now, *Dad*? I'm still hungry."

In answer to his business partner's sarcasm, Sebastian hurls a bagel his way. "Get your asses back in here." As the guys enter, he nods to them. "Calder, you and Elijah will scout out the area around the hotel for cameras. Talia and I will talk to the police to confirm with them that the car belonged to Regan's mother. We'll also try to determine if the burned body is Regan's with the DNA sample we have. It should go without saying that, with so much going on, tomorrow will be a workday. Everyone plan to come in the office." Cutting his gaze to me, he continues, "In the meantime, *nothing* better happen to my sister. Not a hair on her head. And you're not leaving here with her until I know your address."

"Understood," I say, nodding to Mina and Talia as they walk in with the map printouts.

When Mina and I walk out to my car a couple hours later, a note had been left under the wiper on the driver's side. I glance around to see if someone is watching, then scan it quickly while Mina gets in the car.

Yes, I know where you work. The tabloids love the Blake family. I will call you later. Unblock me and answer your damn phone. If you don't, I'll show up at your house next. Nice brownstone, by the way. I'm trying to be the friend you obviously think I'm not. But if you're going to blame me, the least you can do is hear me out.

Hugh

Bloody bastard. Crumbling the paper, I unblock the bastard on my phone, open my car door and get in. The fact he came to my place of work is too damn close for comfort. I don't want him anywhere near my home. I'll let him speak his peace and be done.

It's late afternoon before we arrive back at my place, and the moment I open my door, I get a text from Hugh with a place to meet. As Mina walks into the kitchen and asks if I'd like a cup of tea, I text him back that I'll pick the meet place and let him know when and where later. I won't text him until I'm already there. No way am I letting him set a trap for me.

"Is everything all right?" Mina lifts the teakettle as I slip my phone back in my jacket pocket.

"Everything is fine, but I just realized that I need to pick up some food for dinner."

"Oh, okay." Mina sets the kettle down and gives an apologetic smile. "I guess I've been eating all your groceries. Let me get my coat on and I'll go with you."

"That's not necessary. The sky is getting darker by the minute. It's going to rain soon. Stay and enjoy your tea. The market isn't that far." When an uncertain look flickers across her face, I re-button my coat and nod toward the door. "My home is very secure, Mina. You'll be safe here. No one but Sebastian and Talia know where I live."

"It's not that," she begins, then shakes her head.

"Would you like me to call Theo to watch from outside?"

"I know you prefer your privacy, Den. And, Theo might be part of your team, but that's just one more person who'll know where you live. Don't worry about me. I'll call Josi and enjoy some tea while you're gone."

"I'll be back as soon as I can," I say, ready to get this meet with Hugh done and over. I want him gone from my life once and for all.

The sky has turned completely dark by the time I arrive in the East Village. I text Hugh to meet me outside

Village Venue, then park a street down from the club. Double-checking my gun, I tuck it away and walk up the street, keeping an eye out for Hugh.

He's standing in the shadows, leaning against the corner of the building as I approach.

Casually unbuttoning my wool coat, I try to gauge if he has a gun. The way he's pressed against the brick wall, it would be uncomfortable as hell if his weapon is tucked against his back. But his thick jacket could easily hide its bulk.

"I'm here," I grumble. "What do you want?"

Hugh blows on his hands to warm them against the brisk night air, then glances up at me as a light rain starts to fall. "We could've talked inside where it's warm."

I snort and cross my arms as I step between the buildings, but keep my distance against the opposite wall. Folding my hand under my jacket, I grip my gun tucked in its holster. "You've grown soft in your old age." Rain begins to pelt my face, but I ignore it. "I don't plan to be here long."

"Then I'll make this quick." Hugh sighs and folds his arms too. "Seven months ago, someone drugged my drink at a bar. I woke up tied to a chair in an abandoned warehouse where three masked men beat the shite out of me. Several cracked ribs and bones later, I could barely take a breath or see from the blood dripping into my swollen eyes. A fourth man, obviously their leader, steps into the light. It was Edgar Stewart."

I tense, recognizing the name from one of our cases. Edgar's younger brother, Jonathan, was killed in a Tube explosion during a multi-faceted, coordinated terrorist attack throughout the city of London. At the time, Edgar's father was just getting involved in politics. "What did Edgar want?"

Hugh's exhale sounds so tortured, I frown as I wait for him to speak.

"Revenge, Den. It was always about revenge for his brother's death."

"*What* was always about revenge?" I ask, frowning.

"Edgar gloated about how clever he'd been to orchestrate all the deaths. To make them look like the acts of nature, accidents, and gas leaks people thought they were."

My pulse jacks like a bullet train in my ears. It's raining harder now, but despite the cold, my chest feels like it's on fire. "What are you talking about?" I snap, my hand tightening on my gun.

Hugh's gaze meets mine, pain and sympathy swirling in the dark depths. "Zeke's son, my Sarah and our unborn child, and..." he pauses, then continues, "Bren and Enya. That sick fuck was responsible for all of it. He wanted the men from our team to experience the kind of pain he claims he feels every day. The pain of living without family. He said, 'The palace shouldn't have been our first priority that day.'"

"It fucking wasn't!" I roar.

"I know that and you know that, but with multiple terrorist attacks and explosions happening all at once, his perception was very different, especially since Buckingham got locked down so quickly. Remember, his father had just left the palace that day. We were fucked no matter who we got to first."

Indescribable rage fills my heart. "How is the bastard still alive after you learned what he'd done to your family?"

"With my throat punched to hell, I could barely speak, but I tried like hell to fight. The men easily overpowered me, yanking me upright. I couldn't even stand on my own two feet, so the bastards held me in place while Edgar put three bullets in me before they opened the warehouse's sliding door and tossed me in the Thames like a piece of trash."

Hugh pushes off the wall and steps closer. I take a step forward too, gravitating to his unbearable pain, feeling it just as deeply. "The only thing that stopped me from drowning that night and kept me motivated to fucking survive these past months, is that you deserved the truth. I clawed my way back from death itself."

I blink at him. "Does Edgar even know you survived?"

The moment Hugh says, "No one does," a bullet whizzes between us, striking me in the upper arm before hitting the Dumpster behind me.

Hugh and I spring apart, stumbling back to opposing walls deeper in the alley.

Guns drawn, we snarl at each other, "You fucking set me up!"

"I set *you* up?" Hugh's eyes widen in disbelief, then narrow.

"I'm the one with the wound, you lying bastard!"

Our gazes glitter with fury and distrust for several seconds in the darkness, but neither of us is willing to pull the trigger. Instead our attention shifts back to the front of the alley where the shot came from.

After a full minute passes, we nod to each other and default to the teammates we'd been for almost a decade. I point skyward to show him the angle of the shot, which means the shooter has to be on the rooftop to our left across the street. Motioning for Hugh to wait for me to make my way around the building, I mouth that I'll text to let him know when to draw more fire. We've worked together long enough that he knows I need to pinpoint exactly where the shooter is.

When he nods his agreement, I make my way to the back of the alley. Shedding my soaked overcoat to allow better freedom of movement, I grit my teeth as I tie a piece of it's lining around my arm to staunch the flow of blood, then climb through a window and land on a low shelf in the storage room at the back of the club. Loud music thumps down the long dark hall, muffling the sound of my footsteps as I quickly move down a back hall and find the exit on the opposite side of the building, slipping outside in the darkness once more.

An awning at the front of the adjacent building provides shelter from the rain, but also a way to see without being seen. I text Hugh.

Ready.

My eyes widen as the crazy idiot rushes out of the alley in a full run into the pouring rain. Wearing my overcoat with the collar turned up, he succeeds in attracting the shooter's full attention.

Of course the bastard takes his chance. While he pops off a couple of rounds, doing his best to take "me" out, I quickly lift my weapon and fire.

The second the bloke drops out of sight, I tuck my gun away and take off across the street. Shouldering my way past the doorman at the entrance of the building, I ignore his threat that he'll call the police, and scan the small lobby until I see the sign for the stairwell.

Vaulting upstairs, I push the rooftop door open to see a guy about five-ten in a hoodie. The moment he sees the light where I've opened the door, he jams a gun in his jeans, then takes off across the rooftop. I only caught a profile but no discernable features, but I chase after him, knowing my long legs will overrun the short bastard quickly. The last thing I expect when he runs out of roof space, is for him to jump onto the roof's edge and take a crazy leap over to the next building's rooftop.

When he lands and stumbles forward, then catches himself and keeps running, I stand in the rain staring after him, my fists curled in anger. *No fucking way am I risking jumping between buildings.* I might be long-legged, but I'm not superhuman, nor crazy enough to attempt it. He barely made that jump himself.

Turning in disgust, I start to walk away when the toe of my shoe hits something hard on the ground. I pull the handkerchief out of my suit jacket's pocket, then wrap the dry part around the phone. At the sound of sirens in the distance, I quickly tuck it away in my inside pocket before climbing down the fire escape.

After I return to the alley, Hugh is gone. I don't see him anywhere, so I head for my car. Grabbing the first aid kit and my gym bag from the back of my car, I quickly dress my wound, then change into shorts, a t-shirt and a zip-up jacket. Once I pull on my trainers, I use my dry towel to carefully retrieve the phone out of my wet jacket. Of course the shooter has a lock code on his phone, but once the lock code screen disappears, I stare at the screen-shot of my license plate the bloke had apparently put as his lock screen for quick access.

The motherfucker must've tracked me through traffic cams. That's the only way, because I disabled the GPS tracker in my BMW the moment I bought it. At least Mina's safe. I made sure there weren't cameras anywhere near my home, so they couldn't have tracked me there. But where did the shooter get this photo of my plate? I zoom in on the image, then exhale harshly when I recognize the unusual brick color of the edge of a building.

This shot was zoomed in on my car as I sat outside Eastend waiting for Mina. Was the shooter part of the clean-up team tying up loose ends? Or did Hugh, in his determined quest to tell me the truth, lead one of Edgar's men straight to me? It's not like Hugh to not spot a tail.

A text from Hugh comes through on my phone.

Did you get him?

Playing human decoy wasn't smart.

I've cheated death already. It worked, didn't it? So did you get him?

No, but he dropped his phone, which is locked. For now, stay clear. I'm not sure if he followed you to me or not. I'll let you know if I learn anything.

Irritated that I can't get into the shooter's phone, I shut it completely off so no one can remote erase it, then drop it in the passenger seat. With the rain, we'll be lucky if we can get prints off of it.

I text Elijah.

Any camera feeds around the hotel with Mina on

them? If you haven't gone through them all yet, take a break and look at the feeds from quadrant four to see if my car shows up. Check that same quadrant to see if Mina is seen as well.

As I set my phone down, my chest tightens. I want to get home and check on Mina.

CHAPTER TWELVE

DEN

The last thing I expect is to find Mina curled up asleep on my couch. When she doesn't stir as I set the takeaway down on the counter, I survey the room as I walk over to her. The kettle is moved onto a trivet and a spoon is sitting next to the tea she brought with her. Half a cup of tea is left in the mug on my coffee table. It doesn't look like she ate anything though.

I hate that I was gone much longer than I expected, to the point she'd fallen asleep so deeply. Sitting on the couch next to her, I touch her shoulder, anticipating it'll take more to wake her. Instead, she sucks in a scared gasp and swings, punching me in the jaw. "Stay back!" she screams and crab-crawls backward on the couch to get away.

"It's me, Mina," I say, but she's looking at me with wide, fearful eyes that don't really see me at all.

The moment I clasp her hand, she seems to come out of her sleep trance. Confusion flickers in her gaze as she glances down at my shorts and sweat jacket, then toward the dark sky outside. "You went for a morning run? I can't believe I slept all night."

Chuckling, I tuck her wavy hair behind her ear, loving her bedhead hair and appealing lavender and vanilla smell. "No, it's only six in the evening. I brought takeaway for dinner. I hope you like Italian." I pull her to her feet, and as she untangles herself from the throw she's pulled over her, I say, "Though I admit to being surprised to find you asleep, since you slept pretty late this morning."

Mina attempts to fix her hair, looking embarrassed. "I —well, I don't sleep very well."

I frown. "Is this all the time? Were you dreaming like you did last night?'

She exhales and looks away. "Yes."

"Talk to me," I say, touching her chin to pull her gaze back to mine. "Have you always dreamed like this?"

She looks up at me and tears fill her eyes. As they spill down her cheeks, I don't want her to feel like she's so alone. Cupping her face, I brush the tears away with my thumbs. "It's okay, Mina. I'm here."

She nods and takes a deep breath. "I haven't always had these crazy nightmares. At first they were just dreams, but then the last couple of months, they've gotten worse, turning into horror freak shows."

"What do you dream about?"

"My mom." Blinking back a new rush of tears, she continues, "She's always in my dreams. Chasing me down, reaching out, trying to get my attention. And it's a version of my mom all burned up, Den. And then later..." She pauses and shudders. "She literally explodes. It's horrible."

"Have you ever tried visualization techniques?" When she shakes her head, I release her and nod. "Try to do them before you fall asleep. If you can learn to do that, it could help you realize that your dreams are just that. Then you can try to control the outcome instead of feeling pulled along by it."

"I'll try anything at this point. If only you had a suggestion for the real world."

"What do you mean?" My brows pull together. "Are you seeing something upsetting when you're awake too?"

Biting her lip, she nods slowly. "I've seen my mom a few times the last couple of months. Or at least a woman who reminds me of my mom. It's freaky and probably why I have the crazy dreams I do."

I clasp her shoulders, concerned. "Where have you seen this woman who looks like Isabel?"

"Several places I frequent in town."

"I'd like you to write them down so I can check them out."

"For a ghost?" she says, snorting. "I know I sound crazy, Den. You don't have to humor me."

I release her and smile. "Weren't you the one who said how seriously I take my job?"

Mina's amusement fades and she takes a step back. "Yes, I did say that. Thanks for being thorough."

Her demeanor completely changed. *How did I manage to muck up the rapport building between us so quickly?* "We should probably eat before the food gets cold."

Walking away, she glances over her shoulder. "And you can tell me how you ended up changing clothes while on your way to a corner market you never made it to."

Apparently she has no issue calling me out. I follow her into the kitchen. "I bought lasagna and salad."

Lifting a box out of the bag, she shifts her gaze to my attire. "What's up with the new outfit?"

"I got soaked," I say as she hands me my two boxes.

"No umbrella?" Mina locates the plastic forks down in the bag and hands me mine, then sits on the stool, digging into the pasta. "You're the one who told me it was going to rain."

"I don't have long, gorgeous hair to worry about." I sit beside her and take a bite of my lasagna.

A hint of a smile flickers as she jabs her fork into her salad. "What made you decide on take out?"

"I assumed you'd be starving by the time I got back, so I decided to bring something ready to eat to save time."

"That was thoughtful of you." Giving me the side-eye, she takes several bites of her lasagna, before turning to face me. "So what did Hugh have to say?"

Despite my surprise, I keep my expression even and only raise my eyebrows while chewing on a bite of salad.

"Before you left you were irritated and tense. I've only seen you act that way when it came to your friend."

I can't believe she read me that well. *Maybe I'm the one going soft*. Grunting, I shove another forkful of food in my mouth so I don't have to answer her question.

"Did you at least resolve your issues?"

Damn, she's not giving up on this. "He's still an arse," I say, digging into my pasta.

Her laughter fills my heart, making me wish I had something else amusing to say so I can hear it again. Unfortunately, that's not the case. "But because of Hugh's presence, I think it's best for you to stay with Sebastian at this point. You'll be safer with your brother."

"What?" Mina drops her fork into her salad and slides off her seat to stand in front of me. "I'm not going anywhere. I feel very secure here."

"You're going, Mina." My tone is clipped, intended to end the discussion.

She folds her arms, her heart-shaped face settling in stubborn lines. "You'll protect me."

I stand and scowl down at her, hoping my honesty scares some sense into her. "I lost one family. I will not lose another!" I brace for her to throw arguments at me in rapid-fire ammunition fashion, so I'm taken aback when she steps close and wraps her arms around my waist, pressing her head to my chest.

"Then don't push family away. Don't push *me* away," she says softly.

Bloody hell, she's a perfect fit against me. My arms instinctively fold around her petite frame, and the overwhelming urge to protect her rears up, clamping my chest tight. "Mina, this isn't about pushing you away. It's about keeping you safe." My voice is gruff. I know I should set her away, keep a professional distance between us, but after today's attack, our time together has to end.

Sebastian has the resources to keep her fully protected. As much as I like to think I'm the best at what I do, I can't be everywhere at once. Even though I know it's the right thing for her, I don't want to let her go. She's a bright spot in my regimented, soulless life. And after holding her last night and feeling her curves pressed against me, I can't stop myself from selfishly locking her close. Lowering my head, I push my nose to her hair and silently inhale her sweet smell.

One last time.

She sighs against my chest, then turns her head, lifting luminous brown eyes to me. "I don't want to leave, Den."

She's biting her lower lip, waiting for me. Her sexy sweetness loosens the tightness in my chest. I have to know. Tilting her chin, I press my mouth to hers.

Soft. Fuck me, she's so soft. Moaning against my mouth, Mina pushes up on her toes and slides her hands along my back muscles, tugging me closer. Every part of me hardens, and my hands wind into her hair. The supple waves entwine around my fingers and I grunt my pleasure and tug, tilting her head to give me deeper access. I have to feel her yield, my body craving hers to fully submit, to give herself over. When her lips part, deepening our kiss, I clasp the back of her head and twine my tongue with hers, floored at the intense desire rushing through my veins and roaring in my ears.

It's one thing to know the chemistry building between us wasn't my imagination, but another to experience how fucking shockingly real it is. I want to tear her damn clothes off and feel her skin against mine. A feral rumble stirs just below my chest, demanding that I stake my claim. That I take her to bed and taste every delicate curve, then devour her essence over and over until she begs me to drown myself in her and make her fully mine.

Holy shite! I have to stop this. She's my charge. What the hell is wrong with me?

I break our kiss and take a step back. "I'm sorry, Mina. That was a mis—"

"Don't you dare say that was a mistake, Dennet Barasa." She's shaking and the brief look of hurt on her face before she crosses her arms twists my heart. "Noble Brits don't lie."

Do I regret it? Hell no. Was it a bad idea? Yes, because I won't be able to stop wanting her. She's robbing me of my ability to think straight. With her hard stare zeroing on me, I suddenly feel like I'm under a heat lamp. Instead of answering, I quickly unzip my jacket and yank it off, tossing it onto the counter. "I'm your guard, Mina—"

"What happened?" Concern briefly replaces the anger on her face as she reaches for the bandage showing under the edge of my athletic shirt's sleeve. Her brows pull together, anger renewed. "Did Hugh do this to you?"

I pull away. I can't let her touch me again. I don't know if I'll be able to stop the next time. "No, he just wanted to pass along some information."

"He was right." Her gaze latches onto my wound, worry flickering. "Trouble has found you."

I still don't know the source, and until I hear back from Elijah, I can't rule out the clean-up team doing a sweep of any potential witnesses. I just hope Mina isn't visible on any of those video feeds. But right now there are too many unknown variables that could put her at risk. "This is why you're not safe here," I say gruffly, following her gaze to my arm. Grabbing my jacket from the counter, I pick up my gym bag where I'd stashed my wet clothes. The last thing she needs to see is a blood-soaked bullet hole. "I won't discuss it further. You should get some rest. Tomorrow, I'll take you to the office. You'll be safe there until you pick Josi up from church and head to Sebastian's place."

"So that's it?" Mina throws her arms wide, her features scrunched, voice shaking. "You're ditching me like yesterday's newspaper?"

"Mina..." I call after her as she turns and walks up the stairs. She reaches the top, but her only response is to walk into my bedroom and shut the door firmly.

Brilliant bloody job, mate. Exhaling my frustration, I retrieve my ruined suit and bury the clothes under all the rubbish from dinner, then tie the bag up and take it out to the bin in the garage.

When I come back in, I have a text from Elijah.

Yep, there's a shot of your car from that quadrant, but I didn't see Mina at all. Still looking through the extra feeds we found. I'll let you know if we see anything.

Thanks.

I set my phone down and think about the shooter's phone sitting in my car. I hope Elijah can figure out a way to turn it on and try to crack its encryption without allowing the guy the chance to erase it. I need to know who the hell ordered that hit on me.

After I turn off the lights and sit alone in the dark, that's when I finally allow myself to acknowledge the truth about my wife and child's deaths.

Their murders.

My hands begin to shake and I fist them on my thighs. Edgar will pay. I will find a way to insure he feels their pain.

Every last fucking bit.

Gritting my teeth, I shut my eyes tight against the moisture that threatens, then lower the dam around my mind, letting the pain I've bottled up for years flood in.

I miss them both so much. The little things: like listening to Bren read me her poetry and watching Enya's endless energy. The way my wife smiled, how she supported my long work hours just as much as she sometimes over-mothered our daughter. Enya's tittering laughter, and how she saw the world. She was full of wonder and awe, never negative or sad. Not my Enni. She was always smiling. They didn't deserve what happened to them. None of our families did.

I approach the cabinet next to the fireplace and stare at the drawer where I'd put the bracelet Mina returned to me. I can't bring myself to open it and look inside. My chest hurts too much, especially after learning the truth today.

I walk back to the couch and sit down, letting the

darkness fan my misery until it feels as if the room is closing in on me from all sides, crushing my chest.

A sliver of light snakes across the room, then suddenly the whole living room is filled with dim light. Mina had reopened her door, and now the light consumes the space, pushing dark thoughts away and leaving sweet memories intact.

Only love and vengeance remains. Those, I can deal with.

My heart twists as I glance upstairs. Even from a distance, as long as she keeps the door open, Mina's presence chases away my demons. I miss her warmth, her exuberance, our debates, and how she seems to read me so easily. The idea of coming home to this place alone tomorrow leaves me feeling unsettled.

Empty.

My gaze lands on her leftover tea. The one thing I forgot to clean up. Craving the closeness I feel with her, even something as simple as sharing a drink of hers, I grab the mug and down its contents in one big gulp.

That's Earl Grey? Pulling back, I frown my displeasure at the empty mug. *Maybe it's because it's green tea.* I roll my tongue around the strange bitterness in my mouth, then shake my head a couple of times. The taste is just not right. I blink in the darkness for a few seconds. My head feels light, airy. Clearing my throat, I stand and walk over to the tins of tea she brought.

I flip one lid open and inhale the mixture. Then do the same to the other. They smell different, but they both have a similar underlying scent. I lift my gaze to the window and try to focus, but my vision is softer, a bit blurred and my body strangely relaxed.

What the bloody hell? I quickly gulp down three glasses of water in an effort to dilute the strange sensation.

CHAPTER THIRTEEN

MINA

"I can't believe you took away my teas," I say as the elevator dings at the BLACK Security office.

"They didn't taste right." Den takes off his shades and steps into place beside me as I walk toward Sebastian's office. "If there's one thing Brits know, it's good tea. I'll replace your tea with better blends. Who did you say gave them to you?"

"My friend Laura. She left them at the door for me." I stop in the hall and look up at him. "I like my teas just as they were. Perfectly mature, sophisticated, and well-blended."

His voice softens as his gaze locks with mine. "It's for the best, Mina."

"I think I know what tea I like," I say, my back stiffening.

"Not when drinking it might hurt you."

We both know we're no longer talking about tea as we stare at each other. His golden gaze probes my face, his broad-shouldered stance tense, dominant. Standing there in his dark custom suit, crisp white shirt, and silver and black striped tie, he's so handsome my heart aches. I inhale deeply to soak in his appealing aftershave. All I want to do is step closer, press myself against his hard chest, and run my fingers along his clean-shaven face.

Last night I slept fitfully. The tease of his hands in my hair, his hard body folding me close and the pressure of his lips claiming mine played over and over in my mind. I can't believe the infuriating man and his sense of honor left me reeling with want.

As the office buzzes with conversations and general morning routine happening around us, I kind of love that none of Den's co-workers have a clue how much passion lies beneath his cool exterior. And the fact I'm the only one who does, makes me want him even more. Even now, the palpable intensity between us hasn't waned, yet he's determined to pass me off to my brother and pretend it never happened.

"Isn't that the whole point of living, Den? Taking risks on things that could hurt you?"

"When it comes to you?" He starts to lift his hand

toward me, then tucks it into his pants pocket. "The risk is too great."

Are we still talking about what happened between us? Or is this about something else entirely? I want to ask, but his next comment throws me.

"I'm pretty sure there was something laced in your tea. Whatever it was, my mind felt spaced and my muscles relaxed, which wasn't right. Based on the thoughts in my head, I should've been very tense."

Was *he as worked up as I was?* Then it hits me what he's saying and my gaze widens. "Are you saying my tea was drugged?"

He nods. "I think they both were. I'm meeting with Travis later today. He should have the results of the blood sample he found at the hotel and Regan's DNA. I'm going to have him do a chemical break down of your teas. I want to know what's in them."

"There's no way Laura would do that. She didn't even drink all through high school and college."

He frowns. "People can change."

"Not her. She's a gem. Teas are kind of her specialty."

He shrugs. "Someone did this, and we need to find out who. Didn't you say the teas were left at your door? How do you know they were from Laura?"

"Yes, they were definitely from her. I know because each package had a ribbon with a peppermint design on it. Peppermint is an inside joke between us."

"No one else knows about this inside joke?"

"Regan knew," I say, my heart sinking. "But since she's gone, that only leaves Laura."

"Travis can tell us what's in it. Then you can call your friend. If it was unintentional, she should know about the teas she's buying."

Just as I nod my agreement, movement in my periphery draws my attention. My brother is in his doorway, arms crossed. Eyeing Den with a purposeful gaze, he inclines his head, indicating he wants to talk to us.

As Den and I walk into his office, Seb moves behind his desk. Stacking several folders neatly next to his closed laptop, he pushes his chair up. "Talia and I have been summoned to the police station. Since we spent months looking for Regan in the hopes of trying to recover the money stolen from BLAKE Industries, they want to question us about her death."

"Her death?" I ask, my chest tightening. While I've been pretty certain the person in the hotel was Regan, it's still hard to hear it confirmed. "Was that her body in the burning car?"

When Seb nods, Den says, "I should get confirmation from my friend today as to whether or not the blood he found at the hotel matches Regan's."

"For now we have to assume that it does, which means you should continue to protect Mina."

"That's what I want to talk to you about—" Den

pauses as Talia walks into the room from her adjoining office.

"We need to double Joey's security."

Seb steps to her side. "Why do you think she's in danger?"

"I just got off the phone with the warden at the prison," she says, her forehead creased in concern. "He said earlier this week someone attacked Simone. Which is probably why she risked getting caught when she called here asking us to help get her moved."

My brother cups her shoulder, massaging it. "It was probably a well-deserved beating. You know as well as I do that nothing out of Simone's mouth can be trusted. Hanging up on her was the right thing to do. But what does that have to do with our daughter's security?"

Talia clasps his hand, holding him in place. "While getting a follow up exam late yesterday, Simone knocked the doctor out. She used her appointment time to give her enough lead-time to escape. She's in the wind."

Blood rushes to my ears, the sudden anger buzzing so hard I can barely hear. "The woman who killed my mother is now running around free?"

Talia nods solemnly, then looks at Seb. "Until they find her, I don't want Joey out of our sight. We should set a security protocol for the entire family."

"I'll do that. Alert your father too in case she tries to reach out to him," he says. "I'll have Teresa bring Joey to the station while we talk to the police." Looking at Den, he continues, "I'd like you to escort them and meet us at the precinct. Calder can relieve you once he gets back from his breakfast meeting."

"Understood. I need to speak to Elijah before I leave for your place." Den turns to me. "You'll be safe here. I'll be back soon."

My brother waits until Den walks out and Talia goes into her office to retrieve her purse to speak to me. "Den's a seasoned operative, but he'll only stay on top of his game if his head is fully in it. Do you understand?"

I start to speak, but Talia walks back in, so I just nod. There's no point in telling him that Den has already made that decision for me. I'll let Den tell Seb he's bringing me to his place later today.

The BLACK Security office feels suddenly quiet once Sebastian, Talia, and Den leave. Theo is at his computer, typing up a surveillance report. I'm sure Elijah's holed up in his office, and I don't really know the two other guys Den spoke to before he left.

Everyone is busy and I'm stuck here under guard and unable to work, feeling completely useless. There has to be something I can do to help. I wonder what turned up in the camera angle surveillance Elijah compiled around the Eastend hotel.

I knock lightly on Elijah's doorjamb just as he leans back in his chair and slides his hands through his short dark hair. He smiles as he lowers his hands back to his laptop and pulls the screen down, closing it slightly. "Hey, Mina. What's up?"

What's he working on that's so private? I walk into his office and nod toward his laptop. "Did you find anything in any of the surveillance footage around the hotel?"

He shakes his head. "Other than the shot Den asked me to confirm of him sitting in his car, I didn't find any sighting of you or of your car in any of them."

"That's good to know." I exhale in relief, then furrow my brow. "Wait, so there was footage of Den?"

"It's just the shadow of the back of his head." Elijah pushes his laptop back and quickly toggles from the video he was watching to another video clip. "See," he says, pointing to the screen. "You can't tell anything about him. Though...hmmm." He taps the screen, his brow furrowed. "The make of his car and his license plate are visible."

Opening another screen, he clears his throat as he logs in. "You're not seeing this, got it?" When I nod, he types in a search in the DMV database for Den's license plate, then checks that address on the Internet. "The address he used at the DMV is actually for a real estate agency. Gotta give the guy props for keeping his home off the grid."

What are the chances there's a connection to the fact that Den drove us to the office today in his Bentley sports car? At the time I accepted his comment that his car was acting funny last night and that's why we came here today in the special car he kept under a cover in his garage. *What else is he keeping from me?*

"I'm sure Den will be glad to learn you weren't in any of the footage," Elijah says, drawing me out of my musings.

I nod. "I certainly am. Did you find anything else while scrolling through the clips around the hotel?"

He shakes his head. "The clean-up crew must've known exactly where all the cameras were. I didn't see anything out of the ordinary while watching. Certainly nothing that looked like a body was being moved. Unless they snuck her out via another blind spot area."

"Did you find anything else while you were out walking around the hotel looking for more cameras?"

He smirks as he queues up another video. "In my online search of the hotel's records, there's no documentation that anyone stayed in that room the same day you went, so I decided to go in person and inquire about the room rates. The goal was to see if there was also a paper record kept at the desk."

He pulls up a video of someone talking to the guy at the hotel's front desk about room rates. It's not the bookworm guy I saw that day, but I recognize the person's voice asking questions and cut my gaze his way. "Where'd you hide your camera? It's hard to tell from the angle."

Elijah retrieves a pair of sharp looking, black-framed

glasses from his desk drawer. Pushing a button on the inside of the frames, he puts them on my face, then hits a few keys on his keyboard. In my periphery, his handsome face pops up on the computer screen. The moment I look at the screen, I see myself in the glasses and smirk. "I don't look half bad in these. I'll bet they can really come in handy."

He nods. "What's nice is they have built-in memory chips along each side, so live is possible, but not necessary. Recording can happen inside the glasses and be downloaded later."

"Who knew BLACK Security had such great spy stuff. While you were at the hotel, did you find a paper register?"

When he shakes his head, I sigh and absently push the glasses up into my hair while his video of the hotel's front desk keeps playing over and over in my head. "Would you mind letting me see the clip you took again?" He queues it up, and after a couple minutes, I point to the screen. "Can you zoom in on that spiral book on the counter? The one to the right that says, 'Guest Comments'?"

When Elijah pauses the video and enhances the page, I point to the screen. "Look, see there. That's the date I met Regan and her room number. And that's absolutely her handwriting where is says: Clean room, very private."

He stares at her signature scrawl. "That doesn't say Regan Crawford."

"Knowing people were trying to find her, of course she signed in under another name, hence the name..." I squint once more. "Elisabeth Vivus."

"That last name sounds like a female body part," Elijah says, snorting.

I roll my eyes and shake my head. "Seriously? Are all men perpetually twelve?"

"Come on." He gestures to the screen. "Using a name like that in a pay-by-the-hour hotel is just asking for attention."

"You're right," I say, rubbing my forehead in frustration. "It doesn't make sense for someone determined to stay under the radar to sign in at all."

"So why did she?"

"I honestly have no idea."

He jots down the name, then starts switching letters around, trying to make other words out of it. Underlining Elisabeth Vivus, he sets the pen down, then nods to the cell phone on his desk. "After I figure out how to safely get into this phone, I'll try and see if I can make sense of her fake name. It could be that she meant it exactly how it sounds, like a porn star."

Sighing that I'll never know what Regan wanted to say to me, I glance at the phone. "I thought you could crack anything. Why is that particular phone such a challenge?"

"Since I have to crack it without turning it on."

"Huh? Um, it's electronic. How are you expected to do that?"

Elijah laughs. "Exactly. The issue is...if I power it up, the second I break the code to get in it, I won't have time to shut off the data being sent/retrieved, since it'll instantly connect to the closest cell tower. It's feasible that the guy who owns it could remote erase it before I can get to the data."

"Ah, sounds like you need a mommy closet."

He gives me the side-eye. "What's a mommy closet?"

"You know, that one safe space that your kid can't find you. They keep looking, but you've hidden yourself so well, they can't see you. My mommy closet is behind the tall clothes in the guest bedroom closet. Now I only use it when we're playing hide and seek. She *never* finds me. Ha! But when Josi was way beyond the age that she should be sleeping through the night, I would sometimes go in there for some peace and quiet. The clothes muffled the sounds of her crying to be picked back up the moment I put her to bed. If I couldn't hear, it was easier to resist the urge to give in. That blissful quiet time saved my sanity and finally helped my daughter fall into the sleeping rhythm she needed."

"Mina, you're brilliant!" Elijah barks out a laugh, his

eyes lighting up. "Your mommy closet is the equivalent of a Faraday cage."

"What's a Faraday cage?"

He stands and grabs a couple of cords, then picks up another laptop on the desk behind him. "A faraday cage is a grounded metal framework that conducts electricity, creating a shielding effect that blocks outside electrical interference. And do you know where we get absolutely no cell or Wi-Fi reception?"

I snap my fingers. "The service elevator, right? The couple of times I had to use it, my phone didn't work in there."

Grinning, Elijah picks up the phone. "I'm off to crack this baby open." Before he walks away, he lifts his chin toward me. "Keep this up and you'll be a BLACK Security team member in no time."

With Elijah off working on his phone project, I sigh. Who knows how long that's going to take. At least while he discussed video clips with me, I was distracted.

But now that he's not, I cut my gaze back to the doorway, then sit at his desk and try to find the video he was looking at when I walked in. Instead, I end up at a folder named *Mina's Walks*.

I click the folder to find five video surveillance clips pulled from various sources that show me running errands and shopping around the city. When I see the labels of the video locations, I realize every place was one I had mentioned to Den. Elijah was probably checking these at his request.

Two of the files are flagged with a red dot and one with a blue dot. *What do the colored dots mean?*

I watch the two red-dotted videos. In both, a woman with blond hair and wearing sunglasses is in the background. My heart jerks with relief to know I wasn't crazy! I stop each one, zooming in on the stranger's face. She looks so much like my mother that my stomach ties into knots. I click open the third video. It's a dreary day and the same woman is wearing regular glasses. Now that I can see the shape of her eyes and the thicker sunglasses aren't obscuring the bridge of her nose, I know she isn't my mom. She must live in the area and happened to be around the same time. At least I wasn't going nutty. At a glance, she does really favor my mom. It's amazing the rationalization the mind can manufacture.

Glad to know my sanity is mostly intact, I start to shut out of the last video when the familiar colorful store sign of Tara's Trinkets & Teas in the background snags my attention. Seeing proof that I've walked past the place where Laura works at least a half dozen times and never stopped in to say "Hi" ratchets my guilt, especially considering she brought tea by for me twice. I've really been a crappy friend. Maybe I wasn't as deserving of Regan's loyalty as I thought.

With that depressing thought, I close the videos and the folder, then shut Elijah's laptop.

The last thing I need is time on my hands to think about the fact Regan is gone...and someone murdered her. Everyone else might need Den's friend to prove the DNA match from the blood in the hotel, but as far as I'm concerned, her handwriting in that book proves it was Regan. A part of me had hoped that I was wrong, and Den's first impression—that I was wasted that day—was right. Now that I know the truth, it would be easier to accept I'd somehow manufactured the whole scenario in that hotel room in my head than to have to acknowledge my friend was murdered. Even now I can't explain why I got so wasted off a half glass of wine that day.

Then again, considering Den's comments about my tea, it's possible Laura might have a clue. There's no better time than the present to make up for being a crappy friend, and at the same time I can ask her about the tea.

I stand, intending to head out, then pause and bite my lower lip. Sebastian and Den will be furious if I go anywhere without back up, even though Elijah couldn't find any proof of me near the hotel. But, so neither of them blow a gasket, I'll ask Theo to keep an eye on me.

WITH THOUGHTS of Regan tumbling around in the back

of my mind, my steps are determined as I walk along my regular errands' route. I've lost one friend. I don't want to lose another, certainly not because I've been so wrapped up in dealing with my own issues. It has been at least a week since I came this way, and I actually miss the routineness of it.

The crowd waiting for the light to change tightens around me, and I'm bumped on my right by a man in dark dreads with a guitar case, and then on my left by a woman in a pixie cut, tats, and round, wire-rimmed glasses. "Sorry, lovely," she says, her nose ring shining in the light as she glances down at me. I nod my acceptance and start to slide a hand through my hair when my fingers snag on Elijah's glasses. Oops, I can't believe I forgot to take them off. Putting them in my purse, I quickly glance around, until I spot Theo leaning against the building no more than twenty feet away.

If I didn't know better, I'd think he was just a bear of a man waiting for his wife to finish up inside one of the shops. With his hands jammed in jeans' pockets, his jacket zipped up and his baseball cap's bill curled just right, the guy's got the bored-husband-ready-to-go-watch-sports face down pat. Thing is, those guys who wait for their wives are special unicorns. Theo's going to make someone a very good husband one day.

Trying to picture the type of woman it would take to make Theo wait outside for her while she shops, I follow the crowd across the street, then pull open the door to Tara's Trinkets & Teas and walk inside the crowded store.

I spy Laura at the register helping a customer. Post cards, stationary, greeting cards, figurines, picture frames, trinket boxes, papers, pens, and specialty gift boxes fill every corner of the store, while the spicy scent of autumn hangs in the air. Is that a candle or a new tea blend? It sure does smell good.

It looks like business is booming. That makes me happy for Laura. She's the one who convinced Tara to add the "tea" element to her store. Now the entire back wall is covered with select teas, specially designed tins, and various teapots from glass to cast iron. I don't think Tara would've had the courage to expand her business without Laura's encouragement and creativity. And the tea element...it sure does add a homey stick-around-for-a-while feel to the store.

With her hair worn in gorgeous shoulder-length black ringlets with golden highlights, creamy light brown skin and a ready smile, Laura has always been classically beautiful. But now that she's in her element ringing up customers while also encouraging them to attend an upcoming blend-your-own-tea party, she's practically glowing.

I spin the cardholder rack and my heart twists a little as my gaze lands on the placard behind the register: Owner - Tara Combs, Manager - Laura Eller. *How did I not know this?* While I'm glad to see Tara recognizes just how awesome Laura is, I feel horrible that I've been so out of touch I didn't know about my best friend's promotion.

Last I heard, she'd proposed the tea idea to Tara and the owner loved it. Laura's smart, business savvy, and very hard working. She deserves all the kudos. The last thing I want to do is throw any kind of negativity on what she's building here with Tara by questioning the tea I was given. And honestly, for all I know, Den's taste buds could be way off.

"Mina!" Laura calls when she glances up and notices me. Coming around the counter, she weaves her way through display tables and past customers to wrap me in a warm hug. "Welcome to the new digs."

"Congratulations on your promotion. You totally deserve it!" I hug her tight and pull back, chuckling. "And you smell like peppermint."

Laura laughs and folds her hands around mine. "I was working on perfecting the Christmas tea blends earlier. Peppermint kind of lingers on you."

"Just only for *all* our lives." We share a laugh and I smile. "Seriously though, I'm super proud of you and what you've accomplished here. Please tell me you'll have time in your schedule next week for me to take you out for a proper congratulations dinner?"

Laura nods. "I'll have to check the store schedule and

text you, but I'd absolutely love to catch up. I'm so happy to see you looking well. I've missed your face so much."

"The same, girl. Truly." Glancing around, I notice a line forming at the register, while her other employees are too busy helping customers to notice. I feel bad for taking up her time, so I squeeze her hands once more. "I just wanted to stop by and ask about dinner. You've been such a great friend, being patient waiting for me to come out of my funk. Thank you for checking on me and for dropping off the teas to cheer me up."

"What teas?" she says, her brow puckering slightly.

"Laura," a girl in her early twenties with wide eyes and a pixie haircut says, "This customer is asking about the autumn blend and I need to ring some people up. Can you take over?"

My stomach churns that Laura seems confused. When she turns back to me, I say quickly, "You know, the teas you left at my door."

"I didn't drop off any teas." She shakes her head. "I mean, I planned to, but since I didn't know exactly what you'd like, I thought I'd wait until you felt better."

"Ah, no worries. My sister-in-law must've left them. I know you're busy. Go help your customers. I'll probably check out the teas myself before I head out. Don't forget to text me after you look at your schedule."

"The new autumn blend is divine." She lifts her cute, freckled nose in the air, sniffing as she backs away. "That's what you're smelling. I can make it for you with a green tea instead of black, if you like."

"Go," I say, shooing her. She grins and kisses the air twice before heading for the tea section to help the waiting customer.

I tried not to let how freaked out I was show when Laura said she wasn't responsible for the teas I received, but honestly, I can't breathe. When I think back on it now, I never said, "Thank you for the teas" in my texts to her. I just thanked her for thinking of me. She had no idea I was referring to the teas. And I've been drinking those blends from some stranger non-stop for a couple of months! My lungs feel like they're collapsing. I need some air. Turning to head out of the store, I run right into a woman standing close to the card rack.

"Excuse me—" I stare at the familiar face. She's the same blonde who starred in those clips Elijah captured. I'm on-the-edge already, and the fact this woman is in the exact same store at the same time I am, can't be brushed off as coincidence a *fourth* time.

"Who are you and why are you following me?" I demand.

"Keep your voice down, Mina," the woman says in a low tone that's entirely my mother's voice.

CHAPTER FOURTEEN

MINA

As I gape at her and whisper, "Mom?" the woman angles herself slightly away and quickly turns the card rack.

Looking at the cards, she hisses in a low voice, "I know it's hard to believe, but you need to at least pretend to look at the cards while we talk."

My face pales and I jerk my gaze back to Laura to see she's still talking to the lady about tea. Raising a shaky hand, I pull a card from the rack. It flops open in my palm, but I don't see what it says at all. "What happened? How is this possible?"

"It's fairly obvious, Mina dear. I faked my own death."

"And changed your face too," I snap, my stomach churning as I return the card and pick a new one. Fighting back tears for all the pain and angst I've gone through since she died in that explosion, and then thinking I was losing my mind seeing a woman who seemed so much like my mom, my hand clamps closed around the card, creasing it. "You left us!" I say on an angry whisper. "Wh—why did you do that?"

"Of course I changed my face. I'm supposed to be dead." Amending her curt tone, she sighs heavily. "As for why I did it, my past sins would eventually catch up with me. It was just a matter of time. And I knew he would always hold it over me. When I discovered an opportunity, I took it."

"You're talking about Seb." I shake my head, embarrassed to call her my mom. "How could you do that to him? And then his poor mother got caught in the crossfire?" I cast a quick glance her way, needing to see her reaction.

"I see Sebastian ratted me out the moment I was in the ground," she says, her mouth pressing together like she just tasted a lemon. "I'll bet he couldn't *wait* to tell your father."

Underneath her bitterness, she sounds tense, but she keeps her gaze averted. It seems she cares more about what my father might think than what I do after learning what she did all those years ago. I return my gaze to the card in my hand and smooth it out. "Sebastian is a man of honor. Dad still doesn't know and he never will. What possessed you to send a hit man after a teenage boy?"

"I was protecting my children. You, Damien, and Gavin were the Blake legacy. Not some bastard child Adam fathered before he married me. You're a mother now, Mina. You should understand the lengths a mother will go to protect her children."

Not like this. Not at all! I'm speechless. All I can do is stand there, frozen in place while my mind races with questions. We saw her get in that limo. We buried a body. "Who burned in that limo?"

"It was just a cadaver, Mina."

When my eyes widen in disbelief, she frowns, then glances around to make sure no one is looking at us. "Instead of judging me, you should consider the fact that, by getting in their limo, technically I saved Talia and Sebastian's lives that day."

"But why—" Clamping my eyes closed for a second, I refuse to let her see how upset she's making me. "You know what...I don't want to know about the past. Why come out of the shadows now? Why have you been following me for weeks?"

"You're my daughter. I miss you. I've been waiting for the right time to approach you. I understand I might not be able to be your 'mother,' in public, but maybe I can be a close friend? Someone you met and clicked with? We can meet for lunches, maybe go to the movies together. Don't worry, I'll dye my hair to a dark shade before we're seen together. No one will ever have to know."

"*I* will know!" I snap under my breath.

She sighs beside me. "You're in shock. You'll come around once you think about it. I want to see my granddaughter."

Not going to happen. "How have you been living all this time?"

"Regan." Her low chuckle grates my ears like a dentist's drill. "It's unfortunate she got caught and had to go on the run, but she always was a social climber."

Regan must've shared some of the money she stole from Blake Industries. That explains how my mom could afford expensive plastic surgery, but not why my friend wanted to meet in a crappy hotel. This woman with a different face is saying things I can't reconcile with my mom. Where did Isabel Blake go? It's like my mother died twice. I blink back emotional tears. "Why did Regan help you?"

"Regan was always about helping herself first." Mom shrugs, then waves her hand dismissively. "I saw her name mentioned on the news today. Something about a burning car found at the park?" Her lips twist. "Seems she got what she deserved in the end."

I can't believe my mother orchestrated her own death, let her entire family mourn, and now she thinks she can waltz back into my life, and not only will I accept her, but I'll keep her secret too? I press my lips together and shove the card back in the rack. "I can't do this."

My mom tries to grab my arm, but I dodge her grasp and bolt out the door. The moment I'm on the sidewalk, I take off in a fast run.

The worried look on Theo's face as he races across the street to be by my side makes me feel bad, but also relieved. As long as he's with me, my mother won't attempt to continue our conversation. Thankful I wore jeans and comfortable low-cut boots today, I slow my stride to a regular walking pace and give him an appreciative smile. "You sure are fast."

"Are you alright?" His eyebrows pull together under his baseball cap, his gaze scanning the crowd. "You were booking it like you were being chased."

"Everything is fine, Theo." I clench my purse's strap to keep my hands from shaking. First, I find out some stranger has left teas—potentially laced with God knows what—for me to consume, and now my dead mother isn't really dead. And, oh yeah, she and Regan schemed together to solidify that lie.

More than a bit paranoid, I glance around to make sure no one appears to be watching me. It takes everything inside me not to look back to see if my mom's following us. If she knows what's good for her, she'll keep her distance. "I'm just ready to go back to the office now."

CHAPTER FIFTEEN

MINA

"Why do you carry a phone if you're not going to look at your messages?"

Den's standing just outside the elevator at BLACK Security, a deep scowl on his face.

"I had it on silent mode." I tilt my chin so I can see his angry gaze. "I was in a store and didn't want it going off."

"What were you thinking leaving here without me? Now's not the time to go gallivanting around."

"Weeeell, then. Looks like it's back to paperwork for me." Theo shoves his hands in his coat pockets and walks away, leaving me to Den's annoyance.

"I'm waiting for an answer, Mina."

He hasn't moved, nor has the frown on his face.

"Then you'll be waiting awhile," I say and stroll around him, heading for my brother's office.

Den's right behind me, his muscular build and six-five height rumbling the floor under my feet as he follows me into Seb's office. Once he shuts the door, brackets form around his mouth while he folds his arms and waits for me to answer.

"And as I recall, you planned to hand my security off to my brother. You no longer have to worry about me. I'll just wait here for Seb."

"Sebastian and Talia are still at the police station, giving the police all their documentation on potential leads as to who might've killed Regan. After what she did to Blake Industries, she's bound to have a few skeletons in her closet." He unfolds his arms and sighs. "Waiting for Sebastian is a moot point. I'm your security."

"What?" I blink my surprise, my heart racing "What made you change your mind?"

"With Simone on the loose, your brother has enough to worry about," he says, rubbing the back of his neck. "I'll continue your security until she's back in prison. It's just a matter of time before they find her."

My heart sinks a little that his decision to remain my guard had nothing to do with us, but before I can say anything, he continues, "Elijah told me that he couldn't find any clips of you anywhere near the hotel, so we'll pick Josi up after the church event, then head over to your place—"

"No," I say quickly, shaking my head. The last thing I

want is to bring my child home right now. Now that she's made contact, I know my mother will show up on my doorstep the moment I'm alone. "I'm going to ask my father and Helena to look after her for a couple more days." I need some time to figure out how I'm going to tell my mother she has to stay dead. For all our sakes. But I can't tell Den about her. I can't tell anyone. It's bad enough what she did to Sebastian in the past, which died with her, but this revelation could implode our family.

"What's going on?" Den steps close and rests his hands on my shoulders. "Elijah said you're in the clear. Your place should be safe for you and Josi."

Even the thick sweater I'm wearing can't keep his warmth from spreading through to my skin. It's hard not to wrap my arms around him. All I want to do is inhale his masculine scent and lean into his strength, but I take a deep breath and straighten my spine. "I know you wanted me to wait, but I needed to know. I went to see Laura."

"What did she say about the teas she left you?"

"That's just it. She didn't leave them." When he frowns, I sigh. "For all you know, Regan could've dropped off those teas."

"Or someone else knew about the peppermint connection, and they used that information so you'd trust who the tea was from."

"If it was Regan, I have no idea why she would've done that. And if it was someone else, I'm a bit freaked.

Who was it, and *what* have I been drinking all this time? Did you give my tea samples to your friend?"

"I went to see him after Calder showed up at the police station and relieved me. Travis will get back with us later today."

Sebastian and Talia walk in, pausing our conversation.

"I'm glad you're here," Seb says to Den. "Did you get the lab results on the blood your friend uncovered in the hotel?"

Den walks over and hands him a piece of paper from his suit's coat pocket. "It appears to be Regan's, but as you know, blood itself isn't enough to prove she was killed there. For all we know Regan could've been in that room before and the blood is there for an entirely different reason."

"The fake name and room number written in their customer comment book proves she was there. I'm sure they erased her booking in the computer, but I'm so glad I recognized her handwriting."

Talia looks at me, auburn eyebrows raised. "Sharp eye, Mina. You're right. The on-line records showed no one had booked the room for that day."

"Elijah caught a clip of it when he went to the hotel. I just happened to catch it while watching the playback. By the way, the name she signed in the book sounded a bit um...yonic. He wondered if she was just being ironic with that choice or if it was some kind of anagram."

"Yonic, huh?" Talia says. "That'll definitely get your attention. Well, two heads are better than one. I'm going to call Elijah now to see if it was meant to be figured out."

"If you need any help deciphering, I'm happy to take a look," Seb says as she walks toward the connecting door to her office.

Pausing at the open doorway, she turns back to catch his smirk. "I've got it covered, Mr. Nosy Pants. Don't forget, the police won't take into account that correlation doesn't mean causation."

"What did she mean by that?" I ask.

Seb sighs and nods. "She's saying that even though the evidence we have so far places Regan in a dangerous scenario in that hotel just hours before her body ended up in a burning car, we're not going to share that part with the police."

I gape at him. "Why not?"

"We don't know for sure if she was dead when you saw her, Mina. To Den's point, we can't assume that's where she died."

"It's where she was stabbed many times and lost a *lot* of blood," I say, flinging my arms wide in frustration. "My friend was murdered. No matter her sins, she deserves justice."

Seb walks up and places firm hands on my shoulders. "You're the only witness who can place her there. You're the last person to have contact with her, the last one she called. As far as we can determine, she's had no contact with any other family, and with no suspects—of which the police have none right now—by sharing what we know, we'd be giving them one. *You*. Until we know more, I don't want to do anything that could help them implicate my sister in her murder."

"I didn't think of it that way." I swallow and look at Den, who nods his agreement of Seb's assessment. "I understand what you mean."

I know for a fact that I'm not the only one who has seen Regan since she went on the run. Mom had to have contacted her at least once for Regan to give her some of the money she took. Which begs the question, why would Regan help my mom? It's one thing to try to get in her good graces like she always did, but another thing entirely to share stolen money with her. Did my mom figure out what she was doing and blackmail her for a cut? And what's really bugging me is: how did my mother fake her own death? She's not strong enough to lift a dead body. And where did she hide it? In the trunk of that limo at Seb and Talia's wedding rehearsal? To do all that, she had to have had help.

We saw her getting into the vehicle right before it pulled away from the curb. Footage around the church proved that. But before the car got very far, it blew up. Holy shit, it just occurred to me: did she actually cause the explosion and not Simone? But how did she get out without us seeing her? Regan wasn't included in the wedding party that day, so I guess she could've helped prior to the event, but my mom was alone in the car. Wait, the limo driver was there too. He had easy access to the vehicle. Is it possible he helped?

"Earth to Mina." Seb waves his hand in front of my face. "Theo mentioned that you raced out of a store earlier today. Is everything okay?"

Pulled out of my chaotic thoughts, I blink at him. "Sorry, yes. I was at Laura's store. She's been promoted to manager there. I was just in a hurry to get back."

He shakes his head, his mouth quirking. "You know you could've had a driver take you straight there instead of walking several blocks."

"I wanted to walk. It felt good to get back to my old routine for a little bit. Speaking of drivers, whatever happened to the limo driver that you saved from that explosion? I know he survived and was in the hospital for a long time. Is he all healed now?"

Sebastian shakes his head, his mouth turning downward. "He recently died, due to an unexpected complication after a successful surgery. It was a sad outcome, considering every indication was that he would make a full recovery after months and months of surgeries and rehab." He pauses and holds my gaze, frowning slightly. "What made you think of him?"

I can't believe the man died after all that. I glance at

Den, then back to Seb. They're looking at me with curious gazes, making my heart race. I want to say something about Mom, but I can't. Ugh, my stomach is churning. "It's just that...since the explosion, I haven't felt comfortable using a driver, not for my own personal use anyway."

My brother gently clasps my shoulders and looks down at me. "You know that Simone was responsible for all of that. She's taken enough away from us, Mina. Don't let her take away your peace. Live your life."

"Unfortunately, she's out there again," I say, grimacing. Before he can respond, I put my hand up and continue in a calm tone, "Which is why Josi's staying where she is for now and Den will continue to watch over me."

"Simone will be caught and returned to prison." Seb speaks with certainty even as his worried gaze scans my face.

"I know you'll do what you can to help make sure that happens."

"We'll use every resource until she's caught. I wish you'd agree to come stay with us."

I appreciate that he's not commanding me this time, so I give him a confident smile and gesture to the doorway where we can see Teresa taking Joey, with her mop of adorable red hair, into the office to see her mom. "You need to focus your energy on protecting your family. Den will keep me safe. Truly."

When Seb sighs his resignation, I shift my gaze to Den. "Once I confirm with Dad that he's okay to keep Josi for a bit longer, we'll have to stop by my apartment and get some more things for her before we pick her up from church. I want to spend some time with my little girl, getting lots of hugs in, before I take her to my father's."

CHAPTER SIXTEEN

MINA

Den is standing just behind me as I wait for Josi to run up to me just outside her Sunday school classroom. She looks so grown up with her blond curls bouncing around her ears, and her green eyes sparkling with exuberance, but it's the way her whole face lights up when she sees me that's worth every bit of sacrifice I have made, and will make, all her life. That part, I do fully understand what my mother means. There's nothing like the protective nature a mother has for her child.

"Mama!" she squeals and barrels into my waiting arms.

Picking her up, I stand and hug her close, whispering in her ear, "I've missed you so much, Josi-Bean."

As I walk her out of the building, her little arms squeeze my neck tight, then she holds my face and smacks wet kisses on my cheek several times. "I've missed you sooooooo much, Mama."

I set her down on the sidewalk outside, then squat to her level as other parents and kids stream past, heading to their cars. "I hear you're having a lot of fun at Granddad's house." Tickling her belly, I continue, "Just so you know, my father was too busy growing the family business to do tea parties with me, so count yourself lucky that he's doing them with you now, young lady."

Josi grabs my fingers and tries to take a breath between giggles but fails, gurgling through her laughter instead. Her predicament makes me snicker and I finally stop the sweet torture. I've just missed hearing her giggles so much.

I realize she's gone quiet because she's staring up at Den with wide questioning eyes. "Josi, do you remember Den?" I say as I stand and gesture toward him standing there, looking handsome and intimidating to anyone who might dare to get too close. "Den used to work for your Granddad, but now he works for Uncle Seb's company. He helps keep a watchful eye on your cousin Joey and Aunt Talia. He's helping out today and taking us for a ride. Isn't that great?"

Josi gives him the side-eye, then tries to hide behind me, saying in a loud-whisper, "He's so big, Mama."

Before I can answer, Den says, "Do you want to see why I can do my job so well?" He smiles and holds his hand out, his tone understanding and gentle. "Let me show you what it's like."

Unsure, Josi looks at me. I smile and squeeze her hand. "Let him show you, Josi-Bean."

As soon as Josi nods, Den quickly hoists her up onto his shoulders. Josi squeaks and grabs hold of his ears, yanking on them like a horse's reins.

To his credit, Den doesn't wince. He calmly tells her to hold out her hands and take his. When she does as he asks, she smiles and kicks her little legs in delight.

"You see, Josi...to be good at my job, I have to be tall. Look how much more I can see up here? Up on my shoulders, you're even taller than me. I'll bet you can see all the way to the other side of the playground back there, can't you?"

When she nods with avid enthusiasm, he starts walking down the sidewalk. "Tell me what else you see?"

"Slides, swings and spin, spin, spin-y things. In red, yellow, blue, purple, green!" When she looks down at me, her eyes fill with excitement. "Tiny Mama," Giggling, she releases one of Den's hands to wave her fingers for mine. "Up, Mama."

Laughing, I pat her leg. "I'm pretty sure I won't fit on Den's shoulders, but from that view, I know you can see many beautiful things."

As she nods vigorously, Den glances my way and says quietly, "So many beautiful things."

It's dark by the time Den and I return to his home. He insisted that we take Josi out for dinner before we dropped her off at my father's, which made me truly appreciate his thoughtfulness on a whole other level. It's like he somehow knew Josi needed more time. Nothing was cuter than seeing my daughter tug on Den's pant leg to get his attention while he talked to my father, except watching him bend down to her level so she could whisper in his ear.

My Dad's look of surprise when my little girl insisted on giving Den a hug goodbye while I hugged Helena before we left, made me smile. Having this bit of normalcy among the chaos that has been my life the last few days was exactly what I needed, not only to reconnect with my daughter, but also to distract me from having to think about my mother. I don't know what I'm going to do on that front.

Den sets the duffle I packed with a couple more sets of clothes down on his coffee table, pulling me out of my musings. Now that I'm alone with him, I hate that all I can think about is my mom. I don't want her consuming my every thought; the guilt of knowing, but not being able to share, is tearing me up inside. A part of me wants to tell Den, but will he keep it to himself? I just don't know what to do.

"Thank you for being so wonderful to Josi today and taking the extra time for dinner. It helped put my mind at ease to see how well she's doing with all the changes."

"Distracting Josi was my pleasure. Every child should feel safe. The extra time to reassure her that the most important person in her life isn't going anywhere felt right. Keeping some routines are important. Speaking of which..." He leans over and unzips the side pocket on my duffle. My heart jerks as he retrieves my notepad. I know I didn't put it in there. He must've slipped it into the bag while I was in my bedroom making sure I had everything.

As he flips through several pages of drawings: Josi licking an ice cream cone, a woman walking and her umbrella turned inside out against the wind, children playing in a fountain, an old man sitting alone on a park bench, leaves swirling all around him, an old dog licking his equally old owner's face...my face flames with embarrassed heat. I curl my fingers by my sides so I don't yank the pad out of his hands the way I want to. Instead, I force myself to wait for him to say something.

"These are excellent. Gallery worthy." Den's golden gaze lifts to mine, his brow furrowed. "The last drawing was dated a couple months ago. Why have you stopped creating your art?"

"Art? They're just sketches." Snorting, I take the notepad and close it. "It helps me decompress, but ever since my sleep patterns turned more erratic, I haven't been able to focus enough to be inspired."

"I recognize talent when I see it, Mina. Don't ever discount yours." He nods toward the wall behind me and I turn to stare up at the gorgeous painting. "That's my mother's. Her paintings sold out wherever she showed. Of all her work, this one was my favorite. When she passed, I donated the rest of her collection to be auctioned off to various charities, but this one...I couldn't bring myself to part with it. It comes with me wherever I go."

"Why this one?" I ask, stepping closer to admire his mother's skill. Every blade of grass, every intricate curve of a leaf, every bend and sway of each tree flows into the whimsical fog hovering over the land. The expertly crafted scene draws you deep into its peaceful, lush world, convincing you that true magic exists underneath.

"The art world said my mom had superior talent for the fanciful." His gaze sliding over the painting, Den folds his arms, his muscles evident even in his tailored suit. "Her talent was indisputable. My father supported her from the moment she picked up a brush. And while I invested in the gallery where she had her third showing—that was the beginning of a lucrative business in real estate for me—it wasn't until I saw this one piece of art that I finally understood what all the fuss was about. The imagery makes a convincing argument that there's more to this life than one plane."

"Exactly! Her painting gives the impression there's something special hidden underneath." Gesturing toward the painting, I continue, "All you have to do is wait for the fog to lift."

He chuckles, amusement dancing in his gaze. "Are you saying she left everyone hanging on purpose?"

I nod, folding my notebook against my chest. "Yep, in a perpetual state of hope."

Den looks down at the book in my hands. "Like the emotions you convey in your art?"

Other than my mother, no one else knows about my drawings. I never thought of them as art. They were scenes from my day, rambling thoughts. My mind's eye, come to life. But for some reason, I don't mind that Den knows about them. I mentally flip through all the images I've drawn over the years and smile. He's right. I captured emotional moments in time. Every single one. *Why had I never noticed that about my own work before?* Maybe because my mother said my scribbling wouldn't pay my bills and I should focus on something practical, which is why I got my degree in marketing.

As my thoughts once again shift back to my mother, my frustration with her actions of putting me in an untenable situation only strengthens my respect for the rest of my family. They have consistently done everything to help and support me. My father and brothers, Sebastian, Talia, Calder, Cass. All of them. Their loyalty to family is ingrained in them. And even though he's not a Blake, Den has shown that same allegiance. Maybe he can help me decide what to do. But how do I ask without revealing my mother's existence?

When he glances at his phone, I nod toward the screen. "Is that Travis with the results on the tea?"

"Not yet." He tucks his phone away and looks at me. "I'm sure you were glad to discover Laura had nothing to do with it."

"I was so relieved, but I have no idea who else would know about the peppermint connection."

Den rubs his jawline. "Did you ever mention it to Derrick?"

"Not that I remember, but I guess it could've come up at some point. Why would he send me laced teas?"

"Has he been trying to get you to let him see Josi more? Maybe he thought the tea would make you more agreeable."

"He has, and he also wants me to tell her he's her father. Using drugged tea to accomplish his goal would be a pretty shitty thing to do to me."

"I'm not saying he did it. I was just trying to think through the people in your life who might know that kind of specific detail about you and Laura." Den rubs the back of his neck. "But if he did, it wouldn't be the first time a family member manipulated another to get something they wanted."

"He's *not* family!" I snap. Then I immediately think about my mother's manipulative action when she hired someone to take out Seb when he was a teenager. "I honestly don't believe Derrick is conniving enough to do something like that to me. But for argument's sake, if it were true...what would you do? Would you cut him off? What about Josi? He technically has a right to see her, so if I cut him off, he could legally start the process to petition for half time with her, and I'd lose the current control that I do have."

Den steps close and clasps my shoulders. "You have to do what serves your family best, Mina. Sometimes doing so isn't always the easy path, but it's the right one. You must fight to protect the ones you love at all cost."

Even once he learned what my mother had tried to do to him, Seb didn't tell my brothers or me about our mother's betrayal. He kept the secret to protect my memory of her. It was only because that secret almost destroyed my relationship with Seb that Talia finally told me the truth.

My brothers, Gavin and Damien, also know what Mom tried to do to Seb, but we all agreed that since our mother was dead, our father should never learn of it. The guilt over Sebastian's crappy teenage years at Isabel's hand would crush Adam Blake. And now...I can't tell anyone about my mom. If my brothers found out, they would be furious, but my father? He would be devastated to learn about her actions, both about Sebastian and that she faked her own death. Nothing good would come of telling him. Oh God, even worse...if the news got out that my mother didn't actually die, that could shorten Simone's jail time—well, once she's finally back behind bars again.

To protect everyone, I have to keep my mother's secret. For what she did to Seb, and then faking her own death to avoid being held accountable for it, she deserves jail time. Yet despite all that, I don't believe she would physically hurt Josi or me, but how do I keep my distance from her? Would threatening to turn her in to the police be enough to stop her from trying to see us?

I sigh and nod, bringing my thoughts back to Den's theory about my ex. "I know you're right, Den. It's just hard, because I want to protect Josi. I don't want Derrick to play dad for a couple months, then get bored and move on to other interests. But if I don't tell her, I know one day Josi will want to know about her father. She has a right to know who he is, and I don't want to be the reason that doesn't happen. I could lose her anyway because I held back."

"Children are far more resilient than you think, but I understand your concern, especially with his track record. Always choose family first. Protect Josi as long as you can, until you think he's earned the right to be acknowledged as an important person in her life."

His advice could easily be translated to my mother: She will never earn the right to become a part of our family again. No one would forgive what she did to Sebastian. *I* don't forgive it! But news of her existence would only bring pain and grief on so many fronts. She needs to remain dead. For all our sakes.

Feeling better about my choice to keep Mom's existence to myself, I tilt my head and smile. "You sure give good family advice for a bachelor."

Den stiffens. "I was part of a family, Mina."

"I didn't mean it like that, Den. Of course you grew up in a family."

He shakes his head, the muscle in his jawline twitching. "That night I helped Hugh. You asked me what I lost?" When a flood of emotions scroll across his face, my stomach knots. I take a breath and wait for him to finish. Den's pained gaze scans mine. "I lost my wife and daughter in that explosion. If I hadn't stopped to help Hugh, if I had put them first and gone home to my family, I might have saved them. If I had—" He rubs his forehead and exhales a harsh breath.

He lost his family? The supreme guilt in his expression makes my heart hurt. My eyes mist as I take his hand. "I'm so very sorry about your family. I can't even imagine the pain..." A tear slides down my cheek, and I take a deep breath to keep from sobbing. "But I know this, it's in your DNA to help others. You saw a friend in need and you helped." I fold my fingers tight around his. "You have to forgive yourself, Den. Your family wouldn't want you to carry around so much regret. You're an honorable man with a big heart. You shouldn't keep it all to yourself."

His fingers flex, then cup my and completely. "I don't feel it anymore."

I'm so emotional, my pulse thrums as I take his hand and flatten it over my own pounding heart. "It feels like this."

My heart thumps harder when he curves his thumb around the edge of my breast. I swallow and lift my gaze to his. The hunger swirling in his golden eyes sends a rush of air through my lungs. "This is dangerous, Mina," he rumbles, but doesn't stop himself from sliding his thumb across the tip of my nipple.

His reverent touch draws a molten line of want from my chest to my toes. As my legs weaken, my racing heart is conflicted. Dangerous is an understatement. This is a bad idea. He has an entire past he hasn't even come to terms with—so much so, no one even knew he had a family—yet I can't help but want to be so very *bad* with him. Knowing how much Den has held inside just makes me want him even more. Like me, he holds pain and loss close, wears regret and guilt like a suit of armor, and lives in the heavy shadow of it all.

"You saw me." I touch his tie, then tug on the knot. "Better than anyone ever has."

Den captures my wrist before I can unravel the knot. His hold is firm, his jaw tense as his gaze slides leisurely from my mouth, to my neck and chest before returning to my face. "I'm a big man. I don't want to hurt you."

I really hope he's worried he'll be too rough with me, because if he thinks he'll hurt my heart, now *that* would break me. All I know is, this beautifully layered, complex man is worth the risk of finding out. "In case you weren't paying attention, I prefer my tea bold, boiling, and bottomless."

His lips quirk as he cups the back of my neck and pulls me against his chest. "It's good to know so many B words are on the table, but I was referring to size."

With his very impressive size already pushing against my belly, I'm left with little doubt as to what he meant. Lifting my gaze to his, I reach for the knot in his tie once more and pull it free. I've never wanted to be with a man as much as I want Den. "Did I forget to mention bountiful? I like my tea *very* bountiful."

Barking out a laugh, he grips my waist and lifts me off the ground until we're at eye level. "I meant my *height*, sweet Mina." The moment I settle my hands on his shoulders, his expression sobers. "While I want nothing more than to explore all twenty-six letters of the alphabet with you, you're so tiny I'm concerned that I might hurt you."

"Don't you know dynamite comes in small packages?" When the worry in his gaze doesn't dissipate, I wrap my jean-clad legs around his trim waist and clasp his handsome face between my hands. "I'm not made of glass,

Den. I'm a flesh and blood woman. Size doesn't dictate the heat level of my desire, the limitation of my wants, or the depth of my pain tolerance. For that matter, how do you know I won't be the one telling you that you're not being rough enough?"

Raw desire flashes through his eyes and his fingers flex on my waist, pulling me closer. "Is that a promise or a tease, Lady Mina?"

The tension in his hold makes me flex my thighs around his waist as I take his lower lip between my teeth and slowly pull free. "Ladies always keep their promises. Though I do hope you can keep up, my Noble Brit. I've got all this *youthful* pent up energy to expend."

"You think you can outmaneuver me?" Cocky amusement tilts his lips before he nips at my chin, then my neck. "Nothing beats experience. Not even youthful enthusiasm."

His confident promise turns my insides to jelly, but I drop a quick kiss on his lips as I slide my fingers along the back of his neck. "Maybe you should take me to bed and show me the benefits of all those years of experience you've got on me. How many is that again?"

"You're welcome to try to guess later." His hands slowly slide to my ass, his firm grip on my cheeks sending heat to every part of my body. "Fair warning," he whispers against my mouth, his warm lips taunting me with a brief kiss that jacks my pulse as he starts walking us up the stairs. "As far as I'm concerned, proper manners don't belong in the bedroom."

I swallow my excitement, but can't help challenging him the moment we reach the landing. "Are you saying no *pleases* or *thank yous* are allowed?"

Turning the lights on a low glow, Den sets me on the bed and slowly pulls off his tie. When his golden gaze slides possessively over me as he removes his shirt, I start to question whether I have what it takes to challenge him in the bedroom. Our verbal repartee and the chemistry it evokes is through the roof, but as I try to unbutton my own shirt while Den unveils his gorgeous upper body, my hands begin to shake. It's hard not to gawk at the exquisite beauty of his cut physique.

I've never seen chest and ab muscles as deeply defined as his. Maybe it's the play of light bouncing across his dark skin, but he appears as hard as stone. I know his job demands that he work out to stay in top form, but I'm also well aware his internal drive to protect is as much a part of his DNA as his fit body. From his broad shoulders to his powerful arms, every movement he makes is fluid and controlled. His upper body alone is so beautiful, I know the rest of him will make me feel even more inferior. God, I can't believe I'm suddenly afraid to remove my clothes. I've never been body shy before.

"Come here, Mina," he says in a low purr. I swallow

my nerves and push up on my knees to face him. Even doing that, I still have to look up at him.

Why do I have a feeling he's about to turn that adage "age before beauty" on its head? I bite my bottom lip, but hold my ground as his fingers pull my shirt's buttons open one at a time. I swallow, hoping to calm my nerves, but it only jacks them higher. Insecurities surface, and all I can think about are those fine silvery lines along the lower part of my belly. I thought I came to terms with them as part of the "new me" after I lost the baby weight and got my figure back, but now it's like my stretch marks are an outward reflection of the imperfections churning around inside my mind.

Now that I know she's alive and can explain why I was seeing my mother in random places, that doesn't explain why I've been dreaming such horrific dreams about her. Why was my subconscious doing that? Den deserves to be with someone who has her act together, someone who doesn't let her dead mother manipulate her. He needs a strong woman like him, so she can help him move on from his own past.

I clasp his hand as he reaches the last button on my shirt. "You're right, Den. This was a bad idea."

His hand stills on the material. "I said it was dangerous, not a bad idea." Lifting my chin, his steady gaze bores into mine. "There's no denying the chemistry between us. What are you afraid of?" I try to look away, but his hold stays firm, his tone unyielding. "If you no longer want *us*, I want to know why, Mina."

He's towering over me, his heat permeating my skin. I want him so much, my heart aches. As infuriating as it is that he's making me fully own my decision about us, I completely respect him for it too. When he releases my chin, my body instantly wants to reconnect. To stop myself from capturing his hand, I slip off the bed and move to stand in front of him.

"You're the most interesting man I've ever met." I search his gaze, looking for a sign that he understands what I'm trying to say, but he doesn't let me off that easy. All I get is a raised eyebrow. *Is that sarcasm?* "Honorable, forthright, loyal, a lone protector in a team of protectors. You've got all these wonderfully intriguing layers, and I've enjoyed every second of trying to unravel each one."

"Enjoyed?" His jawline hardens. "We aren't *past* tense, Mina. Not bloody at all."

"I know we don't have a past. And maybe it's for the best that remains true." I take a deep breath, hating that I'm not strong enough for someone like him, but at least I'm self-aware enough to admit it. The old Mina would never have questioned if she was enough for *anybody*, but I have too many cracks in my armor now. There's just too much crap going on in my head, yet I can't resist touching him at least once. Stepping closer, I rest my hand on his muscular chest. He's as hard a steel, but so incredibly, deliciously warm. "You deserve someone equally as wonderful. Someone perfect, who's fully whole—"

Den clamps a hand over mine on his chest, his fingers folding firmly around it. "I want you so much I can already taste you, Mina. I want to feel your nails digging in my back and hear the sounds you'll make in the many ways I'll make you come. When I've worn you out and all you want to do is sleep, understand this, I'm a relentless lover. I plan to bathe in your scent all night long. It's all I can think about."

For a man of few words, that was incredibly arousing. Adrenaline and desire shoot to every nerve center in my body in record speed. "Den, I—"

"No one is perfectly whole." Cupping my neck, he pulls me so close only a breath separates us. The heat of his skin arcs to mine as his fingers fold into my hair, his touch both tense and reverent. "We all have dents and dings, maybe even a few chunks missing. But all that roadmap-of-life damage is what makes us who we are." Lifting my hand from his chest, he presses a lingering kiss to my open palm. As the sensation tingles all the way down my arm, he moves lower, warming my wrist. "I want to explore every part of you. Every beautiful dent, ding, and missing chunk."

I'm speechless as he nips at my skin, then lowers his hands to my bare waist above my jeans. "What's your answer, Lady Mina?"

My throat tight with emotion, my answer is to shrug my shirt off my shoulders. I start to unhook my bra, but Den's hand covers mine. Brushing my fingers away, his voice is gruff. "Let me unwrap you."

I swallow and the instant I nod, he tugs on my hand and turns me around. My skin prickles when his mouth connects with my shoulder and warm fingers slide my bra off. I hold back an involuntary gasp of pleasure as his big hands fold fully over my breasts, but it's the sensation of his bare chest and abs completely heating my skin from shoulder to waist that makes it hard to take a breath. He's right that he's so much larger than me, but my concern isn't for my safety. It's not being able to measure up. I've always considered my C cup breasts my best asset. For my size, they're more than ample, but his hands completely dwarf them. "When you told me you've got me covered, I didn't expect you to mean that quite so literally."

Den's low chuckle actually comforts me. At least he's not letting go. Instead, his fingers tighten, his hold more dominant and possessive. "They're truly perfect."

My confidence bolstered by the appreciation in his voice, I tuck my hand around his neck and pull him down to my level, whispering in his ear, "I sure hope you plan on doing more than covering them back up, handsome."

"Along with the rest of you, these gorgeous breasts are going to get a hell of a work out." Pulling me fully against him, he slides a hand down my belly and deftly unbuttons my jeans.

"On that note." I clasp his hand, needing to face my worries head on. Turning in his arms, I take a breath and step back to shimmy out of my jeans and underwear. When I'm standing naked in front of him, I take a deep breath, then clasp his hand and touch his fingers to my stomach. "These stretch marks are a part of me. I don't have a perfect body, not anywhere near." Lifting my gaze to his, I shrug and offer a trembling smile, hating how vulnerable I feel. "Might as well get the uncomfortable stuff out of the way."

Den's gaze drops to my abdomen and I swallow my embarrassment as his fingers slowly feather across the marred skin. Lowering his hand, he says, "You mean like these?"

When he turns around and I see a four-inch diagonal slash along the lower right of his muscular back, I lift shaky fingers to the marred skin. "Is this a knife wound?"

Den nods. "It took almost losing a kidney to remind me to never let my guard down."

As my gaze travels to the new wound on his shoulder, I frown at the scab forming. That's a pretty deep gash. *What happened?* My stomach churning, I take in the canvas of his back and pick up three more scars, some deeper than others.

Just as I brush my fingers over another scar, Den turns

and pulls me close. "Dents and dings, sweet Mina. They just mean we've lived our lives."

In Den's arms, I feel invincible, perfect and whole. And now that I'm up close and personal, I can't help but notice another mar on his chest. *Oh God, was that from a bullet?* I touch the perfectly round scar on his right pectoral, then press my lips to it. "Some of us have lived much harder than others."

Den hooks his finger on my chin. Tilting it up, he lowers his mouth to mine, murmuring, "Right now all I want to do is live *with* you."

Pushing up on my toes, I accept the press of his mouth and part my lips to show him I'm all his. Den rumbles his primal approval and buries his hand in my hair, fisting it tight as his tongue thrusts deep, tangling with mine in an aggressive dance of dominance.

When I start to unbuckle his belt, he grips my waist and quickly lifts me up onto the taller bureau to his left. "What are you doing?" I ask, not wanting to let him go.

"Spread your legs," he says, his hands moving to free his belt from his pants.

Den's gaze drops to my clenched thighs and my sex throbs harder as I watch the golden color turn a molten bronze shade when his hands move to his zipper. Sitting on top of a dresser is not what I expected, but I'm willing to take this intriguing journey with this man. Lowering my hands to my knees, I use them to help spread my legs wide and say innocently, "You mean like this?"

Den's nostrils flare and he rips his zipper completely apart as his gaze locks on my exposed sex. I've never been more thankful that I kept my laser removal appointments than I am at this moment. They might've been just for me, but the look in his eyes makes it totally worth it.

When Den pushes his pants and boxers down, then steps out of them, I lose a bit of my siren's swagger. He's much bigger than I expected.

Just as I release my knees, Den steps forward and lifts one of my legs, draping it over his shoulder. His voice is guttural with want. "Put your other leg around me," he says and clasps my bare ass.

I yelp in surprise when I'm yanked to the edge of the dresser and his tongue thrusts deep inside me.

Unable to do anything but feel, I grip the back of the dresser and fold my leg around his shoulder, arching against his hot mouth.

Den rumbles, his hands digging into my ass. "Bloody hell, you taste like honeysuckle."

My stomach flutters at the very personal compliment, but the moment he finds my clit, I shudder and my legs start to tremble against him. Gripping the edge of the dresser, I pant and rock hard against his mouth. "God, Den...don't stop!"

He grunts against my body, then makes my head loll

when he slides two fingers inside me and curls them forward. Stroking me, he pulls me even closer to his hot mouth. "I can't fucking get enough," he husks then clamps on to my clit, sending waves of pain and pleasure rocketing through me.

I shiver and shake, my vision blurring as my orgasm takes over my body, consuming all of my senses, not once but…twice. I haven't even stopped vibrating when Den hoists me up on his shoulders, one hand supporting my ass and the other splayed along my lower back. While my brain floats somewhere in lala land and my ability to reason temporarily ceases, all I can do is grip his head tight and clamp my legs around his shoulders as I speak in incoherent gibberish, asking for more.

Den nips lightly at my sensitized sex as he walks us to the bed, then drops to his knees to lower me down onto the mattress. The moment I'm free, I wrap my arms around his shoulders and accept all his weight as he lowers himself to the bed over me with dominant intent.

"Condom," he rasps against my mouth, but I shake my head and kiss him silent, loving that his fingers are already sliding deep inside me once more.

"I'm on the pill. I have never climaxed back-to-back like that before. I've—" I pause and swallow. "I've clearly been missing out."

"Any man who didn't take the time to make this delicious body of yours sing through an encore should be shot." His voice sounds strained as he kisses my throat. "I wanted to prepare you so you're not too sore tomorrow, but holy hell, Mina. I've never tasted anything so arousing. You're pure sex with heavenly nectar mixed in."

"I loved how you proved me wrong."

"Wrong?" he murmurs as he lifts my thigh over his and drops a kiss on my lips.

"Yep, apparently I fit on your shoulders really, *really* well." As he chuckles, I smile then kiss his jaw, my fingers digging into his shoulders to pull him closer. "And for the record, I only taste like I do, because I want you so much." Undulating my hips, I press my sex against his erection. "I want more, Den. Don't hold back."

He captures my jaw, his gaze searching mine. "I might have years on you, but fuck if you aren't everything I need right now."

The look in his eyes matches the ache in my chest. I slide my hand between us and guide his thick erection to my sex. "I'm pretty sure I'm right, but show me just how good we can be together."

As he slides inside me, Den takes my hand and presses a kiss to my palm. Closing his eyes briefly, he tenses, then exhales slowly and slides deeper.

I swallow past the tension while my body resists, then welcomes him, adjusting to his size. Tingling all over, I embrace the flood of desire rushing right behind it. We begin to slowly move together, and when Den groans and fully seats himself inside me, I arch against him, biting back the last pinch of pain.

He slides his fingers in my hair, his breath rushing against my cheek, harsh and full of need. "I'm sorry, Mina. I wanted to take this slower. You're just so addictive."

When he takes a couple of deep breaths as if he's afraid to move, I slide my fingers down his shoulders and dig my nails into his back at the same time I squeeze my lower muscles around him. "I want all of you."

Den's back muscles tense and his grip on my hair tightens just before he pulls out, then jerks his hips forward. His next thrust is harder, like he's trying to imprint himself on me from the inside out. I gasp and meet his aggression with a welcoming roll of my hips. He fucks with fluid, strong movements, and the brutal tenderness makes me feel completely possessed and necessary for his pleasure. My head swims with emotion as waves of euphoria flood through me. We chase each other in a dance of need and want until I cry out and arch against him. When I moan and shudder through waves of pleasure, he roars through his own release.

Our bodies tangled together, hearts pounding, it's hard for me to catch my breath. I'm exhausted, but hearing his heavy breathing makes me feel strong and confident. "That was incredi—"

Den clamps his mouth over mine, male satisfaction rumbling in his throat as he rolls me fully under him.

Clasping my breast in a firm hold, he lifts his head, his golden gaze locking with mine as his thumb teases my nipple. "We're nowhere near done. You're all mine tonight."

Before I can respond, he dips his head and latches onto my nipple, then bites down with such aggressive passion I completely forget my next thought. Instead, I dig my heels into his hard butt muscles and pull him closer, wanting more. All I can think about is reaching that same bliss with him again and again, until we fill every dent and ding between us.

CHAPTER SEVENTEEN

DEN

Mina's laying across my chest, her hair a gorgeous tangle down her back. I smile at the wavy bedhead she'll have in the morning as I run my fingers through the silky golden strands. Every movement releases her floral scent, making me both hard and relaxed at the same time. It's a strange sensation I've never felt and I'm not sure how to unpack my thoughts on it. The fact I broke my own rule about never getting involved with a client, and the shit I'm going to get from Sebastian at some point don't weigh on my mind as much as the fact that what I have with her is so intense. I didn't think I had it in me to be connected to anyone or anything ever again.

One thing I know for sure, this woman is pure decadent pleasure. With a sexual appetite that matches—maybe even surpasses—mine, she surprised the hell out of me. She was insatiable in her desire to experience everything she could. While a part of me loves that I introduced her to new positions and experiences she'd never tried before, the idea she might later do them with other men splits every atom in my brain.

My fist tightens in her hair and I wrap the ends fully around my hand. Bringing the strands to my nose, I inhale deeply. She is everything I didn't know I wanted. Perfect for me in every way.

I glance down at her angelic face. Even just watching her sleep, my body stirs to life all over again. As promised, I wore her out until she fell into an exhausted sleep, but the truth is as much as I enjoyed meeting her every desire, I just couldn't get enough of her. I release her hair and lift her limp hand. Pressing my lips to her palm, I smile that her fingers twitch against my cheek as she sleepily murmurs, "Now you're just being a glutton, Dennet."

Chuckling, I lay her fingers on my chest and trail mine across her bare back, enjoying how soft her skin feels. I pause my movements when I realize that I don't want to stop touching her. My brow creases at the thought. Mina loves teasing me about being older than her, but would she feel differently if she knew that I was older than Sebastian by more than a couple years? For that matter, would she even want more than this one night of phenomenal sex? How the hell could she not want more? What happened between us transcended any relationship I've ever had. This, from a slip of a woman I can pick up with one hand. I grin at the aptness of her earlier comment: dynamite indeed comes in a small package. Her wit and debate skills draw me in, keeping me on my toes, but the fact that I can hear every single heartbeat when I'm with her...that's what fills my soul.

As I tuck a strand of blond hair behind her ear, a text message pops up on my phone. I lift my phone from the nightstand to see it's from Travis.

You were right. The teas were laced with the same drug, which explains why you felt completely relaxed. It has a THC base (from marijuana) and some other natural drugs that mimic a lower dose of Rohypnol (roofies). As for reactions, this kind of cocktail would make the person feel a pleasant high and also be much more pliable, possibly even suggestible. Depending on the person and how much they consume, they could also experience hallucinations.

I frown, then quickly type a response back.

Would the response be stronger if mixed with alcohol? What do you mean suggestible?

It would absolutely be enhanced with alcohol. What I mean by suggestible is the person who ingested this could be more easily influenced and do things they might not under normal circumstances.

Worry tightens my chest and I slip my fingers in Mina's hair once more as I type my next question one-handed. It'd better bloody only be a few hours.

How long would this cocktail of drugs stay in a person's system?

Depends on the person, but it could stay in their system up to five days.

Five days? I scowl at the screen. Fucking hell. Could what just happened have been influenced by the drugs still in her system? I don't like thinking that Mina would possibly have made a different decision about us. Not at all.

I splay my hand across her back, pressing her closer as I reply to his text.

Thanks for running the tests. I owe you.

CHAPTER EIGHTEEN

MINA

My pencil slides quietly across my notebook as I sit cross-legged at the end of the bed and sketch Den. He's sleeping on his back with one arm above his head, his chest and abs fully exposed, one leg out of the covers. Even in this completely relaxed position, his muscles reflect just how powerful his body is.

With my first really good night's sleep in ages—probably due to sheer physical exhaustion—I take advantage of the morning sun streaming through the window while it lasts. Casting soft light on Den's darker skin, the sun highlights where his muscles bulge with spots of bronze. He's a beautiful study of relaxation. One I'll never get tired of capturing, for many reasons, but especially because I'm the only one he has allowed to see him this way.

I spend time on his jawline and mouth, then move

down his shoulders, forearms, and hands to add more detail. My body tingles all over as I remember his possessive grip, the movement of his hands warming my skin, his mouth burning a hotter path right behind.

Getting the shading just right is a priority. It takes time and attention to detail to make an image pop. I lower my gaze to the paper, smudging, then erasing to achieve the right amount of negative space. I'm determined to capture his rich bronze highlights to perfection.

"You're drawing," Den says in a low tone, capturing my attention.

I close the notebook, not ready to let him see what I'm working on just yet. "It feels good to sketch again," I say, smiling. "It has been a while since I've been inspired."

Crawling to the head of the bed, I pick up the full mug of tea from the nightstand and hold it out to him. "I got so into my art, I forgot to drink this. Would you like mine? It's not super hot, but still warm."

"I'll always want your tea, no matter the temperature, Lady Mina." Smirking, he sits up and fluffs his pillow, then takes the mug.

When his golden gaze locks with mine over the mug's edge as he takes a long sip, I realize his comment has nothing to do with morning beverages, and my face blooms with heat. What we shared last night was indescribably passionate—just thinking about it, my body warms to the memories—but the confident look in his hooded gaze is a stark reminder that the moment he touches me, he has this uncanny ability to tap into a wild side within me that I didn't know existed. *That* Mina's desires are a bit embarrassing in the light of day.

"That wasn't me, Den," I say quickly, hoping he doesn't think I'm this sexually free with every man I'm with.

Lowering the cup, his brows draw together. "Was there some other woman in my bed last night?"

When his gaze drops to my bare legs underneath his t-shirt, I quickly pull the sheet over them in an effort to regain some decorum after last night's sexy adventures. "That's not what I meant. I um...well I just wanted you to know that I'm not usually so forward—"

"Do you regret it, Mina?"

His crisp tone and tense jaw surprise me, but I don't know how to answer him. If I tell him that I enjoyed everything we did—Every. Single. Decadent. Moment—will he respect me? Or will my honest answer put a fast end to whatever this is before it even gets started? Some guys can have weird double-standards about women who aren't afraid of sex. They don't mind fucking them, but that's all they want. I don't want to be his hot lay. I want to be the woman he's proud of, the one he wants to show off, who also happens to be adventurous and uninhibited in bed. So how do I learn which kind of guy my stoic Noble Brit is without screwing this up? Honesty is best. If nothing else, he would appreciate that. "I was there, remember?"

"The fact you're giving me non-answers says you might." Before I can respond, he holds up his hand. "We'll talk later. For now, since I'll be out of the office a fair bit today, you should probably stay here."

Who doesn't have concerns or insecurities the first morning after? Even when—no, especially when—the sex was freaking fantastic? When more is on the line, because *this person* could truly break you, your response could detonate your new dynamic. "Den," I reach for him, but he slides out of bed.

Walking, in all his naked glory, toward the bathroom, he says in a low tone, "I have an early meeting."

The door shuts, cutting off our conversation and my view of his perfectly muscled ass.

I SPEND the next couple hours, trying to finish my drawing and not let the distance Den put between us get to me, but of course my brain won't stop churning. I finally close my notebook in disgust and pace the living room. The more I think about how he shut down and didn't say much before he left, the angrier I get. No way am I letting him ignore me the entire day. The only reason I'm still here is because we don't know who sent me those tea packages. For all I know, the tea is perfectly fine. Picking up my phone, I send him a text.

I know we got off track last night, but did Travis get back to you about the tea?

The teas had a mixture of marijuana and other drugs in them. The combination would definitely relax you, but it could also make you suggestible as well as hallucinate. Assuming you had some that morning, I believe the tea was the reason you seemed high from one glass of wine on Friday. Your building's security cameras don't store recordings more than forty-eight hours, so we won't be able to determine who left the tea that way.

I can't believe someone tried to drug me! But his comment about possible hallucinations makes me wonder and I quickly send him another note.

Did your friend say anything about nightmares?

He didn't, but if the tea can cause hallucinations, then it could also be the cause of nightmares. If you follow the pattern I've seen since we've been together, you usually drink a couple cups in the evening before bed.

I'm pissed that someone drugged me, but I'm so relieved that those drugs could potentially be the source of my horrible nightmares the last several weeks that my gaze blurs with tears. Thankful to think I'm not losing my mind, I reply.

I wonder if the peppermint ribbons were just a fluke and had nothing to do with my connection to Laura?

I don't believe in coincidence, not something this specific. For now, I'm having Elijah check for any other cameras that face your building. If he can find some that go back to the day you said you received the latest gift of tea, we'll have you review them to see if you recognize anyone entering the building.

Okay.

When he doesn't reply, I try not to let it get to me that he's keeping our interactions all business. Maybe the woman I was last night was truly more than he bargained for.

My heart twists at the thought, but I don't want awkwardness to replace the wonderful rapport we had before mind-blowing sex complicated things. I miss my daughter, so for now, it's probably best if I pick her up after daycare and bring her to his place tonight. Hopefully we'll uncover the person who drugged my tea quickly, and then I can go back to my apartment, my job, and my single life with Josi.

She and I were doing just fine without any men in our daily lives. It's time to get back to just depending on *me*. Decision made, I dial the daycare.

"Briarwood Daycare," a younger woman says in a perky tone.

She must be new. Where's the older lady who usually answers the phone? "Hi, this is Mina Blake. I just wanted to let you know that I'll be picking my daughter, Josi, up at the end of the day instead of my father."

"I'm confused, Ms. Blake. I have the note you sent letting us know your mother would be picking Josi up today. She signed her out earlier."

What in God's name is my mother doing? While ice cold worry rushes through my veins, quickly followed by mind-numbing fear, I try not to let panic come through in my voice. "Sorry about the misunderstanding. What time did my mother pick Josi up?"

"Right before lunch. She said she was taking Josi to a place that used to be your favorite lunchtime spot. Can I help you with anything else, Ms. Blake?"

I know exactly where Mom has taken Josi. "No, that's all. Thank you for letting me know."

I hang up, then quickly pull off Den's shirt and step into a pair of jeans. Tugging a sweatshirt over my head, I grab my jacket and purse. The moment I rush toward the door, I realize I don't have a car. "Dammit!" As soon as my steps slow, I remember Den's other car.

Pivoting, I head for the built-in cabinet next to the fireplace and open the drawer I saw Den tuck the other set of car keys into. The last thing I expect to find is the braided bracelet Den had used in my hair. It's lying on top of an eight-by-ten picture of a blue-eyed, curly-haired brunette and a young child about five years old with light brown skin and a mop of dark ringlets around her sweet face.

My gaze snags on the bright colored bracelets they're all wearing. His wife's braided one is blue, red and white. Den's is orange, green, white, red and black, and when I see his daughter's bracelet has all the colors of Den's and his wife's, I realize that each bracelet must represent their nationalities' flag colors. *Did his daughter make them?* My heart hurts for Den's loss of his beautiful family. I want to examine every nuance of his wife and child's features, to appreciate the woman's smile who stole his heart so completely that he married her and had a little girl with an impishly pert nose and golden eyes like her father's. But I have to get to my own child right now. Grabbing the keys, I close the drawer and turn toward the garage door with determined steps. *My mother is going to wish she never came back from the grave for pulling this stunt!*

I'm surprised, but so very thankful the car starts up easily. Did Den really have an issue with it? I don't have time to worry about why he wasn't driving it. All I can do is hope it gets me to Central Park. As I back out of the garage, it hits me that I shouldn't keep the truth about my mom to myself. Trying to deal with dodgy people on my own is what got me into the horrible Regan mess in the first place. She might be my mom, but she's made her share of bad judgments, including the line she just crossed by taking my child without my permission.

The last thing I want to do is pull Seb into this. I don't want him to learn that my mother faked her death. Finding Simone needs to be his top priority so he can keep his family safe. I'll call Den once I'm parked. No matter what's going on between us, I know Josi's safety matters to him.

CHAPTER NINETEEN

DEN

This morning, while Mina was in the shower, I pulled the tins of tea from the cabinet I'd hidden them in and dumped most of the tea down the disposal in the sink, save the bit I gave to Travis to test. When I turned, intending to bury the tins under the rubbish in the bin, that's when I noticed the logo imprinted on the bottom inside: Come back to Tara's Trinkets & Teas to get your next tea fix!

Standing outside of Tara's Trinkets & Teas, I watch Laura open up shop and walk into work. According to Mina, Laura would never try to hurt her, but the tin in my hand tells a different story. The metal container bows as my fingers cinch around it. Determined to get answers, I start to walk across the street, when a text comes through. Mina's asking for the lab results on her tea.

It's like the woman has a sixth sense. Shaking my head, I answer her question with Travis' findings, but I don't volunteer where I am. There's no point in upsetting her unnecessarily. I need more information.

My fingers hover over my keyboard. I consider telling her to be ready to talk tonight, but that might put her on the defensive. The conversation we needed to have was more than a five-minute one. I left to give her time to think. I can only hope allowing her space wasn't a mistake. Putting my phone away, I head for the store.

The bell rings when I walk in, and I instantly recognize Laura from working security at Josi's christening. She looks up from doing paperwork at the register. "Good morning! Can I help you with something in particular?"

I approach the counter and set the empty container down. "You can tell me why you tried to drug your best friend."

"Pardon me?" Once the shock of my comment fades, Laura takes the tin and glances down inside it. "Yes, this is one of ours, but I don't know why you think I tried to drug anyone?"

"I'm referring to Mina." I cross my arms and give her my most intimidating look. "I'd like to know why you lied and told her you didn't give her this tea, which was laced with a cocktail of marijuana and other drugs. Mina's been through enough this past year. What exactly were you hoping to accomplish by drugging her?"

The door's bell chimes when a new customer enters. I turn and say to the young woman, "The store is still closed. Please wait outside until she tells you to come in."

Blond eyebrows hike and she points to the door. "But it had the Open sign—"

"Turn it to Closed on your way out."

Her eyes widen, but she nods and scoots toward the door. "Um, okay."

"How dare you treat my customer like that!" Laura says the moment the woman walks out. Reaching for her cell phone, she glares at me. "If you don't leave, right now, I'm calling the police."

I unbutton my overcoat and jacket, then slide my hands into my pants pockets, making sure she sees my holstered gun. "Be my guest. I'm sure the police would love to know the store you manage is selling drug-laced teas. No wonder you're doing such brisk business."

"Who are you?" she says as she sets the phone back down with a shaky hand.

"I take care of the Blake family. That's all you need to know."

"I have no idea what you're talking about with drugs in our tea. I mixed the batches myself, so I know for a fact, there wasn't anything like that in it! And I would never try to hurt Mina in any way. I love her dearly." Losing some of her bluster, she continues, "I can't believe someone tried to drug Mina. Please tell me she's okay?"

I ignore her question and drill further. "Not only did this tin come from your store, but when it was left at Mina's door, the packaging had a peppermint ribbon on it. So did the first package of tea she received in the same manner. Why don't you tell me how these two things pointing to you and your unique connection to Mina would look to an investigator?"

Laura's gaze widens and her bottom lip starts to tremble. "Both packages had a peppermint ribbon?" When I nod, she shakes her head. "I have no idea who would try to point the finger at me, but I promise you, our teas aren't laced with anything but tea and natural herbs that are listed on the label. Nothing else."

When she glances toward the door as someone knocks impatiently on the glass, I stare her down. "The sooner you help point me to the person who did this, the sooner you can re-open your store."

"Please tell Mina it wasn't me. I feel so horrible." Rubbing her forehead, she sighs and picks up the tin, her bangle bracelets clinking on her arm. "This particular batch was a seasonal one. It was for a special promotion we ran in the store. I believe I made ninety."

"I'd like the list of purchasers."

"Of course. Anything to help my friend." Nodding, she taps on the computer screen, then looks up. "If you only had the other tin, I could—"

I pull the second tin out of my overcoat pocket and set it down on the counter. "I want both purchase lists."

Elijah's on the phone when I walk into his office. "Sometimes, you two have your own married couple's language." Snorting, he shakes his head. "Yeah, I can't believe this fake name is stumping us. Maybe Regan really was being ironic. That place was the epitome of a dive hotel."

I step up to his desk and set the two lists Laura gave me on his keyboard in front of him. "I need you to compare these purchase lists and get me a name."

He raises his eyebrows and sighs into the phone. "Let me call you back. Den's in my office, commanding my attention."

Sebastian's grumble of annoyance comes through loud and clear as Elijah sets the phone back in its cradle. "Now that you're here, you've saved me a trip." He pulls out the phone I asked him to try to break into and hands it back to me. "I was able to decrypt the passcode, but unfortunately it was a dead end. All I got off the phone was a burner number that sent the person that picture of your car and license plate. And before you ask, I tried to trace the number, but the phone went dead after that day. The owner was probably smart enough to ditch it."

"What about this phone? Can you tell where the person had been?"

"The phone was activated that day," Elijah says, shaking his head. "There wasn't any history on it to scrape. Oh, and one last thing, you had me check on Edgar Stewart." Elijah taps on his keyboard and scrolls down. "There's no Edgar Stewart listed as having arrived in the US. Does this have something to do with that phone?"

I shake my head. "They're unrelated. Please be sure to inform me the minute he steps foot on US soil."

"Will do. Though I have to warn you that when it comes to diplomats, they're a bit harder to track."

"Understood." If Edgar hasn't arrived, he most likely isn't responsible for the shooter. Since I haven't made any enemies in the US that I'm aware of, it very well could be the sweep team from the hotel going after possible witnesses. "Thanks for doing that, Elijah." I pocket the phone, then point to the two lists I laid on his desk. "When you're not actively searching for Simone, this is next on your list. Someone on these two lists bought teas and dropped them off at Mina's door as a gift. They were laced with drugs. These lists are from two separate purchasing days the teas in question were bought. I believe it's the same person, and I could use your ninja skills to get me a name and hopefully an address."

"You know if they paid cash, they won't be on this list."

I nod. "It's still worth comparing the lists to see if a name pops up in both."

"Got it," he says, then frowns. "Is Mina okay?"

"She is, but whoever did this needs to be caught and charged." Which reminds me, I pull my phone out and turn it back on to check in with Mina, when an alert pops up that she has left me a voicemail. I step outside Elijah's office to let Talia enter and hit Play.

"Hey, it's Mina. I'm at Central Park. Sorry, but I had to take your car. I couldn't wait around for you to come get me. In retrospect, I know I should've told you this sooner, but I didn't know what to do with this information and now..." She sighs and continues, "The bottom line is, my mother didn't die in that explosion."

My gaze jerks to Talia who's talking to Elijah. She's saying something about Latin, but I glance away to concentrate on Mina's voicemail.

"I know it sounds crazy, but Mom's very much alive, with a new face, thanks to Regan's stolen Blake money. At least I know I wasn't going completely crazy seeing a woman who looked like my mom. With sunglasses on, Mom can kind of pass for her old self, which she used to her advantage to pick Josi up from daycare today. That's why I'm at the park. When I was little, Mom would take me out of school for a special lunch where I could feed the ducks. I'm sorry if I'm rambling. I'm not really sure why I'm telling you all of this. Yes, I'm a bit freaked out that she took Josi without my permission, but I truly don't believe she would hurt her or me. I guess I just wanted someone to talk to about all of this when I get back with my daughter. It's not like I can tell anyone in my family. Thanks for listening and I'll see you later."

I immediately try to call her, but her phone goes straight to voicemail. My pulse races as I check to see how long ago she called. Ten minutes. *Bloody fucking hell!*

Just as I tuck my phone away, Talia says, "Hey, Den, we think Regan's fake name was in Latin, which roughly translates to 'Elisabeth living.' Care to join us on brainstorming what that could possibly mean?"

"Can I talk to you?" I curtly nod toward her office, when what I really want to do is rush out the door.

"Of course." Talia follows me into her office and shuts the door. "What's going on?"

I glance toward the open doorway between her office and Sebastian's. Once I hear him talking on the phone, I lower my voice. "My guess is *Elisabeth living* means Isabel is alive."

"What?" Talia's green eyes widen. "How did you come up with that?"

"Isabel is a variation of Elisabeth. Also...because it's true." I quickly explain the voicemail Mina left me. "Mina truly believes her mother would never hurt her, but after everything the woman has done, down to faking her own death, I don't trust her. I'm going over to make sure everything goes smoothly. Mina doesn't want her family to know about Isabel, but her safety is my utmost concern. There's yet another layer of danger she's unaware of. I know we couldn't find Mina on any of the tapes around the hotel, but my car showed up. And I think that it's possible the team that took Regan out might be looking for my car that Mina drove to the park."

Talia's brow furrows with worry. "Is that why you've been driving a different car?"

"Yes, someone took a shot at me the other night. I originally thought it had something to do with my past, but I just got confirmation that isn't the case. And since the one lead I had about the shooter went cold, I would like backup to cover the bases. I know Mina will want to tell Sebastian about Isabel herself, so could you ask Theo to head over just as a precaution?" When she nods, I continue, "Once I leave, please have Elijah ping the traffic cams near Central Park to look for my car. I disabled the GPS, so that'll be the only way to locate it. I need to know where to start looking for Mina. I think she may have turned off her phone."

"Where do you want Theo to meet you?"

"Once Elijah finds my other car on the camera feeds, give Theo that location. He can stake out that car and look for anyone who seems interested in it. My vehicle is all the shooter had to go on before. My tag isn't tied to my house, so he must've looked for my car via street cams. He has no other way to trace me. I'll make sure Mina doesn't go anywhere near the vehicle. She'll ride with me. When we get back and Mina's safe, finding this anonymous shooter will be my next priority."

Talia nods her agreement. "Sebastian won't like not being called in on this, Den."

"It's not optimal, I know, but I'm honoring Mina's wishes while doing my best to keep her safe. If Sebastian came, he might recognize Isabel, and you know how well that would go over."

"I do." Talia briefly grimaces, then tilts her head. "You really care for Mina, don't you?"

I hold her questioning gaze, an unspoken truth passing between us. "I don't want her mother to hurt her all over again."

"We'll debrief later." She grips my arm before I turn away. "You're right to not trust Isabel, especially now that we know Regan left behind a message. There's a reason she decided to tell Mina the truth after all this time."

On the outskirts of Central Park, I shut off my engine and start walking through the crowded street at a fast pace. The smell of exhaust fills my senses and car horns blare as I check the text Theo sent.

Stuck in traffic. Be there soon.

When I turn down the street where Elijah said my car

should be parked, a bloke with a bleached buzz cut is using his body to block people's view, while another bloke in a hoodie pockets a tool, then quickly opens the passenger door on the car Mina drove.

The car appears to be empty, but what if Mina's in it and I just can't see her? Fury rises as my worry amps. "Hey," I yell and start running toward them. When the hooded one turns around, his gaze narrows with murderous intent, and he barks something to his friend.

I glare at them and increase my speed, but the second they both pull guns from their jackets, I barely have time to dive behind another car on the street before a barrage of bullets hammer the vehicle. The *ping, ping, pings* absent of loud gunfire are oddly more disturbing.

Yanking my gun from its holster, I call Theo. "I've got two firing at me with silencers. Possible professionals. I'm pinned down. Call Sebastian and the police."

"On it! I'm just pulling up and see them. Others must have already alerted nearby police."

Sure enough, the blare of approaching sirens ends the gunfire. I chance a look over the car's hood to see the two shooters running in the opposite direction. Jumping up, I tuck my gun away and take off after them. No fucking chance are they getting away!

The bastards are fast and already have a good start ahead of me. When Theo steps out from behind a parked van and stiff-arms the blond one, I grunt my approval as the bastard goes down. The guy tries his best to recover, but Theo hammers him in the chest with his meaty fist twice, then nods that he's got him, so I zoom past, not breaking my stride. Hitting the pavement hard, I dig in and focus on the dark-haired one, his hoodie now flying behind him.

The second shooter reaches a busy crossroad. He tries to step out, but blaring horns and cars weaving in and out of lanes force him to stop. He turns down the street and I pivot to follow, knowing his goal is to get across when he can.

I push myself harder to reach the punk before he can turn.

The instant there's a break in the traffic at the next light, he starts to bolt, but I reach out and grab hold of his hood, yanking hard.

When he lands on his side, sucking wind, I don't give him a chance to catch his breath. "Who sent you after me?" I roll him over and slam my fist against his jaw, getting right in his face. "You're going to tell me every single name!"

He moans in pain and tries to pull away, so I haul him off the ground by his hood until he hacks for air. "Names!" When he nods, I grunt my satisfaction, then lower him to the ground, winding my fist in his hood to assure his cooperation. *Never underestimate a man with a family to protect.*

CHAPTER TWENTY

MINA

Once I leave my message for Den, I get out of the car and immediately wind my way through the crowds of people on the sidewalk before heading for the spot my mother used to take me in Central Park. Despite the cooler weather, I'm sweating underneath my coat. My heart races as I walk at a brisk pace, my gaze scanning the busy park. Everyone is watching the water, staring at the ducks. Ah, I remember now, there's a colorful Mandarin duck that has decided to grace the park with his presence yet again this year. Frustrated at the crowds, I peer past the people until I spot Josi's blond curls as she throws a piece of bread to the ducks. Exhaling a sob of relief, I run toward her.

The moment I reach her side, I quickly swoop her up into my arms. "I'm here, Josi sweetie!"

"Want down, Mama," she says on a frown and lifts the bag of breadcrumbs up. "Ducks!"

"Put her down, Mina. Let her have fun," my mom's voice calls from behind me.

Turning with Josi in my arms, I narrow my gaze on my mother, who's sitting on the bench farther away than I would be from Josi. "You should be closer with her around water!"

Josi squirms against me, craning her neck to see the quacking ducks behind me. "Down, Mama!"

Sighing, I set my daughter down, then zip her jacket all the way up against the cold air. "Remember what I said about staying back from water, Josi? Don't get anywhere near the ducks. Understand?"

She looks at me solemnly and nods. "Water bad."

When I nod, she smiles, her face lighting up. "Ducks good?"

"Only if you stay back from them," I say, giving her a half smile. "You can throw the food. Otherwise, if they get too close, they might nip at your fingers."

Her green eyes widen slightly and she jerks her little hand behind her back, shaking her head. "No, nip-nip!"

"That's right. So listen to your mom. I'll be right over there on the bench watching you, okay?"

As I approach my mom, I keep looking back at Josi. Mom smiles, like she's meeting a friend, not like she just took my child from daycare without my permission.

Thankful that Josi is distracted, I curl my hands into fists and walk straight up to my mom. "Don't you ever, and I mean *ever*, take my child from her daycare again!"

My mother frowns behind her sunglasses. "Sit down and keep your voice low, Mina. You're making a scene."

"I will not sit down," I say in a lower tone, narrowing my gaze on her. "This isn't shock talking. I can't forgive what you did in the past to Sebastian and his mother, and I sure as hell don't forgive what you've done to our family, to *me*, by faking your death. You wanted a new life? It'll be one without *any* of your family. The only reason I'm keeping your secret is because I don't want to break Dad's heart, but if you try to see me or my child again in any capacity, I *will* call the police and have you arrested."

Mom presses her lips together briefly, then sighs. "We both know you'll do nothing of the sort, Mina." Gesturing toward my daughter hopping up and down as she tosses several bread pieces to the ducks, she continues, "Josi's having a blast. Take a seat. There's a reason I'm here and why I picked Josi up. You're in danger."

"What are you talking about?" Heart racing, I instinctively glance around as I sit down.

Mom sets her purse on her lap, fiddling with the designer emblem. "It all would've worked out if Regan hadn't grown tiresome. I was biding my time until I thought you could handle seeing me, hoping that tea would help you to remain calm when I finally approached you—"

"Oh my God, you're the one who gave me that drugged tea?" I stare at her with disbelief.

"Of course I did. I bought some of Laura's special blend teas and added top dollar ingredients to help relax you, then wrapped them in a special bow."

"Those peppermint ribbons were the perfect way to get me to not only accept the gifts, but to use them," I snap, getting angrier by the moment. "Did you know that those *special* ingredients also cause hallucinations?"

Surprise registers in my mother's gaze. "I was assured it's perfectly safe. Just something to relax you."

"It gave me nightmares, Mom!" I say, swinging my gaze back to Josi briefly. "Awful, burned-in-my-retinas imagery. I thought I was losing my mind."

"That wasn't the intent, Mina." A twinge of regret flickers across her face before she sighs. "But we're talking about how Regan screwed everything up."

I'm suddenly worried what she means by that. At this point, I wouldn't put anything past my mother. I hardly know this person. "*What* happened?"

"Regan wanted me to share more money with her." She shrugs. "I disagreed."

I shake my head. "What do you mean she wanted you to share more money with her? Regan's the one who stole all the money."

Mom snorts. "Who do you think she stole it for?"

I keep an eye on the crowd stepping forward to get a better look at the Mandarin duck floating by in the water. I don't want them to get too close to Josi. "According to Sebastian, Regan stole money over a period of time. With *my* sign-in! And you condoned this?"

"Don't look so surprised, Mina. Regan was only in it for herself." Mom curls her lip in disgust, but keeps her voice low as people stroll by behind our bench. "She wanted a much larger chunk of the pie and thought she could blackmail me by threatening to reveal my existence. I couldn't allow her to do that."

More people pass; everyone's getting in their steps, yet I'm sitting here, my heart pounding like I'm running a marathon. My lungs feel like they're closing, so I take shallow breaths to try and calm my heart. "What did you do, Mom?"

"I protected the Blake family name, of course." She finally glances my way, her expression matter-of-fact. "Like I always have."

I can't believe she doesn't see that she's the cause of all of this. She's so delusional, but I have to know exactly what my mother is capable of. "Did you hurt Regan?"

"Mama, Mama," Josi calls out in her sweet voice as she throws her tiny body against me. "See the ducks!" She's so excited and out of breath, her green eyes full of innocence. I pull her into a tight hug and kiss the curls on top of her head. "I see them, Josi-Bean. You can feed them for just a bit longer. Remember, stay back and where I can see you."

She beams, then runs off once more. The bag of bread bits dangling from her hand.

"Regan threatened the family name." Mom's stares after Josi, her gaze locked on her granddaughter. "I couldn't have that."

I think back to Talia's comment about Regan's choice to kill herself by stabbing. She'd said it was an odd choice and such a painful way to die...as if she were punishing herself. Talia's analysis makes even more sense now. "*You* killed Regan in that hotel room and hired a cleanup team to get rid of her, didn't you?"

Mom looks at me, her ice-blue eyes unfazed by my accusation. "You had no reason to trust Regan. Not after what she did to the family. I wish you hadn't gone to that hotel." She exhales, her gaze regretful. "The team I hired did their job, but they also fiercely protect any threats to their business. A potential witness is seen as a threat."

"But I didn't see anyone," I say, shaking my head. "I can't possibly be a threat to them."

"Regan placed a phone call to you right before she died. These people have traffic footage of your car approaching the hotel just before they made it there. The fact you can place Regan in the hotel and not in a burning car where the police found her, makes you a threat. They have ample leverage on me, so they don't see me as one. I've tried to call them off, but they've already been paid and won't be deterred from their path."

My gaze swivels to my daughter, worry for Josi's safety rushing to the front of my mind. "I can't believe this is happening. That you put us all at risk like this...and for what? Money?"

"For the Blake name to endure, Mina. If you haven't learned anything else from me, know this...I have always done everything I have to protect this family. Even from myself." As I bring my attention back to her, Mom tilts her head, giving me an intense look. "You have to leave with me today. These people aren't to be trifled with. They work in the shadows and are very thorough in cleaning up loose ends. If you had just stayed away from Regan, you could've gone on living your life here. Now, you don't have a choice."

"Is this seat taken?" a woman in a slouchy beanie cap says at the same time she plops down on the other side of Mom.

"Do you mind?" Mom says in a cold tone. "We're having a private conversation."

"Oh, but I do mind." Sliding fully against my mom's side, she clamps an arm around her shoulders and holds her in place.

Worried by this strange woman accosting us, I try to pull my mom free of her hold, but she grips Mom's shoulder harder. "I wouldn't." She *tsks* and briefly drops her gaze to the sharp knife she has jammed against my mother's side.

The moment I realize our attacker is Simone, an involuntary gasp escapes. I stare at her in shock and recognition. She's the same woman who bumped me in the street across from Laura's store. She looks so different from the Simone I remember at Talia's baby shower. With short, red pixie hair poking out of the hat, pale skin, kohl-lined eyes, and a nose ring, I hardly recognize her. But changing her looks can't cover up her psycho mind. I jerk a fearful gaze to Josi, hoping the ducks continue to entertain her.

"As selfish as you are, I knew you couldn't stay away from your granddaughter. It was only a matter of time before I found you," the escaped convict sneers at my mom. "All you had to do was make sure Talia and Sebastian got into the right limo that night. I thought we were of like minds, but instead, you fucked up my plans with your own agenda."

"Let me go!" Mom hisses and tries to break free. "You're not going to do anything in public for God's sake."

Simone pinches Mom's shoulder painfully and adopts a cold smile. "I was willing to bide my time in prison. Sitting on useful information that I knew could come in handy one day worked for me, but the moment you tried to have me killed in my cell, well, I just couldn't let that slide." Jamming the knife deep into my mother's side, she leans in and exhales an eerie, satisfied laugh in her ear. "Looks like that new face didn't help you after all, did it, Isabel?"

I cover my mouth, holding back my scream. The last thing I want is to alert Josi that something is wrong. I don't want my child to run over and see this nightmare happening. Simone smugly twists the knife in my mom's side several times, while I beg her to stop, tears of helplessness blurring my vision.

"You're welcome, Mina." Pulling the knife free, she casually wipes the blade clean on my mother's coat, before flipping it closed with one hand. "I just did what you couldn't. She would always drag you down. Tell Talia that prison gave me a new perspective. I plan to do whatever it takes to protect *our* family. No matter the cost."

As my mother slumps against the bench and moans through the pain, I reach around and put pressure on her wound, trying to keep her from bleeding out. Dismissing my mother like a bug she just squished under her shoe, Simone slides her attention to my child. "I suggest you quietly get up and take Josi away from here before chaos ensues. She doesn't need to see this."

Simone stands and walks away at a leisurely pace, disappearing into the crowd. Keeping an eye on Josi, I do my best to apply pressure to my mom's gushing wound, while pulling my phone from my purse. "Hold on, Mom," I whisper, but she has already lost consciousness. When my screen doesn't light up, I realize I must've turned my phone off by accident earlier. I try to turn it on with one hand, but the phone slips from my fingers, hitting the pavement.

Tears rain down my cheeks as I release my mother to retrieve my phone as quickly as I can. Applying pressure to her side once more, I power up my phone with sticky, blood-soaked fingers and dial Den's number. Just as I look up to check on Josi, Den picks my baby girl up in his protective embrace.

When she points toward us on the bench, then turns in his arms to stare at the ducks, rambling and smiling, Den's golden gaze locks with mine. He quickly shifts her into one arm so she's facing the ducks, then lifts his phone to his ear to answer my call. "I've got her, Mina. Are you okay?"

His deep voice is the most reassuring sound I've ever heard. I blink to try to stop my tears and glance helplessly at my mom. "I'm okay. My mom's bleeding bad."

"It's going to be okay." He turns to speak to Theo, who's just walking up. "Tell Sebastian that Josi and Mina are safe, but we need him here now. Then please go stand with Mina while you call for an ambulance."

"Thank you for keeping Josi away from this," I say into the phone. My composure crumbling, I let out the sob I've been holding back and lift my blood-coated hand to my mother's slack features. In my heart I know...she's already gone.

"As soon as Sebastian takes Josi, I'll walk over," Den says quietly in my ear.

"Okay." Just hearing his calm tone keeps me from completely breaking down.

Theo calls for an ambulance as he reaches my side. Hanging up, he briefly puts a comforting hand on my shoulder before he turns to stand guard next to me. People have started to notice my mother, their steps slowing, gazes widening at the blood. I realize I'm still on the phone with Den and start to hang up, but he shakes his head, his expression intense. "Stay with me, little willow. I'm right here. Talk whenever you're ready."

I look at my daughter waving to the ducks and renewed fear pushes the words out of me. "Mom hired that cleaning team. They know I was there, and they're looking for me. I'm worried for Josi—"

"We got them, Mina," Den says with a curt nod. "The police are rounding the rest of their crew up as we speak."

"Tell me what happened, so I don't have to think about anything else." The moment he starts talking, I close my eyes, appreciating his comforting voice and the distraction he offers.

CHAPTER TWENTY-ONE

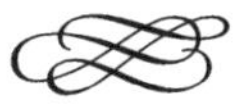

MINA

I pull the covers over Josi in Sebastian and Talia's guest bedroom, tucking her in securely. She's so tired from her outing at the park and feeding the ducks, that she's already asleep. Thankful that she's so resilient, I push her curls away from her angelic face and kiss her cheek, whispering, "I wish I could be more like you, little one."

I've never been so bone-weary in my life after spending several grueling hours doing police interview after interview, where not only was I grieving the loss of my mother for the second time, but I also couldn't stop the truth from coming out about her faking her death.

With Regan's burned body tied to the cleanup team, who were hired by my mother, who was later stabbed to death by Simone for her role in trying to have Simone assassinated in prison...yeah, my mother's tightly woven lies quickly unraveled the moment the cleanup guys started ratting each other out.

I pat the covers around Josi, then rub my eyes and sigh. I know my brother is waiting to talk to me.

I start toward the closed door when I hear Seb speaking in a low angry tone. "You've gone rogue on me for the last time, Den. Your job was to keep Mina safe and me informed, so I'd love to know how keeping me out of the goddamn loop about Isabel's return from the grave was part of that fucking equation?"

"Mina remains my priority. Nothing has changed," Den simply says, but doesn't elaborate to defend himself.

"Not anymore, she's not!" Seb snarls.

Talia says something I can't hear, but my brother charges on. "Your definition of priority and mine are obviously in conflict. All I want to do right now is kick your ass for putting her at risk, but I don't have time. Not only did I get my ass handed to me by the police Chief for withholding information, but I now have the fun job of telling my father the whole twisted truth about Isabel tonight so he doesn't find out when the shit-show hits the news outlets."

"Stop taking your frustration and anger out on Den, Sebastian," Talia cuts in. "Isabel's actions were her own.

And as for Den not informing you, that's not accurate. He—"

I quickly open the door and close it behind me. "I'm to blame for his silence," I say as I walk into their living room. Meeting my brother's angry blue gaze, I step beside Den, showing my support. "Den just learned the truth about Mom today. I asked him not to say anything, because I wasn't ready to share. And honestly, I'm not sure I ever would've told anyone. Like you, I wanted to protect our father from the truth." I spread my hands and sigh. "But that would only work if she stayed dead, and out of all of our lives. Her actions of taking Josi from daycare today told me I shouldn't remain silent."

Anger melting away, Seb pulls me into a bear hug, his gaze sympathetic. "I'm sorry you had to witness what happened to your Mom."

I swallow my emotions and squeeze his waist. Releasing him, I step back into place beside Den. "No one saw Simone coming. Especially not Mom."

Seb scrubs his hand along the scruff on his jaw. "I'm still stumped how Isabel pulled off faking her death. She couldn't have gotten out of that limo without help. The only thing I can think of is that she must've paid the driver to help her escape without detection. Unfortunately, the vehicle was so damaged from the explosion it was scrapped, so there's no way to know for sure."

"If Isabel tried to have Simone killed, I wonder if the

driver's surprising death after surgery was also engineered by her?" Talia muses, tapping her chin. "As for how he helped her, the only scenario I can think of is that the limo had a trap door underneath. I remember thinking it was odd that the limo stopped for a short time just as it pulled away, then it moved forward, driving off. At the time, I thought it stopped because Isabel realized she'd just taken our limo." Looking at each of us, she nods. "While all of you were in police interviews, I reviewed the footage from that night in our database, and yep, there was a manhole just beneath that spot where the limo stopped. All I know is, she took a huge risk on the timing of that explosion working to her advantage."

"Agreed. Then again..." Seb looks at his wife. "We helped her case."

I frown. "No one in our family would've helped Mom orchestrate this."

"Not intentionally." Shifting his attention to me, he continues, "But we did help when we didn't run the DNA test on the burned body in the limo. Skipping the test made sense at the time, since several people saw her get into the vehicle." Seb rolls his head from one shoulder to the other, then exhales. "Regardless of the why of the past, it's done. Now I have to deal with the fallout with Adam."

"I'll go with you to talk to Dad. We can do it together."

He shakes his head. "You've been through enough for one day, Mina. Get some sleep. Go get in bed with Josi and crash."

"Joey's down for the night, so I can go with you," Talia says, then turns to me. "I know you're exhausted. Get some rest, Mina."

As Talia walks over to their coat closet, Seb looks at Den. "I'd like you to stay until we return. After that, your services with BLACK Security will no longer be required."

"What?" Tense with anger, I glare at my brother. "He didn't do anything wrong!"

Den doesn't react at all. Instead, he turns to Talia, who's stopped halfway across the room, coats in hand, a look of astonished exasperation on her face.

"Is that your opinion, Talia?" Den asks.

My stomach tightens with worry when Talia steps forward and hands Seb his coat. Shrugging into hers, she meets Den's unwavering gaze as she buttons hers closed. "You're the best at what you do, Den. Of course I want you to stay. But I also consider you family, so I do have a request." Her gaze pings between the two men. "I want you two stubborn alphas to stop butting heads. Can you please do that for me?"

Den bends slightly at the waist and inclines his head. "I'll try my best."

Grumbling his acknowledgement, Sebastian follows

his wife into the elevator and as the door starts to slide closed, he says to Den, "I expect a full report of everything that led up to today's events, your conversations with the police...all of it, in my inbox before I get back."

The tension in my shoulders eases once the elevator door shuts. "Please tell me you'll write that report," I say, turning to face Den. "I don't want Seb to keep threatening to fire you. I can't take the stress."

Den shrugs. "He fires me on a near daily basis. It's kind of our thing."

"I know my brother, Den. He's not happy with you."

"Sebastian's right pissed for sure. We'll work through this in our own way." Stepping close, he runs his knuckles down my cheek. "You've been through a lot. Are you going to be okay, little willow?"

My heart squeezes and tears threaten at the sympathy in his gaze. Straightening my shoulders, I push the images of Mom slumped against me out of my mind and take a deep breath. "I think so." Tilting my head, I hold his gaze. "Why do you call me willow? I hope I'm the bird variety and not a plant that grows in mud."

Chuckling, he tucks a strand of my hair behind my ear. "Definitely not a muddy plant. It's a small, yellow-feathered bird. When I was young, every spring the willow's song would filter through our kitchen window. As soon as my mom heard it, she'd make tea, then walk outside to her garden and check on each plant's buds about to bloom. With hope in her eyes for a great flowering season, she'd head off to her studio, inspired to start a new project. Now, whenever I hear the willow's soft song, it instantly makes me smile."

"Soft song? Um, you're the amazing singer, not me."

"You're my *hope*, Mina," he says, running his fingers down my hair.

He's standing so close, his intense gaze sliding to my lips. My eyes drift closed and I wait for his mouth to claim mine. After everything that's happened today: betrayal, shock, fear, sadness, anger, terror, and bone-weary tension, I crave connecting with him again on a visceral level. Even if it's here in the living room, I don't care. I just need to feel alive and wanted.

The instant I sense Den stepping back, my eyes pop open. My brows pull together in confusion as he walks to the window and puts his back to me, his hands crossing at the base of his spine.

"You should get some sleep," he says gruffly.

Frowning, I walk over and stare at his profile. "I'm not sleepy."

He doesn't bother to look down at me as he responds. "Reading might help you fall asleep."

Annoyed that his gaze stays focused on the city lights below, I say what's on my mind. "I'd rather spend time with you." When he doesn't respond, I huff my frustration. "So, is that it? Now that the danger is over and the job is done, you're finished with me as well?

"You need time to process. I think keeping my distance is best for now," he says, his jaw muscle jumping.

"Was I *that* much more than you expected?" Leaning my back against the window, I cross my arms and apply pressure to my chest to ward off the hurt creeping into my heart. "I never would've thought anyone could intimidate you, least of all little 'ole me."

Den's laser gaze cuts to me, his brow furrowed. "What are you going on about?

"I'm saying that you're as much to blame as I am."

His mouth thins and he returns his focus to the city. "Which is why I'm giving you space."

"How awfully considerate of you." Stung by his rejection, I turn my sarcasm on full blast as I push off the glass. "Since you're not planning on sticking around, I guess I should thank you for unleashing my inner siren. Someone will absolutely appreciate all she has to offer."

Den quickly steps in front of me and puts a hand on the glass to block my exit. "The idea that our connection last night could be due to lingering drugs in your system is driving me fucking insane!" His tortured gaze searches mine. "Tell me you wanted every single thing that happened as much as I did."

"You think I regret all that primal rawness? That I didn't freaking love every sensual way you made me scream your name?" I blink at him in surprise. "Is that why you've been keeping me at arm's length since this morning?"

He slides his fingers under my hair, his hold tense as he clasps my neck in a firm hold. "I learned about the drugs in the tea after you fell asleep. I didn't want to believe they could've influenced you. This morning when you said you weren't yourself last night, I tried to keep my distance, to give you an out, but..." Pausing, he runs his thumb down my neck. "I'm a greedy bastard."

Relieved he still wants me, I rest my hand on his chest. "This morning, I was worried you might be put off by my, um...aggressiveness. I was actually trying to apologize, but apparently bungled it." Smirking, I continue, "Last night's Mina would've scared the ever-loving-hell out of Derrick."

"The last thing I want to think about is you with your ex." He pulls me against him, and my heart skips several beats as he stares down at me, all broody and intense. "Never apologize for your wild, Mina. If a man can't handle the demanding minx you are in bed, he doesn't bloody deserve you. I covet every gorgeous, petite inch. I want to be the only man you debate with, the only man you cook with, the person you want to share all your stories with, and absolutely the only man who grants every desire your sexy mind conceives."

The fact he's saying everything I want to hear makes it hard to speak. *Me too, big guy. Me freaking too.* Too emotional to form the right words, I push up on my toes to wrap my arms around his neck when Den scoops me into his arms.

As he walks past the couch, I frown. "Where are we going? The leather is perfectly cushy."

He stops halfway across the room and looks down at me, his golden gaze turning a deep amber shade. "I want you always, little willow."

Every muscle in my body turns to mush and my arms tighten around his neck. "I lo—"

"But not tonight," he continues as he walks over and sets me down just outside the guest bedroom door.

"Are you serious?" I say on a low hiss so I don't wake Josi up.

"I meant what I said about you needing to process."

"Oh, I'm processing all right." Narrowing my gaze, I cross my arms. I can't believe I almost told him I loved him. Is there a female version of blue balls? Because if there is, I'm feeling it! And you know what they say about payback. "You won't like what I'm thinking right now."

"Get some rest. Tomorrow and the days to follow will be hard."

"I don't want to process," I argue past the tremble in my lips. His rejection on top of everything else is just too much. "I don't want to think, Den." I put my hands on his lapels. "I want—"

Clasping my chin, he presses his lips to mine in a

dominant, you're-mine-and-yes-I-want-to-fuck-you-just-as-much kiss. The moment I return his affection with all the pent-up emotion swirling through me, he pulls back, his intense gaze glittering with smoldering lust. "It's because I care that I'm telling you *good night*, Mina."

CHAPTER TWENTY-TWO

MINA

While I stuff a stack of mail into my purse, I watch Josi crawl into Den's lap to show him her Halloween artwork from daycare. My heart swells with love and appreciation as he asks about every slash of color and listens intently to her describe and point to her Jack-o-lantern, witch's hat and black cat drawing.

Den's patience with Josi is so heartwarming. It gets to me every time I see them together. The moment he stops by on his way home from work to check on us, she's on him like Velcro. Yet, he's so patient, but also firm with her. Far better than me. After losing my mother for a second time, I've spoiled my daughter more than I normally would've, but now that Josi and I are finally getting back into a rhythm that works without constant fit pitching or foot-stomping bouts, I'm bringing her back to a more structured routine.

The last week and a half hasn't been easy. After the initial news cycle and social media fallout of my mother's duplicity, each of the Blakes dealt with Isabel Blake's actual death in their own ways.

While continuing to search for Simone, Seb uncovered the fake identity my mother had been using, which helped him recover and move the rest of the stolen Blake money back to the corporation.

My brothers, Gavin and Damien, in solidarity with our father, refused to attend our mother's burial, which was set far away from the Blake family plots in another part of the cemetery.

And my father? To Gavin's delight, Adam Blake has spent less time at the office as CEO, because he's been spending more time with Josi. I never thought I'd see the day that my dad would be so involved in my child's life. I've appreciated him more every day. With Helena's help, he has thrown himself into grandfather-hood with gusto. Of course, he also tried to include Joey in some of their outings, but so far Seb is resisting. While I can't begin to understand my brother's reasons for holding back, I appreciate that Seb needs time. Of all of us, he suffered the most and lost so much from my mother's machinations.

For my own sanity from reporters and ugly news reports, I buried myself in Blake Industries work I'd missed leading up to my mother's murder. I had a lot to catch up on, and if it weren't for Den insisting that I attend my mom's burial once her body was finally released from the morgue, no one would've been there when she was put to rest.

Once I slide the gift I plan to give Den into my oversized purse, I start to push my hair back when my gaze snags on the present he gave me just before we picked Josi up.

As we parked the car at Josi's daycare, I glanced down at the sensation of Den's fingers sliding along my wrist. I've missed his touch so much. "I waited until after your mother's funeral, but I couldn't wait any longer to put this on you."

Lifting my arm, my gaze misted over as I stared at the gold willow charm dangling from the matching chain link bracelet he hooked around my wrist. "Thank you for the thoughtful gift. Didn't you say willows are slim? I think my little bird needs to go on a diet."

Chuckling, Den tapped the bird. As it spun in circles between us, he said, "No matter where you are, I'll always be with you."

The sentiment behind the bracelet melted my heart. It was such a sweet gift, I had to swallow a couple of times to hold my tears back. Leaning over, I kissed his jaw and whispered, "Thank you so much, Den."

Coming back to the present, I glance up to see him

staring at me. My cheeks flame with embarrassment to be caught mooning over Den's gift, but I can't help myself. I absolutely adore the little chubby bird, and the big man with the heart of a lion who gave it to me. I hope he appreciates my gift just as much.

Den smirks at the heat in my face, but doesn't get a chance to tease me before my daughter's small hands flatten on his cheeks and turn his head back to her drawing. As she prattles on, so happy to have his full attention once more, I admire his handsome face, appreciating his amazing support as my mind jumps back to my mother's burial earlier today.

"Is it bad that I didn't add a date?" I said as I numbly stared at the headstone that simply read: Isabel. After all, she'd already died once. I knew my internal thoughts sounded bitter, but I couldn't help the way I felt about all the misery she caused.

Den stood beside me, his presence giving me the strength to get through her burial in my own way. "You gave her your heart the first time you buried her. It's understandable to feel betrayed, hurt, and all the other emotions you're experiencing, Mina." He slid his gaze my way, the morning sun turning his golden eyes into warm rays that settle my warring heart. "In the whole scheme of things, a headstone is just a marker."

"Then why am I even here?" I asked, not really expecting an answer.

"Closure, Little Willow." Glancing away, he stared off in the distance. "After my wife and daughter died, I went through the motions for everyone else: family, friends, co-workers, but I didn't speak at their funerals. I couldn't." His attention returned to me, regret swirling. "I've been away from London long enough to wish I had given them a proper goodbye."

"You weren't ready, Den." I understood his emotions more than he would ever know. "Now you are. When you decide to go, I'll stand beside you if you'd like." The frigid wind whipped around us, stirring the clouds in the overcast sky. It was perfect weather leading up to Halloween. I shivered in my long overcoat and stared at the newly packed dirt around my mother's grave, trying to come up with the right words.

"There are so many things I want to say to you, Mom." My voice cracked, but I pushed onward, needing to get the words out. "I'm furious at everything you did: the lies, the deception, your new life without us. And while I will never understand it, I know in your own warped way, you loved our family. I'm sorry for what happened to you. No one deserves to die the way you did. I just wish you could have trusted what the rest of us have always known...that the Blakes will always have each other's backs. No matter what." Tears tracked down my cheeks and Den wrapped his arm around me, pulling me close to his warmth as I finished, "I hope you can rest in peace now."

Josi's voice draws me out of my musings. She's pointing at me, a wide grin on her face. "I draw like Mama."

Den nods, then gently palms the top of her head to turn her gaze back to his. "Why don't you go get ready for your granddad? He'll be here soon to take you to dinner before trick-or-treating."

"Going tricky-tweatin'!" Squealing her excitement, she jumps down and tears out of the room.

When she comes barreling into the living room carrying a black dress with flowing sleeves, her pointed witch's hat perched on her blond curls, and a plastic pumpkin swinging on her arm, Den smiles and adjusts the strap under her chin, righting the crooked hat on her head. After he helps her step into the dress, he ties the back, then lifts the drawing up beside her and looks at me. "This masterpiece shall be called: Life imitating art, imitating life."

As I smile my agreement and Josi claps her hands, the doorbell rings. "It's Granddad!"

I intervene before she can open the door. "Always let me answer it, sweetie. Hey, Dad," I say, opening the door for my father.

"Look at my witchy dinner companion." Walking into

the foyer, he nods to acknowledge Den, then winks at me as he takes Josi's hand and spins her around to see her costume. "I'm going to feel a bit underdressed at dinner tonight," he says, glancing down at his dark jeans and cashmere sweater. "Are you sure you want to go out with me?"

"Helena too?" Josi looks up at him, her green eyes full of hope.

"But of course. She's dressed as a fairy and waiting for you." Dad's blue eyes sparkle with amusement. "Why don't you go get your overnight bag and we'll head out for the evening?"

"Cannnnnndy!" Josi calls out and speeds back to her room.

While Den steps over near the windows to answer his phone, I raise my eyebrows at my father. "Please check her candy."

He chuckles. "I'll inspect every piece, and she'll only get two or three pieces for the evening. The rest will be put away...after we sort each type into their respective piles for trading, of course."

I grin, surprised he remembers us kids doing that. "Thank you so much for offering to take her tonight. It might be a day early, but our old neighborhood always had the best trick-or-treating. But please don't take her to too many houses. We still have to take her around my neighborhood tomorrow."

"You've had a long week." He pauses and I see the unspoken appreciation in his gaze. "The least I can do is give you an evening all to yourself," he says as Josi stumbles into the foyer, juggling her overnight bag and the pumpkin still draped on her arm.

My father hasn't spoken my mother's name since he learned what she did. And I know he never will. She died the moment she betrayed our family, but he's human, so in his own way, he's letting me know he's thankful that I took care of her burial.

I step close and wrap him in a tight hug, whispering in his ear, "I love you, Daddy."

He squeezes me tighter than he ever has, then kisses me on the cheek. "Love you more, Princess." Before he releases me, he whispers in my ear, "Have you told Sebastian about Den yet?"

I give him a surprised look. "There's nothing to tell." Between work, Mom's funeral stuff, and Den working on BLACK Security cases, I haven't seen him for any real length of time except for the funeral today. Casting my gaze Den's way, I murmur, "And, even if there was, it's none of Seb's business."

"Mmm, hmmm," he says, giving me a knowing look. "I know you want to take Josi trick-or-treating tomorrow night, but I'm happy to keep her on Sunday if you like—"

"Come *on*, Granddad." Josi tugs hard on his hand.

Happy that my father approves of Den, I call after

them before I shut the door, "I'll touch base later to say goodnight."

Den's warm hands land on my shoulders, massaging gently. "Are you okay?"

"Today was the closure I needed." I take a breath and turn to face him. The moment we lock gazes, it hits me just how much I truly love this man. Den doesn't let me run all over him. He's his own man, yet he's also someone who listens, even to my crazy ramblings about my dead mother. I guess, sometimes it takes losing yourself to find the right person to put you back together. Den has done that for me in so many ways. "Thank you for coming with me today, and well...for everything. I don't know if I could've done it without you."

"You're stronger than you think, but I would've never let you do that alone." His mouth tilts in a smile. "Would you like to go out to dinner?"

"Can we go to your place and order something instead?" I glance around my apartment and shrug. "I'd rather not be here without Josi."

"Then you'd better pack," he says, sliding his thumb along my jawline. "I'm not bringing you back here until I absolutely have to."

Stomach fluttering, I press a soft kiss to his palm, then force myself to walk calmly to my bedroom. The moment I enter, I glance back at the doorway to make sure he can't see me before I pull the duffle bag I've already packed out from under my bed. My heart might be doing summersaults, but I don't want to appear too eager, so I force myself to unzip the bag and slowly flip through the contents to confirm I have all my overnight stuff. Change of clothes, sleep tee and shorts, toothbrush, face soap, lotion, hairbrush, make up, and birth control. Nodding that I have it all, I re-zip my bag. *Keep your cool, Mina. Don't overthink it. He likes your sexy self, remember?* Lifting my bag onto my shoulder, I walk out and grab my purse from the counter, saying, "Let's go, Noble Brit."

On the drive over to his place, Den and I debate our dinner choices, but it's not until we pull into the garage that I finally convince him the Thai place on Columbus has the very best food. "Unfortunately, they don't deliver," I say, scrunching my nose.

"Now she tells me." He shakes his head and starts to push the button to open the garage door once more, but I quickly open the car door and hop out with my purse and bag.

"While you're getting the food, I'll set the table and be ready to go once you get back, okay?"

My stomach tenses when Den hesitates, but then he pushes a button on his phone to disarm the house system. "The door's unlocked now. I'll be back in just a bit."

I wait until he backs out and the garage door closes before I run upstairs as fast as I can. I have very little time to put his gift together and set the table before he gets back.

Sliding the bag out of my oversized purse, I retrieve the custom picture frame and smile as I run my fingers along the smooth, colorful glass pieces in blue, white, black, green, orange and red. Every color of his family is represented in the thin, braided border a half-inch inside the edge of the honey-colored wood frame. Pleased with how the custom frame turned out, I walk over to the cabinet in Den's living room, retrieve the picture of his family and the bracelet, then lay them on the island so I can take the back off the frame.

Setting the custom cut mat against the glass, I carefully arrange Den's well-loved braided bracelet inside the special rectangular cut out just below where the main braided border will frame the picture, then set Den's family portrait on top before I replace the frame's back to hold it all together.

When I turn the frame around, my gaze mists as I stare at his beautiful family. "I'm so sorry, Den." Sniffing back unshed tears, I walk over to the mantle and set the frame just below his mother's beautiful artwork. I slide the picture frame to the left a bit, then walk back and smile at the end result. "I hope he loves it as much as I do," I murmur just as a phone rings.

Startled by the unfamiliar sound, I turn around in the room, looking everywhere for the source. When I finally find an old-style phone tucked inside the bookshelf next to the kitchen, I follow my instincts and lift the handset.

"Hello?"

"May I please speak with Sir Barasa?" a man asks in a formal British accent.

"*Sir* Barasa?" I say, my voice pitching.

"That is how knights are addressed, yes," he says in a slight condescending tone.

Oh my God, Den's a freaking *knight*? *Has he been inwardly smirking every time I call him Noble Brit?* Beyond speechless, I manage to reply, "He isn't home at the moment. I would be happy to give him a message."

"Please tell, Sir Barasa..." The man pauses and clears his throat. "That his *Queen* requests his presence. It's time for him to come home."

Come home? My stomach drops and my heart stutters, but I manage to answer. "I'll be sure to relay your request."

"Thank you. Is this Lady Barasa?" he asks, sounding suddenly curious.

"No, I'm just a friend." *Who would love an invite to the Palace!* "Thank you for your call." I set the phone back in its cradle and my heart feels heavy as my gaze strays to my bracelet. *Will Den go back for good?* I know he wants closure with his family, but what if the Queen's request means his return home will be a permanent one? I can't lose him now.

The doorbell rings, jerking me from my angsty musings, and I automatically move to answer it. Does Den's neighborhood celebrate Halloween a day early too? Grabbing the bowl of candy Den had prepared—Really? What was he thinking with such a small bowl?—I open the door to a man of medium height in a custom suit with perfectly groomed dark hair and smooth, aristocratic features.

"Hello, are you Mina?" he says in a polite tone. When I nod, my brow furrowing, a somber look crosses his face. "I wish I came with better news, but there has been an accident."

"Is Den okay? Was there a wreck?" Panic sets in as I quickly set the bowl down on the table next to the door and retrieve my purse, reaching blindly for my phone.

He nods. "I saw the whole thing. Den gave me his address and asked me to let you know that they've taken him to hospital. If you don't have a ride, I'll be happy to take you to Presbyterian."

Worry grips me as my fingers brush the glasses I forgot to return to Elijah. Something feels off. I can't imagine Den sending a stranger to his home, yet he does know that I'm here waiting for him. I search my mind for a reason why I feel tense when something the guy said sets alarm bells off in my head. He might sound American, yet he dropped *the* before hospital, like Den does every so often when he's talking fast. Heart racing, I quickly grab the glasses and put them on my face, pretending to adjust them. "Thanks for letting me know, but I've got a ride." Please let that button I just pushed activate a bat signal, or at the very least send Elijah a screenshot of this guy's face and not of my own eyeballs. Glancing down, I reach for the door and start to pull it closed when my body suddenly seizes and a massive Charlie horse takes over every single muscle at once.

Sharp pain radiates everywhere, and the guy quickly pulls a Taser back in time to capture me before I hit the floor. "Come along," he says cheerfully. "That's a good girl." Lifting me as if I weigh nothing, he carries my still shuddering body to a waiting limo and stuffs me into the back seat before he climbs in and shuts the door.

As my captor digs through my purse, snapping, "Where is her phone?" I stare through half-closed eyes at a man curled up on the bench seat across from us, his arms and legs bound with sturdy rope.

I try to speak, but nothing comes out. Ever so slowly, feeling starts to return to my body, but it's like pins and needles everywhere.

Hitting a button on the console, the guy speaks to the driver. "Alberto is meeting us at the planned location. He'll take Hugh. Let's go."

Hugh?

When the guy grabs my floppy arm and uses my thumbprint to open my phone, I curse myself for not using a code instead. Who is the man with the Taser? And what is he planning to do with us? I steal a peak at Hugh, worrying for Den's friend. I'm pretending to be unconscious, but he's completely vulnerable in his unconscious state.

While my captor's distracted with going through my phone, I try to see past the tinted windows to figure out where we're going.

Without lifting my head, I can't see anything but the thick frames on the glasses.

I look at Hugh once more, then slowly lift my hand to my face.

CHAPTER TWENTY-THREE

DEN

The Thai takeaway smells so good my stomach starts growling the moment I get in the car with it. I reach for my phone to let Mina know I'm on the way back, and a text pops up from Elijah. The last thing I want is to think about work when I finally have Mina all to myself, but I can't ignore it. I start to read the text when I notice I also have a voicemail from Hugh. When did he leave that? Clicking on Elijah's text, my brow furrows as I read.

Edgar Stewart entered the country two days ago on a private plane. His diplomatic immunity made accessing his information a bit more challenging, but now you have it. Do you need me to do any other searches?

Tension tightens my shoulders and I immediately dial Mina's number. When my call goes straight to voicemail, I try not to worry even as I retrieve my gun from the console, check that it's ready to go, then text him back.

Inform Sebastian and Talia that Mina needs her own detail going forward. I will fill them in shortly.

Before I send Hugh a "heads up" text, I listen to his voicemail.

"One of my old contacts at the embassy let me know that Edgar is here. Going to do some recon. Will call you with an update later."

Frowning, I glance down at the time he left the message. It was hours earlier while my phone was on mute during the funeral. I start to dial his number when Mina calls me back. Relieved to see her name on my Caller ID, I answer before the first ring ends. "Good call on the restaurant. Food smells amazing," I say, trying to keep the worry out of my tone. I'll talk to her about added security when I get back. "On my way back with it now."

"Such a pity Mina won't be eating with you, Dennet."

The snide British accent knots my chest in fiery anger. It takes every bit of my training not to bellow at him, but I manage a lethal tone pretty damn easily. "You hurt her at all and you will find out why I'm the fucking best, Edgar. There will be nowhere you can hide and no end to the many ways I will rip you apart before I destroy you." I put him on speaker and quickly type a text to Sebastian.

Mina's been taken. On the phone with the kidnapper right now. Trace her phone.

"It's a shame we didn't get to play the 'guess who this is' game? That would've been fun, but alas, since you know who this is, your old colleague Hugh must've filled you in on my last conversation with him. I really enjoyed that one."

If he knows Hugh is alive, that can't be good. "You will pay for what you did to my family, to *all* of our families, you disgusting piece of shit."

"See, this is exactly why I'm here, Den." He sighs dramatically. "It's my heart's desire to give you a second chance, a do-over as it were, so you can make the right choice this time around."

"What are you talking about?" I growl as I start my car's engine.

A message comes through from Sebastian.

Elijah's jumping on to do the trace. Keep him on as long as you can. Do you know for sure he has Mina?

"Not everyone gets a second chance in life, but I guess you're extra special. I have Hugh *and* Mina. Both their lives are precarious, and finite. The question is, which one will you save this time, Dennet? Do you save the woman you care about? Or do you save a long-time friend, who apparently came back from the dead to tell you about me? Don't bother trying; you can't get to them both in time. I've made sure of that, so you'll have to choose. Who will it be..." he sing-songs gleefully.

"You will wish for death before I'm done with you," I snarl into the phone. "Where the hell are they?"

"Such violent promises in your tone! It gives me shivers. Let's just say Hugh's life is on a timer. Dear Mina is stuck with me, and you know how I feel about leaving anyone you care about still breathing..."

"Motherfucker, I'm going to rip you apart with my bare hands!"

"The great thing about diplomatic immunity?" Edgar says in an unruffled tone. "I can be so much more open with my loathing. Tick-tock, Dennet. If you're so fucking *great*, you should find me before Mina meets the same fate your family did. Then again, if you choose to save her, you'll be willfully killing your loyal friend. I hope you make a better choice than you did for my brother."

"If we had saved your brother that day, you wouldn't have your father. You'd have lost either way, you bloody wanker!"

"Between the two of them," he says in a droll tone. "I'd much rather have my brother. Make your choice wisely." Before I can respond, he continues, "I'll even give you a hint to make this interesting. Our location always had an audience. If you decide to try to find Mina first, I suggest you hurry. She'll be my entertainment until you get here. I hope she's up to the task."

He hangs up before I can threaten him again. Fury

boiling inside me, I immediately call Elijah. The moment he picks up, I demand, "Were you able to trace it?"

"The signal dropped in and out a couple of times before going dead. I couldn't get a lock."

"Talia and I are in the office now," Sebastian cuts in, his tone all business. "Bring us up to speed, Den."

Once I fill them in as fast as I can about Hugh, Edgar and his ultimatum for Mina and my friend, Sebastian says curtly, "You know this guy, Den. What's your plan of action—"

"Look at this!" Elijah jumps in. "I opened my other laptop, and the GPS signal from my surveillance glasses is live. The last time I saw those glasses, Mina was trying them on."

"Do you think she could still have them?" Talia asks.

"It's possible," Elijah answers. "Mina's a smart cookie. If the guy took her phone, she might've turned them on to help us find her. Right now, the signal isn't moving. And it appears to be in a building on the Lower East Side."

"Something Edgar said makes me think there might be a timer of some kind, possibly explosives, so take a signal jamming device with you," I say. "It could buy us time if he's using remote detonation."

"Bombs? Motherfucker!" Sebastian growls. "You brought this psycho down on my sister—"

"That's how he killed my wife and child!" I cut him

off with a cold snarl, not needing to hear shit from him right now.

Silence fills the airspace. Most likely shock.

"While you check out the first location, Sebastian," I continue in a calmer voice. "I'll chase down another lead based on some coordinates I have, but I'll need Elijah's help to pinpoint it."

"We'll head out now." Sebastian's tone shifts to all business.

"I'll call the police and have them meet you at the location Elijah gave us," Talia says.

"Okay, Den. Sebastian's on his way. Hit me with what you've got," Elijah's says.

I pull up a number on my phone and read it off. "This is a GPS signal. Lock on it and send me the location."

While I wait for him to find the signal, I curl my hands tight around my steering wheel.

"I'm truly sorry, Den."

I shut my eyes for a second, appreciating Talia's words. She's always known we both suffered loss, but not the details of mine until now. I won't let it happen again. *Could I have done something different to protect Mina from this without smothering her?* Sebastian is right. Mina's life wouldn't be in jeopardy right now if it weren't for me.

"Okay, I got it. It looks like this signal leads to the abandoned Regent Theater in the Lower East Side."

That certainly fits with the hint Edgar gave. "Is Theo or Calder available?"

"Calder's on his way in, but I can help now," Elijah says.

"Sebastian might need you to track another signal if that one doesn't pan out. You should stay there."

"I can do that from the car and coordinate with Talia at the office," he counters. "Mina's family, and you need the backup. I'm coming."

"Bring a jamming device and see you in a few," I say, appreciating the support. "Make sure you answer if Sebastian calls. We're already at odds, I'd rather not give him yet another reason to be pissed at me."

"Got it. Heading out now."

Gunning the engine, I speed out of the parking lot. According to my car's map, I'm six minutes away from the Regent. I won't let this bastard destroy Mina's bright light.

The front of the abandoned theater is dark so I park down the road with my lights off. I don't want to alert anyone I'm here.

The moment I cut the engine, I glance at my watch. I can't wait. Elijah is at least eight minutes behind me. Every minute counts. I check my gun in my shoulder holster once more and make sure it's unsnapped for easy access under my jacket, then grab my knife and holder from the glove compartment. Strapping it at my back, I get out and shut the door with a soft click.

Every streetlight is out, as if the city has written off this section of town just as much as the squatters have. Thankful for the cover of darkness, I pass boarded-up storefronts and tenant housing, all stained with soot and falling apart with disrepair.

No lights, no heat. No heart, no home.

Gone, forgotten, dead.

The cold, dilapidated imagery feels ominous, gnarling a knot of dread in my chest. I inhale quickly to clear my head and swallow the cough as the frigid air fills my lungs. Setting my jaw, I stealthily slide behind a bullet-riddled bench, then a burned out car, before moving on to a bashed-in donation box just a few feet from the building.

Broken windows line the theater's top floor and graffiti-littered boards cover the bottom ones. A puff of cigarette smoke curling in the brisk air gives the lone guard's position away in the shadows to the left of the double front doors.

Idiot.

My gaze narrows on the chain around the door handles. Not an access point. Must be around the side.

First things first. He's in my way.

Crouching low next to the donation box, I pick up a small rock and toss it hard back toward the burned out car.

The rattling ping on the hood captures the guard's attention.

"Who's there?" he barks. Stepping out of the shadows,

he lifts his gun and stalks toward the car, demanding, "Show yourself, motherfucker!"

Not that you'll see me coming. As he passes the donation box, I pull my gun and quickly stand, clocking him on the back of the head.

Stuffing his unconscious body into the back of the car, I move over to the building and stay close to the structure, ducking under the one intact window as I make my way in the shadows to the side street.

When I come upon an idling limo with diplomatic plates, my gaze slits in anger. Approaching from behind, I can make out the silhouette of a single man in the car. Edgar sure has shitty security. This guy apparently decided that being warm was more important than guarding another entrance to the building. I'll take the win. I crouch so I can't be seen in the rearview mirror and unknot my tie. Shoving the cloth into the tailpipe, I wait for the car to stall. Once the car sputters out and the bloke is busy eyeing his dashboard trying to figure out what caused it, I make my way around and wait just behind the driver's door.

The instant he opens the door, I grab him and clamp my arm around his neck, using my height to my advantage. He struggles, trying his best to knock me off him, but eventually he passes out. Once he's tied up and tucked in the trunk of the car, I retrieve my knife and jam it into each back tire with grim satisfaction, then head for the side entrance of the building.

Dank air fills my nostrils, along with the smell of mold and worn wood. I eye the diagram of the old theater in a worn gold frame on a wall in the lobby. It's intended to help the ticket holders find their seat locations, but the image also gives me an idea of what I'm walking into. The bowl-like design is a true relic from the past. With high ornate ceilings for acoustics, hundreds of seats descend in a horseshoe shape from the highest entry point, fanning down to the screen and stage for live performances at the bottom.

A text comes through from Sebastian as I make my way across the trash and leaf littered concession area.

We found a guy strapped to a chair with an arm from a pair of glasses jammed into his eye socket and a suicide bomb jacket lying on the floor. Hugh's not here. Where the hell is my sister? Heading to your coordinates now.

Relieved Hugh apparently got away, I text him back with the current location. *I believe she's here. Approaching building now. Elijah should be here soon.*

Right behind him.

As I quietly open the theater door, I hear Mina before I see her. She's singing the Rolling Stone's Satisfaction song, her voice wavering, pitching high, then low as her fear escalates. I tamp down my first instinct to run to her. Instead, I study the contraption she's tied up in and try to determine the quickest and safest way to get her down. With a rope hanging down from the scaffold currently wrapped around her neck, and two other ropes attached to the scaffold's sides that are tied around her wrists, she's at least twelve feet in the air, perched on top of an industrial looking ladder.

"God, my ears are screaming. Mina, *Mina*! Surely you can do better than that." Edgar calls from a seat halfway down in the seating areas. Settled in the very center of the room for optimum viewing of the stage, he's leaning back with his feet up. "Why don't you try to sing 'Let it Be'?" When Mina frantically shakes her head, he sighs. "No? Ugh, so young...let's see. You have to know this one. Sing 'Another One Bites the Dust' and try your best to do it justice this time."

"I can't sing!" she yells, her voice bouncing around the empty room.

"Not even to save your life?" When he lifts his hand and pushes the toggle button on the device, my gaze jerks back to Mina and I step forward out of the shadows so she can see me. As the ladder lowers slightly, she grabs hold of the ropes tied around her wrists to keep her balance and bites her lip to stay calm and not give me away.

Seeing her raise up on her toes to keep the rope from choking her, eyes wide in terror, rips me to pieces. Sheer fury flashes through every muscle and I quickly step down to the end of the row behind Edgar's. Lifting my gun, I put my finger on the trigger, ready to blow his fucking brains out. Diplomatic immunity can fuck off! "Put down the remote, Edgar. It's over."

He glances my way and shrugs, completely unfazed by my gun pointed at him. "It's about time you got here. This was getting old and honestly...?" He pauses and sucks in air through his teeth, wincing. "A bit painful on the ears." When I shift to a step to the end of his row, he holds the remote aloft. "Ah, ah...don't come any closer. If my finger comes off this remote at all, the ladder will collapse on itself." Glancing back toward the stage, he nods at Mina. "Also, see that lovely metal collar she's wearing just below the rope around her neck? It's tied to me via a cuff on my wrist. If my heart rate goes up at all, yep, signal goes off and...boom, goodbye, Mina."

"What do you want?" I bite out, not bothering to hide my vile hatred for him.

"I want you to suffer." He pushes the button under his thumb and the ladder lowers until Mina's lifting up on the tips of her toes. One foot slips and she screams, but catches herself, her legs shaking.

"Let her go!" I grit out. "I'm the one you want. This is between you and me."

"Because of you, I lost my family."

"Because of *you*, I lost mine, you psychotic murderer!"

"But she's right there," he says smoothly, gesturing to Mina. "You love this woman, right?"

I don't look at Mina. Instead, I keep my gaze trained on him, hoping to distract him from hurting her. He can't know how much I care for her. I want nothing more than to eviscerate him for killing my family, but not at the risk to Mina's safety. "I'm her bodyguard. Nothing more. You went to all this trouble for nothing, when your focus should've been on me."

"Then I guess I'm done here." As Edgar stands and pushes the button fully forward, the ladder drops from under Mina, quickly collapsing into itself.

The sight of the rope cinching Mina's neck guts me. "Pull on the ropes!" I yell, forgetting Edgar as I vault down the stairs in inhuman strides to get to the stage as fast as I can. Jumping up onto the stage, I repeat my instructions once more, right before I fire twice to sever the rope above her head. The moment the cinch rope breaks and her straining arms suddenly bear the rest of her body weight, I secure my gun to grab her ankles and hold her up.

"Feels like I'm being pulled apart," Mina whimpers hoarsely.

Please let this old building's concrete and stone walls help block that psycho's phone signal. Where the hell is Elijah? "It's going to be okay." I keep my tone calm as I shift around her and hold one hand out, palm up. "Put all your weight on one foot on my hand." As soon as she does it, I move completely under her, and capture her other foot. Lifting her up, I fully extend my arms, taking the pressure off her shoulders and arms completely. "Now you can just use the ropes for balance."

While Mina shifts her weight on my hands and exhales her relief, Hugh steps through an exit door at the back of the theater. As he makes his way around the edge of the stage, he assesses our predicament. "Does the ladder work?" he asks, his gaze shifting between Mina, me, and the scaffold.

"No time," I say shaking my head. "Get my knife. It's at my waist."

Hugh retrieves the knife from the holder at my back. As he starts to climb up the left side of the scaffold, Elijah pulls open the main entry door. "Did you bring the jammer?" I call out before he starts down the stairs toward us.

Lifting the box in his hand, he continues down, his echoing footfalls drowning out my next instructions to turn on the jammer. The second he reaches the stage, I growl one more time, "Turn the goddamned machine on now!" I bellow, hating how helpless I feel.

Dark brows pulled together, Elijah quickly sets down the small box on the stage edge. "I'd left it off so you could contact me—" Cutting himself off, he opens the box, flips the switch, then nods curtly. "We should be good now."

I look at Hugh, who's shimmied up the pole to saw the knife against the rope. "Once Hugh cuts the first rope, she might lose her balance. Get ready to support her until I can move over and redistribute her weight once more. We have very little time to get that collar off her before Edgar gets beyond the jammer's range."

Working together, the three of us cut Mina down quickly. Once I cut the ropes from her wrists and try to examine the rope burns on her fair skin, she touches the fat bird on her bracelet and tears fall.

"I'm so sorry, Mina," I say, staring at the angry welts on her arms while Elijah examines the collar for a way to access the electronics.

She turns the willow between her fingers, staring at the dents in it. "The ropes damaged my bird."

Chest tight with worry, I tell her it's okay as Hugh and I do our own evaluations of the collar. After looking at it, we all shake our heads in frustration. None of us have had as much training with sophisticated explosive devices as her brother has. "Where is Sebastian?" I snap, my deep voice echoing loudly in the empty theater.

"Right here," he says as he and Calder enter the theater.

"We have to get this explosive off Mina now!" Elijah calls out to them.

Sebastian bolts down the stairs and jumps onto the stage. Squatting beside us, he turns the collar until he gets the best access to open the door covering the electronics. With a multi-tool knife, he unscrews the cover, then asks

Elijah and me to confirm the colors of the wires before he cuts.

The moment the red light turns off, disrupting the signal, I exhale deeply, the pain in my chest slowly easing. Sliding the collar off Mina, Sebastian sets it down gently, then pulls her into a hug, his voice gruff. "Jesus, Mina! Let's not do this again. I don't think my heart can take it."

Nodding, she croaks, "You and me both."

He helps her to her feet and examines the red marks on her neck and wrists. "I'll have Ben meet us at the office to examine you."

"I'm fine, Seb. A little sore, but—"

"Let Ben check you, Mina," I say, holding her gaze. "He can give you something to help the rope burns and ease your sore muscles. You're going to feel this tomorrow."

Shutting the signal jammer box, Elijah looks perplexed. "Where did the GPS signal you gave me originate, Den? What was the source?"

I lift Mina's arm and tap the bird. Locking gazes with her, I say, "There's a reason the willow was so fat."

"It had a tracker in it?" she asks, her eyes wide.

"I had no way of knowing if Edgar would come after you, so I tried to be prepared without worrying you unnecessarily."

Sebastian's mouth tightens, his tone terse. "I take it Edgar got away?"

"I disabled his car, but he could've left on foot," I say.

"We'll have to fill the police in," Sebastian says, grunting his annoyance. Turning to Hugh, he continues, "With that mess you left behind, they're going to want to talk to you. It's a miracle that man is still alive."

"It was self-defense." Hugh shrugs, turning his swollen eye toward Sebastian. "An eye for an eye."

Snorting at his dark humor, Sebastian shakes his head. "The glasses were meant to be used on the job, but not like that."

"I improvised," Hugh says unapologetically. "If it weren't for Mina, I wouldn't be here. I woke up when she stuffed those glasses in my jacket pocket."

I stare at Mina, both proud and concerned that she took such a risky chance. "Why would you do that, knowing those glasses were probably the only way we could track you down?"

She lifts her shoulders. "He was unconscious. At least *I* knew what was going on. I thought that once he woke up, he could figure out a way to use the glasses to get free. And then he could save me." When we all frown at her, she points to the bird on her wrist, her lips pursed. "Apparently I already had a GPS signal on me anyway."

Sebastian cuts a sharp gaze my way. "Meet us back at the office to form a plan to take this bastard down."

"He'll hide behind his diplomatic immunity," Hugh warns.

"I don't give a damn," Sebastian and I say in unison.

As he and I exchange a look of agreement to do what it takes to get Edgar, Mina moves to my side. "I'm riding with you."

"Go with Sebastian and let Ben look you over," I say, shaking my head. "Hugh and I have to collect Edgar's men that I've detained and turn them into the embassy authorities."

When her expectant expression falls, all I want to do is pull her close and kiss her, but Sebastian is watching us. The last thing she needs is to stress about him flipping out on me. "See you in a bit." I hold her gaze for a second, hoping she understands that we'll talk later.

Calder and Elijah offer to stick around and help Hugh and me escort Edgar's men to the embassy, but I tell them to head back to the office. "Hugh and I are familiar with the embassy. As UK citizens, we have access and rights there that you two won't."

"Where are Edgar's men?" Hugh says once everyone leaves.

"Trussed up in vehicles. Are you okay to help?" I ask, staring at his swollen eye. "You should have BLACK Security's in-house doctor look at that."

"I'll get to it when I do."

I snap my gun into my shoulder harness, but pause on my way up the stairs to exit the theater when Hugh draws a gun from behind his back. "Do I even want to know where you got that?"

"Probably not," he says, glancing down at the weapon in his hand.

"Put that away," I grumble. "We can take these blokes out with our bare hands."

"Promise?" He flashes a smile and tucks his weapon away as he bolts up the stairs ahead of me.

Outside, I point to the vehicle and we silently approach.

When I look inside to see an empty seat, I frown. "I clocked him good. He can't be far," I say and start to reach for my gun.

"Turn around slowly, hands up," Edgar says smugly from behind us.

Our hands slightly raised, Hugh and I turn to find Edgar standing between his two men. While Edgar aims a handgun at us, his two guards are holding semi-automatics. If we'd had our weapons already drawn, that wouldn't have been a very fair gunfight.

"I don't know how you managed to free Mina from that bomb," he says, frowning. "But trust me, I won't make the same mistake next time." Waving his handgun, he continues, "Retrieve your weapons slowly, then set them down and kick them over."

There fucking won't be a next time. Hugh and I don't even have to look at each other. Neither of us is going down without a fight. We've lost too much and need to move forward in our lives. But we have to be smart about our current predicament. We don't need guns. Our training taught us to use something as innocuous as a pair of glasses to defend ourselves.

When I start to lower my hands to comply, the guard I clocked in the head narrows his gaze and hammers the ground at my feet with a spray of bullets.

Edgar laughs and just as he nods for him to stop firing, that guard slams to the ground.

A second later, the other guard goes down in the same fashion.

At the same time I pull my gun, Hugh steps in front of me, retrieving his weapon as well.

As I bark at him to move, Edgar's shot nicks Hugh in the ear before zooming past my neck.

Grabbing my friend's shoulder, I yank him out the line of fire and bellow my fury as I pull the trigger three times. For Bren, for Enya, and for Mina.

Edgar hits the ground hard, and while he's bleeding and whining in pain, he screeches, "I have diplomatic immunity. You're going to rot in prison for trying to kill me!"

It takes thinking about Mina to keep me from filling the fucker's head with the rest of my clip. I kick his gun away and narrow my gaze on him. "You don't have a leg to stand on with your diplomatic immunity bullshit. I'm a

UK citizen who defended another UK citizen in imminent danger from you. The soil we're standing on makes no difference in this scenario. You'll be sent home, where I'll personally make sure you're prosecuted for *all* your past crimes."

Kicking the wounded guards' guns out of the way, Hugh eyes the bleeding wounds in Edgar's knees, then leans over and punches the bullet wound on the man's shoulder. "Ha, you won't have *either* leg to stand on for a long time, you murderous fuck!" Ignoring Edgar's whimpers of pain, Hugh moves to stand beside me and peers into the night, his dark humor subsiding. "Where the hell was that other shooter?"

I glance toward the rooftop that provides the best viewpoint to both entrances of the theater and see a familiar silhouette against the night sky. As he lowers his sniper rifle, I nod to acknowledge Sebastian's help, then reach for my phone to call the embassy.

CHAPTER TWENTY-FOUR

MINA

I'm a freaking mess by the time I arrive back at BLACK Security. At least I am on the inside. Holding myself together and pretending I'm okay is all I can do. I don't want my family to freak out and send me to the hospital. I survived. And while my arms and neck burn a bit from my injuries, they'll heal.

But doctors can't mend a broken heart.

It hurt so much to hear Den say I was nothing more than an assignment, but when he admitted that the bracelet he gave me was a tracking device, it made me want to bawl my eyes out. That meant all the sentimentality I thought his gift conveyed...didn't. I'm so confused. He seemed to truly care for Josi's well-being. *Is keeping us safe all that really mattered to him? Did any of what he and I had mean anything?*

And yet, even though I'm upset with Den for not caring for me the way I thought he did, fool that I am, I can't help but worry for him with Edgar still out there. I was surprised when Seb asked Calder and Elijah to take me back to the office, saying he would meet us here later, but I didn't argue. I was thankful that he decided Den might need additional backup.

I feel numb and broken, but force a brave smile as Cass throws herself around me in a tight hug. "Meeeeena! I'm so happy you're all right. We've been so worried!" Pulling back, she grabs my hands and stares at my neck. "You poor thing."

As she pulls me into a gentler hug this time, Talia smiles. "I think she just gave you my hug too. We're glad you're safe, Mina. Did Sebastian say when he thought he'd be back?"

"No, he didn't," I say, sounding a bit hoarse.

"Okay, I'll text him for an ETA."

Releasing me, Cass says, "Are you hungry? I hope so, because we've ordered dinner and plan to eat in the kitchen. God, all this worry has left me ravenous."

It's on the tip of my tongue to tease her about stress eating, but then I notice the loving amusement in Calder's eyes as he looks at his wife and I suddenly wonder if there's another reason she's so overzealous about food. "I'm actually pretty hungry. In all the chaos, I never got to eat dinner."

"Okay great. I'm off to find out when it'll be here. Theo went to get it."

While Cass walks over to Theo's desk to make a call, Calder and Elijah follow Talia into her office and fill her in on tonight's events.

"Hi, Mina? How are you feeling?" Ben asks as he walks off the elevator.

His brown eyes are so sympathetic, I almost break-down. Instead, I take a deep breath and give him a half smile. "Thanks for coming. I'm sorry Seb dragged you here for me."

"Hey, I'm here for the food," he speaks into the stethoscope hanging around his neck like a radio announcer, then gestures toward an empty desk in the main room. "Why don't you let me check out your injuries?"

Once we're seated in chairs facing each other, I roll my sleeves up so he can get a better look at my wrists. "I know my voice sounds a bit rough, but my throat feels okay. These marks on my arms aren't too bad. They just burn a little. My shoulder muscles are sore, but otherwise I'm fine."

"I can prescribe some muscle relaxers and a salve if you'd like." He takes my pulse, listens to my heart, then tilts my head up to evaluate my throat. Lowering his hand, his dark brows pull together with concern as his gaze flicks quickly back to mine. "That was a close call. Are you sure you're all right?"

"I'm alive. That's all that matters. The salve sounds like a good idea. I don't want any kind of drug-related relaxers. I've had my fair share recently. I'll just take an Epsom salt bath."

Ben shakes his head. "A warm bath is fine, but skip the Epsom salt until your skin is completely healed. I'll give you a script for the salve."

The elevator door opens, drawing my attention as Seb, Hugh and, Den walk into the room. My heart jerks with happiness, then plummets with sadness all in an instant as I stare at Den. This big brave man has ruined me for all men. *How am I going to get over him?*

"Thanks for being there tonight, Sebastian," Hugh says, clapping my brother on the back.

"Yes, we appreciated the backup, Sebastia—"

I gasp when Seb pivots and punches Den in the jaw. "That's for sending me after your fucking friend instead of my sister!"

Den stumbles back from the hard blow, then narrows his gaze and yanks his jacket off. "That's bloody fucking it!" He quickly launches himself at my brother, barking out, "You'd have done the same thing if it was Talia!"

"Stop it!" I cry out and start to go after them, but Ben wraps his arms around my waist. He hauls me off my feet so I can't intervene as my brother and Den tumble over desks, landing on the floor in a tangle of powerful arms and legs.

"That's entirely different, Talia's my wife!" Seb barks out as he scrambles to his feet and swings hard.

Den ducks and lands a punch in Seb's side. "It matters because I love her, you jackass!"

I gape in shock at Den's declaration, while Seb growls and ducks his head. Bulldozing into Den, he lifts him off his feet and slams him onto another desk.

"They have to work out their issues, Mina," Ben says in my ear at the same time Talia, Cass, Calder, and Elijah reach the main room. "Talia," he calls to her. "Come get Mina."

When Hugh curls his hands into fists and moves forward, like he's about to jump in the fray, Calder steps in front of him. "Not a good idea. This needs to happen. Follow us to the kitchen. Food is coming."

I dig my heels in, refusing to let Talia pull me away.

"Go on, Mina." Ben pulls wireless ear buds from his pants pockets and plunks them in his ears. Leaning against the wall, he nods for me to go. "I'll make sure they don't kill each other."

We've only been in the kitchen for a minute or two and the sound of glass shattering and furniture breaking has my stomach already tied into fierce knots. The deep, angry rumble of their voices carries down the hall, but I can't make out what's being said. Unable to sit, I pace the room. This is driving me crazy!

Theo comes into the room a couple minutes later

shaking his head. Setting down the food, he chuckles and looks at Talia. "They're having a good bout for sure."

Calder grumbles, "They're going to destroy the cubicles."

"I'm all for that," Theo replies, snorting. "I'd rather have a true bullpen where we can talk in the middle."

"I like that idea, Theo." Talia nods as she pulls the bags of food to the middle of the table.

When something hits the kitchen wall hard and shakes the whole room, my heart jerks with renewed worry. I turn to the group and snap, "I refuse to stand by and let the two men I care about the most tear each other apart. Don't anyone get in my way!"

"Take my phone," Talia says, handing her phone to me. "Just push the button."

Glancing down at the Air Horn app she has pulled up, I smirk despite my angst, then turn the volume up full blast and walk down the hall with determined strides.

I enter the room to see Seb and Den on their backs on top of collapsed cubicles. Oblivious to the broken office equipment, supplies, papers and folders strewn all around them, Den has Seb in some kind of choking headlock. Yanking back hard, he grates out, "That's ten, Sebastian. Give up!"

When my brother growls his fury and elbows Den in the gut, I cast an accusing gaze Ben's way. He quickly pulls an ear bud from his ear and gives me a questioning look. "What?" I shake my head and lift the phone up, hitting the button. The sound of the blaring horn stops the men before another punch is thrown.

"You two are being ridiculous!" I say once their heads swivel in my direction. "I just want a hot bath and a soft bed. Den..." As he sits up, the sight of the oozing cut on his brow bone and the blood splatter on his torn dress shirt makes me sigh. "Take me home."

CHAPTER TWENTY-FIVE

DEN

Sebastian and I dive across the last standing desk and land on collapsed cubicle walls. While grappling and throwing punches into each other's sides, I grunt at a particularly powerful blow and realize no matter how long this conversation lasts...it's going to be more painful than I thought. At least now we'll finally answer the question: Who wins in a fight: MI6 or SEAL?

"What the hell's wrong with you?" I bellow as we stumble over broken chair parts. Putting our fists up, we regain our footing around the debris, ready for the next round. "Do you think I'm not good enough?" I bite out the question, not sure if I want to know the answer, but needing to hear it nonetheless.

Sebastian snorts as he bounces on his toes. "No one's

ever going to be good enough for her. It's not you. It's anyone. She's my baby sister. But I do think you're too old for her." Pausing, he straightens, head tilted. "How the hell old are you, anyway?"

I rest my hands on my hips and take deep breaths from our exertions. "Old enough to kick your ass. That's all you need to know." When he glares at me, I clip out, "Mina and I are perfect together. Get the hell over yourself. I could say the same to you. Talia's like a little sister to me. Do you see me giving you shit?"

"Yes!" Sebastian throws his arms wide. "Yes, the fuck you have...many times."

I shrug, unapologetic. "You apparently deserved it."

When he narrows his gaze, I glance back toward the hallway and exhale heavily. "Mina's had a hell of a day. This is the last thing she needs right now. We need to call a truce. I love your sister and I care deeply for Josi like she's my own. Their happiness and safety are my priority. That's all you should ever care about. Period."

Sebastian grunts, then nods and puts his hand out. The moment I clasp his hand, I say, "I'm taking Mina to London with me."

He cinches my hand in a bone-crushing grip and grits out, "No the fuck you're not!"

"You don't get a choice." I set my jaw and make him wince with my fierce return grip. "Mina and Josi go where I do."

"Want to make a bet?" he challenges, blue eyes fired up all over again.

I flash a confident smile. "If I pin you for a ten count, I don't want to hear jack shit from you about it."

CHAPTER TWENTY-SIX

MINA

The ride back to Den's house is quiet. He insisted on getting food since we left without eating, so I use the excuse that I'm starving and eat in the car to fill the silence. In truth, I don't know what to say. *He said he loves me!* I'm so afraid to believe it—to let myself be happy with all the bad that has happened in my life lately—that I'm frightened to say anything that might jinx myself. At the very least, anything coming out of my mouth right now would probably sound corny based on the rambling thoughts in my head.

When we walk in, Den strides over to the front door, picks up my purse and returns it to me. "We will get you a new phone tomorrow." He pulls his phone out of his pocket and sets it in my hand. "Why don't you give Josi a call and see how trick-or-treating went? I'll be right back."

I grip the phone tight and it takes major effort not to cry. I can't believe I forgot about Josi trick-or-treating with my father. I'm a terrible mom. Den's a better parent than I am. "Okay," is all I can muster as I watch him walk upstairs. Turning away, I sniff back my tears and dial my dad's number.

"Hi, Mina. How's your evening going?"

"H—hi, Dad," I stutter when it occurs to me that he has no idea what's happened and most likely won't be told. Forcing an upbeat tone, I realize that's for the best. "We've just had a late dinner. You'll have to excuse my scratchy voice. I guess the Thai was extra spicy. I just wanted to see how trick-or-treating went. Did Josi have fun? Were there lots of kids?"

"Yes, little Josi was the life of the neighborhood. She kept giving her candy away to the other kids passing by. It was pretty adorable, Grandad bias aside. Maybe you can convince her to keep more than she gets tomorrow night. Next year you'll have to come and dress up."

"You dressed up?" I ask, snickering my surprise.

"Not tonight, but Helena's really campaigning for me to do it next year. We'll see."

"I know it's getting late, but is Josi awake so I can say good night?"

"She is. She's looking through your old books for a story for me to read to her."

Happy tears spill at the idea of my father reading

stories to Josi. How I wished he had done that with me more than the couple of times that I remember. I'm thankful he's making up for lost time with my daughter. "I wonder which story she'll choose?"

"Helena knows your favorites, so I'm sure—ah, here she comes now. Josi, your mom's on the phone."

"Mama?" Josi says, her little voice filling my heart.

"Hey, baby girl. Did you have fun tonight?"

"Uh, huh. Candy! Grandad said 'only two,'" she says on a pout.

"That's so you don't get a tummy ache," I say, grinning. "If you eat it all up, there won't be any more left. You want to make it last."

"No! Eeeeeeeeat it aaaaaall," she mimics her favorite cookie eating monster voice.

Laughing at her sense of humor, I brush away the tears on my cheeks. "Okay, you little monster. Enjoy story time with Grandad. You'll have to tell me about it tomorrow. Love you, Josi-Bean. Hugs and kisses."

"Huuuugss and kiiiiiisses, Mama," she continues in her monster voice before she hangs up.

Just talking to Josi lightened my heart so much, that I smile as Den walks back downstairs. "Josi had a great time." Chuckling, I continue as I set my purse on the island and pull out the mail I'd brought with me. "She's such a character. I don't know where she got her sense of humor from."

"I know exactly where," he says, giving me a knowing look.

"Me?" Shaking my head, I sift through my mail. "Not likely."

"You're a bright light, Mina. Challenging, smart, and you make me laugh."

When I look up, my heart filling with love for his compliment, he continues, "While Ben stitched up my eyebrow, he told me a hot bath will help with your sore muscles." He glances toward the stairs, bending at the waist. "Your bath awaits, Lady Mina."

"Aww, thank you, Den." My fingers snag on a small bubble wrapped envelope in my mail and I quickly rip into it. When a set of earplugs lands on the counter, I laugh. Still chuckling, I slide them across the counter toward him. "These were intended to drown out your sexy accent, but maybe you'll need them tonight. I have a tendency to sing while in the bath. Since you walked in on my terrible voice today, you know my singing *isn't* pretty."

Den folds his arms and frowns deeply. "Not funny, Mina."

"Too soon?" I respond to his serious countenance.

He sighs, his severe expression slowly melting into amusement. "Like mother, like daughter. Off you go before the water gets cold."

A half-hour later, I feel so much better after my bath,

my body is all warm, my skin supple. Even the angry red marks on my wrists and neck aren't burning any longer, just a bit sore. After I towel dry my hair, I step into my underwear, then walk into Den's room and pull out a clean white undershirt from the tall dresser.

Slipping into his shirt, I walk down the stairs to an empty living room. The sound of water running in his other bathroom tells me he's taking a shower, so I take the time to clean up my mail and tuck the important papers and bills away in my purse along with my notepad.

When I turn off the kitchen light, the only light in the room is from the fire. Den must've turned it on while I took a bath. The mantel is still mostly dark. Did he notice the picture frame I'd set there? I walk over and flip on the spotlight above the fireplace, then step back to admire the photo of his family. I really do love how the frame turned out, but now that the stakes are higher between us, my stomach tightens with worry. Will he be angry that I did this? Will he think I overstepped my bounds? I straighten my spine, not regretting it for a second. I'd do it again if it helps him embrace his past so he can move forward toward his future.

Den steps into place beside me in a fitted soft t-shirt and lounge pants. His hard body is radiating the warmth from his shower and smells of woodsy leather and bergamot. All I want to do is wrap my arms around him and inhale deeply, but I pause when I see he's staring at the frame, his gaze unreadable. *What is he thinking?*

"I found it while looking for your car keys," I say quietly. "You have such a beautiful family, Den. I hope you don't mind, but I thought they deserved a place of honor in your home, to be cherished for the time you had together."

When he swallows a couple of times, I worry that I overstepped, but if we're going to make this relationship work, I need to be fully me. "Are you okay with this?"

Den turns and walks over to my purse. Pulling out my notepad, he flips the pages, then folds the pad open and leans it against the mantle, saying, "Only if you promise to frame this one too and put it beside it."

I stare at the picture I'd drawn of Josi on Den's shoulders from that day we picked her up at church. It's the only drawing I've completely colored in and one of my absolute favorites. I didn't even know he'd seen it.

My throat tightens with emotion as I nod. "I'll be happy to."

Den looks down at me, his golden gaze searching mine. "I meant what I said to Sebastian. I love you, Mina Blake. You brought sunshine into my life. You and Josi." He takes my hand and lifts it, touching the dented bird on my bracelet. "I'll replace the willow."

I turn my hand for a better view. "I don't know, Den. The bird might've originally just been a means to an end, but with all those scratches, dents and dings, it makes me think of us now."

"It was never a means to an end, Mina," he says, clasping my fingers between his to turn my hand. "But you're right, now it's truly unique to us. Are you saying you want to keep it?"

"I do. Even the tracker. Just like you promised, I want you to always be with me."

Nodding, he releases me. "I was going to wait a little bit for this, but I came too close to losing you today. Life's too bloody short to worry about timelines." Capturing my hand once more, he slides an antique, art deco style ring on my finger. "This was my mother's. A gift from a woman who inspired hope in the masses to the woman who inspired hope in me."

Tears stream down my cheeks. My heart swells at his sentiment and the connection of honor he made to his mother. I wish I had known her. I'd love to thank her for creating such a wonderful man.

When he kisses the round center stone surrounded by a cushion-shaped halo of diamonds and says, "I believe it's a fitting ring for a Lady," my heart stutters several beats and my eyes widen.

"Are you...asking me to marry you, Sir Barasa?" Folding my fingers around his, I huff. "I can't believe you didn't tell me you were a knight!"

He stares at me for a beat, surprise in his gaze. "How

do you know that about me?"

"Oh, you know, it's no biggie," I say, shrugging. "While you were out getting dinner, the Queen called to ask you to come home."

Barking out a laugh, he pulls me close, his golden eyes flashing with amusement. "Will you do me the honor of becoming my wife, Mina Blake? Where, among other perks, you will officially be addressed as Lady Barasa when you visit the palace to meet the Queen."

"Are you going to tell me what you did to deserve a knighthood?" I ask, smiling.

He laces his fingers at the base of my spine. "Maybe you can convince me to tell you...*after* we're married. I'm waiting on an answer, Mina."

"Ugh, I shouldn't have to wait to learn the story."

"Me either. Want to elope?"

I flatten my hands on his chest, where the ring captures my attention. "This ring is gorgeous. Thank you for honoring me with such a special piece of your family history. And yes, I will marry you." Tilting my head, I tease, "Maybe you can convince me to run away with you...*after* you tell me about how you became a knight."

"Hmmm, this sounds like a circular challenge I'm up to, Lady Mina." Before I can react, he quickly tosses me over his shoulder and bolts up the stairs, making me sound like a squawking chicken with my crackly squeals of terror.

The moment he sets me down in the bedroom, I wrap my arms around his waist, my excitement sobering. "My family will flip if we elope."

"We can have a celebratory party later." He smiles and cups his hand on the back of my neck, rubbing his thumb along my jaw. "I just want to enjoy time with you and Josi all to myself."

"We will need an engagement period. Not for me, but for Josi and the rest of my family to get used to the idea of us being engaged. Then, we'll talk about the other."

Den cups my face in his big hands, all teasing gone from his expression. "If you want a big wedding with all the trimmings, we'll do that. Just don't make me wait forever for you to move in with me."

My heart jumps all over again. "You want us to live with you here?"

"Absolutely." Pulling me close, he wraps his muscular arms around my back. "I have plenty of room. There's a great park close by. Josi will love it. But I do want you both to go to London with me as soon as possible. And before you answer, just know that I might have to be there for several weeks. There are business things that I need to attend to, but my first priority will be to make sure Edgar gets the punishment he deserves."

"Yes, we would love to go with you." I nod, then grimace when I think about a couple upcoming projects I need to work on. *I hope it'll be possible to do them remotely*. "And if we need to come back before you can, we will."

Den frowns slightly. "I don't want to be separated. But if you need to come home for whatever reason, I'll fly back with you."

"We'll make it work," I say, smiling. "I'm looking forward to seeing London through your eyes." Raising up on my toes, I start to wrap my arms around his shoulders, but wince at the tightness in my muscles.

"Are you okay?" he asks, gently pulling my arms back down.

"I have an idea." Clasping his hand, I give him an impish smile, then pull him into the bathroom and turn on the shower.

While steam fills the room, he tugs his shirt off with an anticipatory smirk. "What do you have in mind, my sexy little minx?"

I pull him in with me, directly under the warm spray and push up on my toes to whisper against his jaw, "This time, I want you to hold me under the water for an entirely different reason, Sir Barasa."

A sensual smile tilts his lips as he runs his fingertips over the wet shirt already sticking to my nipples. Pinching the sensitive tips with just enough pressure to make me gasp for more, he rumbles his approval. "Now *that* I can get on board with, Lady Mina."

As his hands slowly explore my body, plastering the

soaked material to every curve, dip and hollow so he can see all of me, I relish his warm touch and savor each white-hot moment between us. I return the favor with his lounge pants, until I can tell every bit of what he has to offer. Water dripping off his face, Den's breathing heavily by the time I'm done, and as he moves to grip the hem of my shirt, I press a kiss to his jaw and nip at his sexy scruff. "You're going to have to do all the heavy lifting in here, I'm afraid."

"I thought you'd never ask," he rasps and yanks my panties right off me. As I snicker at his impatience, he quickly lifts me up. Pressing my back against the shower wall, he chases away my gasp at the cold tile on my skin as he imprints every inch of his impressive, clothes-soaked erection against me.

The pounding water enhances the delicious heat and friction of his hard body hitting all my erogenous zones. I moan and press my mouth to his, accepting the thrust of his tongue as his hands spread over my ass. Den grinds his hips against me, his grip tightening, spreading me for his entry.

I pull back slightly, my breathy laughter echoing in the shower. "You um, need to take your pants off to complete this transaction, Sir."

He nuzzles my throat, nipping his way to my jaw. Rolling his hips aggressively, his accent is an arousing rasp in my ear. "A lady should know how to disrobe her man, no matter the circumstances. Show me just how inventive you can be."

When he kisses me with intense passion, it's hard to concentrate, but I take advantage of the support his hands provide and dig my toes into the low-slung material at his hips. It takes extra muscle power to move wet clothes, but Den doesn't let me get very far. The moment the tip of his cock is free, he moans his need and pulls me down on top of him, letting the weight of my body strip him free of his pants as he thrusts deep.

Setting me back against the wall, he begins to move, his possession a powerful claiming, not only of my body but also my heart. This man has stolen my soul. My vision blurs, and all I can do is cling to his slick, muscular body, willingly riding the emotional roller coaster between us until waves of ecstasy vibrate all over my body again and again.

I'm on such a high, I don't want to come down, until I hear Den's deep groan of satisfaction. And even then, I never want it to ever end.

"I love you, Dennet Barasa," I pant against his cheek. "Don't ever let me go."

He nips at my throat, then kisses me hard, his breathing just as labored. "Not now. Not ever. You're all mine, Little Willow."

CHAPTER TWENTY-SEVEN

DEN

"Hugh is an excellent guard, Talia. He'll keep you and Joey safe while I'm gone, but you've got my number, so don't hesitate to call if you need anything."

Talia surprises me when she steps around her desk and gives me a hug. "I'll be fine, Den. Don't worry. Have a wonderful time in London."

Before she can pull away, I hug her back and whisper in her ear, "Hugh's truly great, but don't let your guard down. I'll be back as soon as I can."

"So has Hugh hired himself on to BLACK Security too?" Sebastian mutters from the adjoining doorway between his and Talia's office.

I release Talia and shrug. "Only if you find his work up to your standards."

"Oh no...I'm holding him to *your* standards." Sebastian's eyebrows pull together as he strolls into the room. "Which means I'll be shadowing him to make sure he's as good as you say he is."

"We trained together," I say. "Hugh knows the stakes, but I'd do the same as you until I felt comfortable."

As Sebastian grunts his agreement, Mina lets out in irritated huff, then starts typing fast on her phone.

"What's wrong?" Walking over, I rest a hand on her shoulder and squeeze gently.

"Ugh, Derrick just sent me a text saying he's not sure about me taking Josi to England." Her brown eyes snap to mine, full of worry. "Now he wants to 'talk' about it. We're leaving tomorrow. I can't believe he's doing this!"

"He gave up his rights, which is why his name isn't even on her birth certificate," Sebastian says, frowning. "The guy's full of hot air. Just ignore him."

Jerking her gaze to her brother, Mina says, "As much as I would like to do just that, I don't want to give him a reason to suddenly decide to petition to have parental rights reinstated. I—" Her phone starts ringing and she sets her jaw, gritting out, "I don't even know how to respond to this."

"May I?" I say, holding my hand out for her phone.

Sighing, she hands me the phone and says in a low tone, "Be civil, Den. He will be a part of our lives."

Nodding, I answer the phone. "Hello, Derrick. Mina's not available at the moment, but I saw your note."

"Look, *bodyguard*, I don't know why you think it's okay to answer Mina's phone, but this is between my ex and me."

"Actually, it's about Josi. Mina let you know they were going to London. She didn't have to, but she did. At the time, you didn't have any issues, but the day before she's supposed to leave, you suddenly express concern?"

"I can change my mind if I want to," he snaps. "Just like I can have my parental rights reinstated and file for half-custody."

Mina's staring at me with wide eyes, her hands clutched tight around her purse's shoulder strap. My fingers cinch around the phone. "Is that what you're planning to do?" I grate out in a cold tone.

"I'm her *father*. Why am I even explaining this to you? You're of no consequence. Just have Mina call me immediately."

"Let's just have a chat about what that choice will mean for you, shall we?"

"I'm not talking to yo—"

"You will immediately owe Mina back pay of forty grand, which is half of what it has cost to raise Josi so far. The full amount up until she's eighteen will be three-hundred-and-sixty-thousand."

"Are you insane?"

"It might even go up a little if she decides to play sports or other extra curricular activities in the area," I say, talking over him. "And let's not forget about college. Josi's a very smart little girl. I see an Ivy League school in her future. Columbia runs sixty-thousand a year for tuition and fees alone. Your half, once you add in food and housing, will be roughly one-hundred-and-eighty thousand for her four years there."

"What the hell? I shouldn't have to foot half her astronomical college bill!"

"In the state of New York, you'll be legally responsible for Josi until she's twenty-one," I barrel on. "And as bright as she is, my guess is she'll probably go to college at seventeen, which means, you'll be on the hook for her full, four-year college experience. Being a parent means also sharing the financial burden. So is that what you want?"

"I can barely afford my rent. No way a judge will tell me I owe back monies or even the crazy amounts you're quoting."

"Rest assured, you will pay overdue monies owed. If you don't, your bank accounts can be seized, your driver's license and passport suspended, and credit reporting agencies will be informed that you owe back child support. All that can be arranged."

"Just tell Mina to call me when she and Josi get back," he grumbles.

"I'll convey the message," I say, then hang up.

"That was brilliant, Den!" Mina looks at me with awed respect as she hooks her arm with mine. "I'll bet Derrick is wiping his brow right now, thankful he doesn't have any of that financial burden."

"And you didn't even drop the bomb that he'll be dealing with you running circles around him from now on as Mina's future husband," Talia says, laughing. "I kind of feel sorry for the guy when he finds out."

"London for several weeks?" Sebastian cuts in, frowning.

Walking over to her husband, Talia wraps an arm around his waist. "At least while Mina and Josi are with Den in London, you won't have to worry about Simone trying to contact her."

"The fact Simone keeps changing her looks makes it damn hard to pin her down." Sebastian pulls Talia close, the lines around his mouth deepening. "I hate that she's still out there, especially with our best guard traipsing around England."

"Did you say *best*?" A cocky grin splits Den's lips. "I never thought you'd admit it, Sebastian."

Sebastian clears his throat and straightens. "What I meant to say was: You will be back here in two weeks, three max. Got it?"

"Try not to give Hugh too hard a time," I say, nodding.

Wrapping my arm around Mina's shoulders, I kiss her temple, "Ready to go, Little Willow?"

"So ready." Squeezing me, she turns her bright smile Sebastian and Talia's way. "And we're off to see the Queen!"

* * *

Thank you for reading **NOBLE BRIT! If you found NOBLE BRIT** an entertaining and enjoyable read, I hope you'll consider taking the time to leave a review and share your thoughts in the online bookstore where you purchased it. Your review could be the one to help another reader decide to read **NOBLE BRIT** and the other books in the **IN THE SHADOWS** series!

Coming up next is **BLACK AND RED** (IN THE SHADOWS, Book 10), a new Talia and Sebastian stand alone novel. If you're not already, **please sign up for my newsletter** to be informed when retailer preorder links for **BLACK AND RED** are available!

Did you know there are **audiobooks** for the **IN THE SHADOWS** series? The audiobooks bring these stories to a whole new level. You can listen to samples and check them out on Amazon and Apple.

To KEEP up-to-date when the next P.T. Michelle book will release, join my free newsletter http://bit.ly/11tqAQN . An email will come straight to your inbox on the day a new book releases.

OTHER BOOKS BY P.T. MICHELLE

In the Shadows

(Contemporary Romance, 18+)

Mister Black (Book 1 - Talia & Sebastian, Part 1)

Scarlett Red (Book 2 - Talia & Sebastian, Part 2)

Blackest Red (Book 3 - Talia & Sebastian, Part 3)

Gold Shimmer (Book 4 - Cass & Calder, Part 1)

Steel Rush (Book 5 - Cass & Calder, Part 2)

Black Platinum (Book 6 - Talia & Sebastian, Stand Alone Novel)

Reddest Black (Book 7 - Talia & Sebastian, Stand Alone Novel)

Blood Rose (Book 8 - Cass & Calder, Stand Alone Novel)

Noble Brit (Book 9 - Mina & Den, Stand Alone Novel)

Black and Red (Book 10 - Talia & Sebastian, Stand Alone Novel - Coming December 2019)

Note: Mister Black is the only novella. All the other books are novel length.

Brightest Kind of Darkness Series

(YA/New Adult Paranormal Romance, 16+)

Ethan (Prequel)

Brightest Kind of Darkness (Book 1)

Lucid (Book 2)

Destiny (Book 3)

Desire (Book 4)

Awaken (Book 5)

Other works by P.T. Michelle writing as Patrice Michelle

Bad in Boots series

(Contemporary Romance, 18+)

Harm's Hunger

Ty's Temptation

Colt's Choice

Josh's Justice

Kendrian Vampires series

(Paranormal Romance, 18+)

A Taste for Passion

A Taste for Revenge

A Taste for Control

Stay up-to-date on her latest releases:

Join P.T's Newsletter:

http://bit.ly/11tqAQN

Visit P.T. :

Website: http://www.ptmichelle.com

Twitter: https://twitter.com/PT_Michelle

Facebook: https://www.facebook.com/PTMichelleAuthor

Instagram: http://instagram.com/p.t.michelle

Goodreads: http://www.goodreads.com/author/show/4862274.P_T_Michelle

P.T. Michelle's Facebook Readers' Group:

https://www.facebook.com/groups/PTMichelleReadersGroup/

ACKNOWLEDGEMENTS

To my truly awesome beta readers: Joey Berube, Amy Bensette, and Magen Chambers, I can't thank you ladies enough for all your help! You always provide great insights and feedback on my books and **NOBLE BRIT** is no exception!

To my wonderful critique partner, Trisha Wolfe, thank you for reading **NOBLE BRIT** so quickly. You never fail to keep me on my toes!

To my family, thank you for understanding the time and effort each book takes. I love you all and truly appreciate your unending support.

To my amazing fans, thank you so much for your love and support of my IN THE SHADOWS series and characters! Every time you post a review or tell your reader friends about the series, more people discover my series. Which means there will be even more readers to discuss the books with. I appreciate you all so much!

ABOUT THE AUTHOR

P.T. Michelle is the *NEW YORK TIMES*, *USA TODAY*, and International bestselling author of the contemporary romance series IN THE SHADOWS, the YA/New Adult crossover series BRIGHTEST KIND OF DARKNESS, and the romance series: BAD IN BOOTS, KENDRIAN VAMPIRES and SCIONS (listed under Patrice Michelle). She keeps a spiral notepad with her at all times, even on her nightstand. When P.T. isn't writing, she can usually be found reading or taking pictures of landscapes, sunsets and anything beautiful or odd in nature.

To keep up-to-date when the next P.T. Michelle book will release, join P.T.'s free newsletter.

www.ptmichelle.com

Made in the USA
Middletown, DE
12 July 2021

44023969R00203